The R

After working in London for many years, Jérôme Loubry moved to the South of France, where he still lives and works.

Born in 1976, he grew up in a village famous for its book printing business, and his aunt, who worked there, made sure he grew up surrounded by books.

JÉRÔME LOUBRY

The Refuge

HODDER

First published in the French language as *Les Refuges* by
Editions Calmann-Lévy in 2019

First published in Great Britain in 2021 by Hodder & Stoughton
An Hachette UK company

1

A CIP catalogue record for this title is available from the British Library

Paperback ISBN 9781529350579
eBook ISBN 9781529350562

Typeset in Plantin Light by Palimpsest Book Production Limited,
Falkirk, Stirlingshire

Printed and bound in Great Britain by Clays Ltd, Elcograf S.p.A.

Hodder & Stoughton policy is to use papers that are natural,
renewable and recyclable products and made from wood grown in
sustainable forests. The logging and manufacturing processes are expected
to conform to the environmental regulations of the country of origin.

Hodder & Stoughton Ltd
Carmelite House
50 Victoria Embankment
London EC4Y 0DZ

www.hodder.co.uk

For Loan

Mein Vater, mein Vater, und siehst du nicht dort
Erlkönigs Töchter am düstern Ort ?
Mein Sohn, mein Sohn, ich seh es genau :
Es scheinen die alten Weiden so grau.

Goethe, "Erlkönig"

My father, my father, ah! canst thou not see
The Erlking's daughters beguiling me?
My son, I see, be calm now, I pray,
It is but the willows, trembling and grey.

Goethe, "The Erlking"

September 2019

François Villemin opened the door to the lecture theatre assigned to his class by the University of Tours and invited the students to come in and sit down.

"Welcome everyone," he began as he placed his laptop on the desk and connected it to the digital blackboard.

His beige wool suit, thin frame, bald spot, and carefully groomed white beard made him look a lot like a certain famous Scottish actor. Of course, given their age, few of the people in the room knew who Sean Connery was. But the professor cultivated the resemblance nonetheless, delighting in their youthful ignorance.

He waited for them all to get settled and, once he had everyone's attention, turned down the lights and began his lecture. "For our second session, we're going to discuss a case from the 1980s. A case I'm calling 'Sandrine's Refuge'. Like last time, I'll lay out all the facts first, and then there will be time for questions. Just a word of warning: don't bother looking it up on your smartphones or wracking your young brains for any memory of this case. You'll find no trace of it anywhere. And at the end of class, you'll understand why . . ."

"Keep your mind busy . . .
Recite your poem, for example . . .
It'll make things easier . . .
Tomorrow, when your teacher has you
stand up in front of the class,
you'll have me to thank . . .
Come here . . .
Come closer . . .
It'll make things easier . . ."

THE FIRST BEACON
The Island

I

1949

Valery threw the stick determinedly. It flew up into the air, climbing steeply and defying the grey clouds for a moment, before falling back onto the sand with a thud. The yellow Labrador immediately ran over, picked it up in his mouth, and wagged his tail happily as he trotted back to his owner, who was walking along the beach at a leisurely pace.

"Come on, bring it here!"

Valery bent down, congratulated her companion, and threw the piece of driftwood again. The early autumn wind was cool and gentle. The smell of salt and seaweed battered by the surf wafted through the coastal air and the wan light of the recently risen sun filtered laboriously through the low clouds.

Every morning, come rain or shine, Valery and Gus, her two-year-old dog, walked along the beach beside the ocean. And it had now become something of a ritual. But these daily walks didn't just hold the promise of some precious time spent with her faithful friend. Even more importantly, they gave Valery a taste of the freedom that she had been deprived of for so many years.

Valery turned away from Gus to contemplate the waves as they rolled over the sand at her feet.

She closed her eyes and listened.

Nothing.

Nothing but the beating of the surf and the seagulls' cries.

No German Stuka screeching through the clouds.

No heavy silence announcing the deadly descent of a destructive bomb.

No anti-aircraft sirens urging people to take cover in their cellars.

No mumbles of resignation from people gathering in makeshift shelters, people who dared not look up for fear their gaze—heavy with the weight of terror and death—might somehow attract the enemy.

Valery sighed and a smile played on her lips. She opened her eyes and caught sight of an island, just a tiny silhouette out at sea, its outline blurred by the mist. Then she turned back towards the port and its buildings and her face darkened. The weight of painful memories etched lines into her forehead, but she had promised herself before leaving on her walk that she wouldn't cry. The scars left by the war had not immediately healed on the day that France had been liberated. Broken windows, collapsed buildings, caved-in roofs . . . *It will take time, a long time, to repair it all,* she thought as she took in the ruins.

A bark pulled her from her thoughts and from the ball of sadness growing in her throat. A few metres away, Gus was lying still on the sand, apparently cowed by an ominous flock of seagulls hovering over the beach. Every so often one of the birds would dive down towards the sand not far from him.

Valery came over, knelt by his side, and stroked his fur. "Afraid of a few birds, eh?" she teased.

But there were an awful lot of them. She was intrigued to see so many birds plunging towards the beach and then climbing back up into the sky. Usually gulls gathered in small groups of ten, maybe twenty individuals, rarely more. At least from what she could remember. But here she was certain at least a hundred of them had flocked together, filling the air with the sound of fluttering wings and snapping beaks.

I wonder what's over there.

She stood up. "You stay here, you scaredy-cat. I'm going to get a closer look."

The dog whined as Valery walked away, but the laughing gulls drowned him out. She approached the spot with the densest concentration of birds, which was about fifty metres away, right at the water's edge. Out of habit, just as when she had walked through her neighbourhood with her ration book in hand to get food for her mother and brothers, she looked all around her to make sure there was no hidden danger.

The beach was empty.

The surroundings hadn't changed: on one side, the silent ruins, on the other, the cold, apathetic sea and the barely visible island—little more than a small rock. The menacing shadows that had once haunted the dark corners of the town had long since disappeared with the arrival of the Americans. The stares that had followed her as she walked through the streets—at the time it was hard to tell if the observers were hostile or simply frightened—forcing her to hunch down and take up as little space as possible, no longer weighed on her shoulders.

The freedom she now had meant she could stand up straight and walk along the beach without fear. But fear was still her natural reflex.

Valery was now only about ten metres from the gulls.

They took flight suddenly, surprised by her unexpected presence. Then, judging that their business was worth the risk, they carried on diving noisily yet gracefully towards the sand, clearly determined not to be disturbed. As soon as they landed on their mysterious treasure (Valery had thought it might be a tree trunk when the birds had briefly abandoned their perch), the gulls began to squabble, pecking one another with their beaks, opening their wings wide, and screeching their discontent. Watching them, Valery couldn't help but wonder if their intent was to kill each other rather than survive. Maybe the seagulls had learned to war like humans, like the children she often saw playing soldiers in the devastated streets.

Have the birds lost their minds too?

Lying on the sand, his frightened eyes glued to his owner,

Gus remained perfectly still and observed the frenzy from afar. Suddenly, a fleeting glimpse caused a chill to settle at the bottom of Valery's spine. The numbness climbed all the way to her lips, which gasped instinctively, paralysed by the horror she couldn't yet name. *It can't be.*

"It can't be. That's impossible."

Her words had lost all meaning. The notion of impossibility had been violated, mutilated by human nature. Bombs dropped on civilians. Women's bodies abandoned by German soldiers in the wreckage of their sexual urges. Children holding out gaunt arms through the slats of a train carriage . . .

Nothing was impossible any more. Words, too, had been destroyed by the war.

Nevertheless, she said it again, without realizing it. A Pavlovian reflex sparked by primitive distress.

The stick she had been throwing lay at her feet. Trembling, she picked it up and stepped closer. The smell barrelled into her senses so hard that she had no choice but to double over and let her stomach expel its contents. But the spasms brought up nothing but bile. Once the pain had passed, Valery stood up, wiped away her tears with the back of her hand, and stared angrily at the army across from her. *They're just birds,* she told herself, working up the courage to keep going. *You've faced worse and survived. Go on, you have to find out . . .*

She brandished the stick in the air and ran towards the gulls, screaming at the top of her lungs.

Dozens of pairs of wings flapped furiously as the birds took flight, taking refuge on the nearby waves and squawking with envy. A few braver individuals, fidgeting on their skinny legs and staring curiously at Valery, only backed up a few steps and then waited a mere two or three metres from the body that the shroud of feathers had finally unveiled.

"My God," she whispered when she finally saw the maimed corpse.

An arm was missing, as was the bottom half of a leg. The face looked down into the sand. Long, slimy clumps of hair were spread out around the head. The body's translucent skin was dotted with wounds inflicted by hungry scavengers.

Valery stepped back slowly. She glanced to her left, towards the buildings, hoping to see someone. She wanted to shout for help, but she couldn't. Her brain was struggling to convey to her legs even the most basic instruction: to get away from the child's body.

Suddenly, a rapid movement on her right attracted her attention. A movement that had come from the sky.

A gull dived towards the ocean.

Then climbed again.

Valery did not want to find out what was causing this new dance of death. She wanted to flee the beach and block out the hoarse cries that were drawing her gaze out over the water. But she couldn't. Her eyes brimming with new tears, she turned slowly towards the rocky outline of the island and watched the birds.

The flock of gulls had dispersed into several groups and each of them was performing the same dance at various points along the beach. The birds were diving down at intervals to feed, doing their best to enjoy the feast despite the seemingly random movements of the surf, which constantly ferried their prey away from them.

And this was how Valery first realized that there were other bodies floating towards the beach, some more visible than others among the waves, as the birds pecked furiously at the flesh with their hungry beaks. Five, six, nine . . . A dozen bundles of skin and bone finally appeared at the surface of the cold water, all of them swollen from the gas produced by their decomposing organs and half devoured by the scavengers.

"My God . . ."

When a second body—a limbless trunk—washed up on the sand and a spectral face stared up at her with its empty eye sockets, Valery ran back to the port with Gus at her heels.

And behind her, dozens of ravenous beaks broke the silence with their mocking shrieks, echoing the screams in her head.

2

Sandrine

November 1986

In deep shit, that's where I am.

Sandrine regretfully studied her trainers, which had sunk down into a mixture of mud and cow manure. They had been an immaculate white colour when she had put them on that morning. Now, stood in the middle of this field, she could barely make out the brand logo printed on the sides.

"You know, I didn't hear a thing. Nothing at all. They did it at night."

Sandrine turned to listen to the farmer standing a few metres ahead of her (who had cleverly chosen to wear high-topped wellington boots) as he pointed with his thick finger at the herd of cows gathered behind a barbed wire fence.

"What did the police say?" she asked as she took pictures of the animals.

"That it was probably kids. That they were just having fun . . . But what am I going to do about the fair now?"

"The fair?"

"The livestock fair a week from today," he explained with a slight accent. "They're dairy cows. If they were for meat, I might still have sold them, though for less of course . . . But now, no one will want them. Not with *that* on their hides . . . Who's going to compensate me?"

Not with that *on their hides . . .*

Crosses.

Hastily scrawled in spray paint on a dozen cows' flanks.

Hakenkreuze.

Swastikas.

The journalist felt her wrist burn. The stripes on her skin felt like they were on fire. Luckily, they were carefully hidden beneath her thick leather cuff bracelet. She swallowed hard to get rid of the bitter taste the memory had left in her mouth.

"I don't know, Mr Wernst. Your insurance company?" she suggested.

"Right . . . They won't give me even a tenth of their value. Come inside, the clouds are getting low. You've got in quite a mess now, haven't you!"

Sandrine turned her ankles from side to side and rubbed her shoes against a tuft of grass to remove as much of the excrement as possible. She promised herself she would think to leave a pair of wellies in her boot for the next time the newspaper had a scoop for her . . .

To think that just three weeks ago I was wandering the streets of Paris dreaming of becoming a reporter for a national daily . . .

The old man (in his sixties, maybe more, though it was hard to pinpoint the age of a face so weathered by hard work) uncorked a bottle of white wine, pulled a plate of charcuterie from the refrigerator, and placed it all on the solid oak table. The room smelled of sweat and wet clothes, partially masked by the odour of the woodfire from the hearth. Sandrine left her trainers on the doormat as if they were a dog too dirty to be allowed inside. She went and stood in front of the fire to warm up.

"My article will be published tomorrow," she said, listening to dishes clinking in the kitchen. Are you a subscriber?"

"No. And I never have time to go into town," he replied.

"I'll drop it by for you then," she promised. "I hope it will help get people talking."

"Do you really think it will?" Frank Wernst asked doubtfully as he came back into the room with plates, glasses, knives and a loaf of bread.

No, of course not. Not way out here in the sticks. Nothing could get the ruins and corpses here to talk, Sandrine admitted to herself.

"Let's sit," offered Mr Wernst. "This is a good bottle."

She sat down in turn and accepted the glass he held out. She had a strange feeling. The feeling that she had met this man before. Which was impossible since she had only been in Normandy for two weeks. *Maybe at the bakery in town or . . . at the butcher's,* she guessed as she studied the plate of sausages and pâtés.

"You'll need a full stomach to get the cogs turning," he explained when she hesitated.

"It's not even ten o'clock in the morning," Sandrine pointed out.

"Time is relative. For you, it's *not even* ten o'clock. But I've been in the fields since five, so I'm halfway through my workday. It's time for a bite to eat."

Sandrine nodded. She spread a thin layer of pâté on a piece of bread and took a sip of wine, not attempting to conceal her pleasure. Frank chewed ceremoniously. He poured himself a second glass, offered to serve her one too, then put down the bottle with a serious look on his face.

"You know, the war has never really left us. It's still here," he said, pointing to his right temple. "I don't need those little shits to remind me of it by painting swastikas on my cows. It's with me every night. There is no more faithful companion than war. When war crosses your path, you're scarred for life . . ."

"I'm sorry, Mr Wernst."

"I know, I know. We're all sorry."

"How . . . How did you end up here?" she asked hesitantly.

"That's easy. I came to France for the worst possible reason: war. And I stayed for the best: love."

"Really?"

"Yes. A year before the Liberation, I fell for a Parisian woman. But we had to keep our relationship a secret. It was frowned upon—a French woman with a German soldier. We moved around a lot. Then, once the past was in the past and people started to forget, we moved here. That was about ten years ago."

"Do you live alone?"

"Yes," he replied, offering no further explanation.

Sandrine scanned the room: an old sofa, dark wood furniture, a painting, a worn rug, old, framed photographs. No television and no telephone. A few books from the 1920s shelved in a makeshift bookcase. The farm seemed to be in limbo, frozen in time. Like a soldier waiting for a ceasefire, it was scared stiff, afraid to move forwards or backwards, refusing to embrace the present day—contemporary music, Sunday night television, more recent and less bellicose literature—and afraid of the impending destruction foreshadowed by the swastikas on the cows.

Ten minutes later, Sandrine thanked Frank and promised to write him a sensitive article, which would inspire only sympathy in the paper's readers. She wanted to add something more personal, say a few words to him about the importance of memory, the horror of war, and the forbidden love between a soldier and a civilian. But she couldn't work up the courage. Firstly, because she didn't feel she had the right to bring up these topics, which she had only ever encountered second-hand in history class. Secondly, because she still couldn't shake the strange feeling that she had met this farmer before. She didn't know why, but she was certain that the discomforting sensation would only pass once she had left his house.

As she closed the front door behind her, Sandrine bent down to put on her trainers. She stopped short when she saw that the old man had cleaned them, most likely when he had been in the kitchen. His kindness made her smile. She wanted to go back in to thank him.

But suddenly, the feeling of déjà vu exploded in her brain again, like a piece of popcorn in boiling oil. And, although she knew that it was silly and that her fears were unfounded, she forgot all about her laces and ran to take refuge inside her Peugeot 104.

3

Sandrine

November 1986

Sandrine stepped inside the tiny local newspaper office, which was located in the centre of town, not far from the market square. The bell on the door alerted Vincent to her presence. He looked up from his typewriter and took a drag on his cigarette before stubbing it out in the ashtray and standing up to welcome his colleague.

"So, was it a scoop?" he asked with a smile, well aware that driving out to the countryside on an anonymous lead was more likely to be a prank than the story of the year.

Sandrine had taken the time to check it out with the local police station before heading out. "Very funny," she sighed as she took off her coat. "At least I got a real breakfast out of it! And a shoeshine!"

When he had seen her walk into the office for the first time two weeks earlier, holding a suitcase and a piece of paper bearing the address, Vincent had felt something detonate deep in his stomach. He had lived in the village all his life and now this woman's presence had dealt him a brutal blow, a seismic tremor whose shockwaves rumbled towards his heart. His first words had been a jumble of fragments and unrelated thoughts because the shockwaves had also affected his brain. He smiled (at least, he thought he was smiling, but standing paralyzed across from her, he couldn't be absolutely certain his facial muscles were following orders) and held out a hand, concentrating hard on pronouncing his own name without faltering.

Sandrine was flattered by Vincent's awkwardness and blushing cheeks.

In Paris, no one would have ever welcomed her with such enthusiasm.

From then on, Vincent was constantly but discreetly doing nice things for Sandrine to try to attract the attention of the new arrival from Paris (an exotic location for those who had spent their entire lives in this isolated part of the world).

First, he enthusiastically explained how the paper worked (which didn't take long since there were only two employees—Vincent and Pierre, who was in charge). Then he carried on presenting the village and its residents. Vincent shared all the details of daily life: the people it was best to listen to, those to avoid, the best restaurants and food shops, the best bars and cafés . . .

His bachelor's routine suddenly began to change as well. In the morning, he took a bit more time to get ready. Standing in front of the mirror in the bathroom, Vincent now paid more attention to his appearance. The tiny flat he rented above a yarn shop watched silently as he underwent this metamorphosis. He shaved carefully, combed his hair, and the scent of cologne lingered in the air long after he had left for work. He had begun singing regularly and smiling for no apparent reason.

The dirty clothes that usually lay in a heap on the floor now found their way to the laundry basket. The beer bottles that had previously dotted every surface disappeared as if they had been a mirage, though admittedly a rather long-lasting one since Vincent hadn't invited a soul up to his one-bedroom flat for the past year. The iron emerged from the cupboard and the hoover came out of hibernation to suck up the crisp crumbs and long-forgotten bits of loose tobacco that littered the carpet.

At the office, the new Vincent was always watching Sandrine. He would pretend to be typing or pondering a headline for the article he was working on, but he was secretly contemplating the deus ex machina that had come to deliver a happy ending to his tragic love life. This morning, as he watched her leave for Wernst's farm, he realized he still didn't know much about her. They had engaged in pleasantries and small talk, but nothing more. He hadn't yet dared invite her to his flat. *Why don't you come over? We can kiss and then make love on the nice, clean carpet.* He fantasized about saying those words every night before falling asleep.

The little he knew about her could be summed up in a few sentences. She was from Paris, where it was hard to find a job as a journalist. She was an only child. She liked to be alone. The leather cuff bracelet she wore on her left wrist was a reminder (of what? She had carefully evaded the question), and yes, maybe one night once she was settled, she would have a drink with him after work.

The rest was the fruit of his careful observation: she was rather tall, about five foot seven, with fine, light-brown hair cut in a bob. Her features were sharp yet harmonious, her eyes were a hypnotic shade of hazel, and her breasts—which he could just make out despite the thick jumpers she wore—were as firm and round as Normandy apples. He had also noticed her lips. From his desk, he often saw them moving, though no sound escaped them. Sandrine spent her time mumbling silent sentences, as though her mind was unable to accommodate her thoughts, which fled their confinement through the silent and barely visible movements of her mouth. And every time (and this turned out to be rather often), this instinctive dance kindled in Vincent the desire to move closer and kiss them.

"And? The story?" he continued, after realizing he was gazing at Sandrine's mouth like a child lusting after a sweets display.

"Cows grazing in a muddy field with swastikas painted on their sides. The police think it was kids," she replied.

"Look on the bright side: you wouldn't have seen that in Paris!"

This seemed to be his favourite line. He brought it out on every possible occasion: talking about the upcoming livestock fair, the bumpy country roads, the tiny, dilapidated post office in town, and the villagers' boorish manners. The unique goal of this mantra was of course to convince his new colleague to never leave the region—or rather, to never leave him.

"No, that's for sure," she conceded.

"Sandrine?"

Shit, thought Sandrine, *he's going to ask. He's going to ask me for a drink and now I don't have a good excuse any more. Why can't he understand that I just want to be alone? Of course he doesn't understand, silly. He knows nothing about me. At least not enough to suspect anything.* Her wrist burned again, as it had earlier when she photographed the swastikas. She rubbed it discreetly against the pocket of her jeans, as if it were an itchy mosquito bite.

"Yes?"

"Pierre wants to see you. It seems serious," announced Vincent.

Pierre, her boss. Pierre who had offered her the job. One of his friends who worked in the capital had mentioned Sandrine. Pierre hadn't hesitated for a second—real journalists were a rare commodity in these parts.

Sandrine knocked nervously on the door to his office.

Your writing is great, but for the local readership . . .

That's what she expected to hear as she sat down across from Pierre. Her boss was in his fifties with curly hair and round, metallic-blue rimmed glasses, but at that moment he looked grave. She could already imagine herself back in Paris, knocking on doors and hoping for a contract, even as a free-lancer . . .

"How are you, Sandrine?" he asked, cutting to the chase.

She could smell cinnamon, though she couldn't work out where the scent was coming from.

"I'm good, thanks."

"Are you liking it here?" he asked as he pulled a plate of biscuits from his drawer. "I know it's not exactly Paris, but we put out a serious paper that people here really appreciate. Our customs probably seem strange to you, foreign even, but the people here are simple folk, and that can be comforting. Especially when you're used to the big city."

"Things are good. I'm getting used to it all: the onion festivals and Saint John's Eve," said Sandrine, though a part of her knew that wasn't really true. "But I think it will take a few more years before I'm willing to dress up and dance around the sacred fire . . ."

"Don't be so sure! You missed it this year, but believe me, it's rather enchanting!"

Sandrine imagined her boss without his tweed jacket and turtleneck, wearing nothing but traditional knickerbockers and dancing around the fire with a host of fake virgins.

"Here," he offered, holding out the plate of biscuits. "My wife has decided baking is the future of humanity. Every day she makes a new recipe. My blood sugar has reached record highs. I feel like I'm urinating glucose syrup these days."

"Thank you, but I already got to sample some regional delicacies at Mr Wernst's house. Maybe later."

Pierre put the plate down and sighed. He looked Sandrine steadily in the eye as he worked up the courage to speak. "Sandrine, I . . . I don't know how to go about this. The subject is . . . difficult."

Here they were at last. The temporal rift where the present collapses and she is forced back to the past. She'd have to move yet again. Leave this place to seek refuge somewhere else. Flee, again, beneath the unstable grey sky. Feel the burn of the scars on her wrist. Recite an old poem to forget.

"What is it?" Sandrine asked, already imagining his next words. Words she'd heard so many times before.

You're too distant. This job isn't the right fit for you. You should open up. Your colleagues are worried about you. Your work is good, but . . . That was one of the reasons she'd never felt at home in the big city. Too often, her acquaintances couldn't understand why she refused to go out with them in the evenings, why she preferred to be alone. Some of them saw it as disdain. Others as social ineptitude or even misanthropy. She had tried to explain that she was happier nestled comfortably in her solitude reading a book than in bars and nightclubs, but very few people understood. So Sandrine had finally acknowledged that moving somewhere more isolated might be the best solution.

"I'm sorry if I'm going about this all wrong," Pierre said apologetically, "but I got a call from a solicitor this morning."

"A solicitor?"

"Yes, a solicitor who sent you a letter a few weeks ago which was returned to him because the recipient no longer lived at that address. He managed to find out you worked here and sent it again. He also called me this morning to let me know it was urgent."

"What's urgent?"

"Your grandmother."

Sandrine sat back in her chair and went quiet.

Your grandmother. Did he mean "Granny Suzanne"? Her maternal grandmother whom she had never met? According to her mother, the crazy old woman lived on an island and had always refused to leave.

Pierre stood up, walked around his desk, and sat down next to Sandrine as he handed her the envelope. "Here's the letter," he said. "I'm afraid it's bad news. I'll leave you alone for a moment so you can . . . well, you know. I'll be next door if you need me."

Sandrine waited for the door to close, then opened the envelope.

Ms Sandrine Vaudrier,
I regret to inform you that Mrs Suzanne Vaudrier, née Hurteau, born 10th December 1912, wife of Jean Vaudrier and mother of Monique Vaudrier, has died at the age of seventy-three.

The death certificate was recorded on 27th October 1986 by the doctor and police officer present. They asked me to inform you and send you the death certificate at your last known address: 56 rue des Halles in Paris.

*When my original letter was returned to me, I conducted
some research and found your new employer.*

*I hereby inform you that the deceased registered a hand-
written will at my office on 25th October 1986. I thus invite
you to come to the address in the letterhead to learn more
about your grandmother's last wishes.*

In the meantime, I offer my sincerest condolences.

Best regards,

Jean-Baptiste Béguenau

Sandrine read the letter a second time.

She still didn't register any real emotion.

She muttered a quote aloud: "Mother died today. Or, maybe,
yesterday; I can't be sure." *The Stranger* by Albert Camus was
her favourite novel. When her friends criticized her need for
solitude and her lack of interest in the city's nightlife, she had
often identified with Meursault. And it was often in his presence, alone in her bed turning the pages of the book, that she
refuted their disapproval. And now that Pierre had announced
the death of one of her family members, she was, like Meursault,
a stranger to the grief she should have felt. Nevertheless, guilt
urged her to scan her memory for something to bring her closer
to her grandmother. But there was nothing to be found. Not
a single image of Suzanne. The only time she had ever spoken
to her mother about her, her curiosity had been quashed with
easy explanations that were as surprising as they were definitive.
"She's crazy. She'd rather stay on her tiny island than get to
know you, her only grandchild. You've never met her and, trust
me, you never will."

End of discussion. Nothing more to say.

Suzanne's existence had been erased from collective memory.
She had been removed from the family tree and her name
barred from the family dictionary. With just a few words, she
had become a taboo subject, and Sandrine had completely
forgotten about her until now.

"Shit," she mumbled.

She read the letter a third time, trying to persuade herself that it was in fact addressed to her, that there had been no mistake. Monique was definitely her mother's name.

I couldn't care less, she decided as she left Pierre's office. Her boss was standing just outside the door. Vincent's fingers stopped typing when she appeared.

"It's nothing important," she said.

"But the solicitor seemed to think it was . . ." Pierre replied, his voice full of concern.

"I . . . I never knew her. People can't just turn up in our lives all of a sudden. Especially when they're already dead."

Sandrine didn't realize it, but her voice had taken on a different tone, almost childlike, and her eyes were glazed. Her hands trembled slightly as she raised the letter in a rebellious gesture.

"I think you need to go," urged Pierre. "Take a week off."

"But . . . A day or two would be more than enough," she objected. "I just have to collect a stranger's things, nothing more."

"Well, you wouldn't exist without that 'stranger', Sandrine," Pierre reminded her. "Nothing else matters. I don't know anything about your family, but I do know that there is a little of her in you; you can't deny that. Some civilizations believed that when an ancestor died, their descendants lost a part of themselves. Not only in emotional terms, but also physically. That the atoms that come to us from our parents stopped living when they did, resulting in a physical sadness. They argued this was why grief makes people so tired."

"I don't think that—"

"Take a week," insisted her boss. "Nothing interesting will happen here before the livestock fair anyway. Maybe another cow or a pig will be spray-painted by bored teenagers . . . We'll make do without you. Go to that island, take care of your affairs, and come back rested. That's all I ask."

4

So the child recited the poem.

> *Who rides forth to-night, through storms so wild?*

Hesitantly at first.

> *A father, bearing his tender child;*

Then determinedly.

> *He fondly clasps the boy in his arm,*

To escape, to get away.

> *From danger shields him and keeps him warm.*

To be alone on their faraway island.

5

Suzanne

1949

"There it is. It's almost here."

Suzanne saw the boat draw slowly up alongside the island. It bobbed from side to side in the waves like a drunk sailor for a few more minutes. Then its bright green hull grew steady as it moored to the dock. Its noisy motor coughed up a thick cloud of black smoke, then went silent.

Someone took her hand: Françoise, the other governess.

Suzanne studied her friend's face, which was red from the freezing wind. Her woollen hood covered her hair, but a few wavy blonde strands had escaped and danced against her temples. She was wearing make-up. This was a special day. The gardener, Maurice, was there too, standing straight as an arrow. And Claude, the mysterious monocled doctor, and Simon, the handyman. The rest of the staff were already at the site, getting everything ready.

They were all certain they were helping to make the world a better place. That's how the director—who was standing as close as possible to the boat dressed only in his suit despite the cold—had framed their work here on the island. *Working to make the world a better place.* They had all smiled upon hearing that phrase. It might seem exaggerated, slightly pompous and pretentious, but it was so full of hope.

Men tightened the thick ropes around the mooring posts and carefully let down a wooden gangway between the boat and the dock. The director stepped nearer. He had been waiting

for this moment—they all had—for weeks. He already knew
the children. He had met all of them on the mainland, but
Suzanne could tell he was nervous from the way he was puffing
on his cigarette. There was no reason to worry. The camp was
ready. Over the next three months, the children would be able
to forget about the bombs. The deprivation. The fear. The smell
of dead bodies. They would be able to heal.

Making the world a better place.

He's right, it does feel that way.

First one head emerged from the hold and came into view.
Then another. Before long, a flock of children had crossed the
gangway.

Suzanne counted them.

Ten.

None were missing.

She already knew their names, though she had never met
any of them. The staff had received files on the children a week
before their arrival, to save precious time. The director had
thought of everything.

Now he was hugging the first camper. Each of them would
get a hug.

The children had taken their first steps on the island and
were now approaching Suzanne, their eyes on the ground. They
didn't return her smile, but she didn't mind. The war had taught
them to keep their heads down and be suspicious of smiling
adults. But she was hopeful that would change.

The staff and children began their walk to the camp with
the director leading the way. He talked the whole time, trying
to reassure and comfort his young charges with his words as
they took the path that led away from the dock and into the
forest. The children kept quiet. But one bit of information did
get their attention.

"There will be hot chocolate when we arrive!" exclaimed
the director.

Suzanne saw the surprise in their eyes. Their lips parted
gently. Now they stared at the director, hoping to learn more.

It was possible that some of them had never tasted hot chocolate before. But the word was enough to make them feel safe, especially when one of the older children, Fabian, asked, "Really?"

"Oh yes, Fabian, *really*. Unless our dear cook has drunk it all!"

"Thank you, sir!"

"No need to thank me. None of you need to. You're my guests. The war is over, children. It's time to stop growing up too quickly."

Less than ten minutes later, they left the small forest behind them and the concrete walls of the former blockhouse came into view. A few of the children chattered excitedly when they saw the sports field Simon had prepared. He had cut the grass very short and built two goals using old pillars from the dock. He had even managed to mount a basketball hoop on a mast he had salvaged from the mainland. But best of all was undoubtedly the garden Maurice had created. He had planted a bit of everything: vegetables, fruit trees, herbs . . . Everything the cook, Victor, needed. And enough to feed the chickens and pigs, which were housed a bit further down the path, as well. The director had planned it all out. There were dairy cows and a few donkeys for rides around the island. Suzanne smiled when it occurred to her that some of the children were probably seeing these animals for the first time.

As they neared the first building, they were gently enveloped by the sweet aroma of hot chocolate.

Soon they'll see their rooms, Suzanne thought happily. *They'll be able to get back to being children and the simple pleasure of blowing on a warm cup of hot chocolate . . .*

Making the world a better place.

6

Sandrine

November 1986

Sandrine exited the station at two thirty and took a taxi to the centre of town.

She had hesitated for a long time. Her grandmother had never tried to contact her only grandchild, had never tried to find out how she was doing. She had never sent Sandrine a card or even picked up the phone to call her. So why should she go? What could she possibly hope to find on that island? Her mother would have forbidden her to go, she was certain of it. Monique would have tried to convince her, told her again and again that the past is the past. But Monique had never been able to follow her own advice—she had never had the strength to free herself from the anger and disgust she felt for Sandrine's father. So why should she listen to her?

Sandrine realized that her trip to the island would be her last chance to learn a bit more about her grandmother and carve words other than *crazy* on Suzanne's tombstone. And Pierre had insisted. He had told her not to come in for a week . . .

The apathetic grey sky watched impassively as she made her way through the streets, and the seagulls seemed no more inclined to acknowledge her presence. The ocean's muffled roar was the acoustic background to the cacophony of cars and conversations. Halliards bounced off masts as sporadic gusts of wind filled the sails of the pleasure crafts in the harbour. Sandrine was delighted by the din. Noise was what she missed the most since moving to her small village. More than the people. She was used to the tumult of the capital and had never been in a place where cars passed at intervals of many minutes rather than seconds. When she walked to work in the morning, she rarely crossed paths with anyone, and her breath was the only sound that reached her ears. So this walk through the centre of Villers-sur-Mer filled her with happiness. The cheerful bustle soothed her.

After ten minutes of wandering aimlessly, Sandrine decided to ask for directions. A woman pointed her towards a street across from the beach, near the marina.

Minutes later, she stepped into the solicitor's office.

"Ms Vaudrier!" exclaimed Jean-Baptiste Béguenau. He was short and stout and nearly bald. He welcomed her inside with a grave look on his face, as though all wars past and present were his responsibility. Sandrine accepted his condolences and followed him into his office, noticing as she did so that he was slightly cross-eyed—a fact she immediately tried, and failed, to ignore. The place smelled of order and turpentine. A large bookcase full of carefully arranged files occupied an entire wall across from a window that looked out over the ocean. There was no clutter: no family photographs, no cup of cold coffee, and no documents scattered around. The most exotic element in the room was the large green plant sitting on the floor in a corner, as if forgotten. Sandrine had the uncomfortable feeling that she was visiting a show home.

"Please, sit down and thank you for coming all the way here, Ms Vaudrier. I won't keep you long. Just a few signatures and you'll be on your way," the solicitor said as he pulled out a brown file.

His leather chair squeaked when he moved. He placed the documents down on the desk in front of him, examined them one last time, nodding and murmuring in approval as he read, then slid them over to Sandrine.

"Just sign here and here. Do take the time to read every sentence. They're all there, unless one has escaped," he joked.

His muffled laugh echoed for a few seconds, then disappeared. *Carefully judged to avoid seeming uncouth given the circumstances,* thought Sandrine. *He probably practises in front of a mirror though it sounds more like a faulty firework falling back down to earth without exploding than a frank and comforting laugh.*

Sandrine quickly scanned the will and signed where necessary. She wanted to get out of there quickly, especially since there wasn't much to learn. Suzanne had left her some personal affairs in her house and a little money in a bank account, though the amount wasn't specified. That was it.

"What now?" she asked, pushing the papers back towards the solicitor.

"Your boat leaves in half an hour," he replied. "You'll need this."

"What is it?"

"An authorization to visit the island. It's been a natural wildlife reserve for seabirds since 1971, so visitors are normally prohibited."

"You mean it's . . . deserted?" she asked worriedly.

The idea of wandering an abandoned rock with no company but the birds sounded more like a Hitchcockian nightmare than an opportunity to commemorate her grandmother. It occurred to her that a solitary life surrounded by only the sound of the rolling waves and the cries of gulls could at least partially explain Suzanne's madness.

"No, not exactly," he explained. "A handful of people still live there. Your grandmother was one of them. They moved there a few years after the war. And the island's owner couldn't bear to evict them. They're allowed to stay, but no other people are authorized. Except when someone . . . passes. Then relatives can go over just long enough to gather the deceased's affairs and pay their final respects."

Sandrine noticed a slight tremble in Mr Béguenau's voice. When she looked away to avoid his eyes, she realized that the only clock in the room had stopped. Its hands read 8:37, when she knew it was nearly three thirty. And its pendulum was perfectly still. She couldn't say why, but the frozen clock bothered her more than it should have. She was surprised that the solicitor, whose office was exceptionally orderly, would tolerate such an anomaly. She thought back to the farmer's remark the day before: *Time is relative.*

"Your clock's broken," she couldn't help but say.

"Oh, you're right. I hadn't noticed. I always forget to wind it." He changed the subject smoothly. "So, you'll need to show this authorization when you board. You can't make the crossing without it. If the authorities do a spot check and find an un-authorized visitor aboard, the captain would be in serious trouble."

"What . . . What will I find there, on the island?"

"I'm afraid I can't tell you exactly what your grandmother owned. She didn't specify in her will. The house isn't hers, in any case. She was renting it. I think it will mostly be personal effects, maybe old photographs, jewellery, who knows really."

The solicitor spread out a large piece of paper which showed a rudimentary map drawn in black marker. The island was pear-shaped. The dock was located near the bottom. Moving inland, twenty small squares—most likely houses—appeared. The only path from the dock came to a fork. The left-hand branch led to the houses while the right-hand branch led to the forest and then disappeared altogether. Her grandmother's house, marked with a red X, and an adjoining outbuilding symbolized by a rectangle, were the only constructions on this side of the island, just before the path entered the forest.

"It's rather basic, I'll grant you that," affirmed Mr Béguenau, "but it should suffice. The island isn't very big. Only about thirty hectares. But it's quite steep, particularly the northern part, so be careful if you decide to go for a walk."

"Did she give you this map?" asked Sandrine.

"Yes, I saw her once, two days before she died. She came to drop off her will."

"How did she seem?"

"What do you mean?"

"I mean, did she seem 'normal'? Did she have her wits about her?"

"Ms Vaudrier, if I had had even the slightest doubt as to her mental capacities, I wouldn't have accepted the will. I would have asked her to come back with a medical certificate proving her good health. There are rules in this profession. There may be a broken clock in this office, but never a client off her rocker."

"I didn't mean to cast doubt on your professionalism, I'm sorry. It's just— "

"Your boat awaits, Ms Vaudrier," he said, cutting her off as he stood up. "There won't be any others today."

He accompanied her to the door and pointed to the boat in question. It was about ten metres long and a pale emerald green colour, clearly faded from years of exposure to the sun and inclement weather.

"The crossing won't take more than an hour," he reassured her. "The sea is calm. I'll see you soon, Ms Vaudrier. Please feel free to stop by when you get back!"

7

Sandrine

November 1986

When she left the solicitor's office, Sandrine had the uncomfortable feeling that several hours had gone by without her noticing. The sky had grown dark and the sun's dying rays informed her it was the end of the day, though she was certain she had gone into his office around three o'clock. *The meeting only lasted an hour, though.* It was as though an invisible veil had been placed over everything around her to temper its natural colours, as if someone somewhere had lowered the lights on the world.

She walked towards the end of the dock and the boat Mr Béguenau had pointed out. Determined to keep her trip as short as possible, she was already thinking of how she would get rid of her grandmother's things. She would bring nothing back to the mainland. She would invite the remaining residents to her grandmother's house and let them take whatever they liked. Sandrine was certain the idea would ensure the place was empty in record time, allowing her to take the boat back the next day and return to her normal life.

She caught sight of two men loading bags and boxes onto the deck. One of them, the younger of the two, stopped working as she drew closer.

"Are you looking for something?" he asked.

He had dark eyes and Sandrine couldn't help noticing the muscles in his arms. She felt like there was a hint of guilt in his gaze, as if she'd caught him red handed.

"You're going to the island, right?" she asked shyly.

"We are."

"The solicitor told me to give you this."

The young man put down the wooden crate he was carrying and read the document she gave him. Suddenly, his features brightened. His brown irises became friendly, inviting even. Sandrine thought at first that there had been a mistake, that Mr Béguenau had been wrong, that this boat, the *Lazarus* according to the name painted in white letters on the hull, wasn't going to her destination. But the sailor handed back the piece of paper and smiled awkwardly. "So you're Suzanne's granddaughter?"

"Yes."

"I'm sorry for your loss. I really liked Suzanne. She was a kind woman. Really . . ." he said, trailing off and looking down.

"I . . . Thank you. I never met her . . . I'm Sandrine," she said holding out her hand.

"Oh, I'm Paul. I handle supplies with Simon. We'll leave as soon as everything's on board. Look, he's over there," he said, pointing towards the bow. "You'll need to show him your authorization. He acts like a bear with a sore head but don't worry about it. He's a real sailor and has the attitude to go with it. Go ahead, climb aboard and get settled. I won't be long."

Sandrine walked down the gangway and then headed towards the tiny cockpit.

The way Paul had praised her grandmother seemed strange to her. *Maybe he's just being polite? He probably doesn't know how crazy she was and how she neglected her family . . .*

"Can I help you?" asked the sturdy man in a cap who had suddenly appeared in front of her. He was in his sixties and waited for her reply with his bushy eyebrows drawn into a frown. He smelled of motor oil and a freshly smoked cigarette. His huge frame forced Sandrine to look up at him and it took her a few seconds to get over her initial fear. While he waited for her to reply, Simon stood stock still, his lips pursed and arms tensed as if he were readying himself to throw her overboard if what she said displeased him.

"I . . . I . . ." stuttered Sandrine.

"Don't worry, Simon," said Paul with a laugh. "She's Suzanne's granddaughter! You can relax."

Simon's expression didn't change as he held out his hand and Sandrine gave him the document.

"My condolences," he mumbled as he stuffed the paper in the back pocket of his denim coveralls. "Is this all your luggage?" he asked, raising an eyebrow.

"Yes, why would—"

"You're not one of those damn journalists who are desperate to visit the island, are you?" he asked, coming closer. "The last time one of them tried it, I acted like everything was normal, then threw her overboard when we were halfway there."

His abrupt tone and piercing gaze made Sandrine shiver. Did he know that she was a journalist? Should she mention it? Tell him that this was strictly a personal trip?

"I'm only kidding, Miss," he said finally with a satisfied smile that revealed a missing tooth. "The solicitor told us to expect you. Relax. We'll be on our way soon. Paul! Hurry up! I want to get there before dark! You can sit on one of the wooden benches on the deck. It's still warm enough out. If you're going to be sick, don't lean too far out. I don't want to have to stop the motor to fish you out of the sea. Speaking of which, don't forget to put on your lifejacket. It's mandatory."

Sandrine got settled at the back of the boat and put on her lifejacket.

Meanwhile, Paul loaded the last crates, untied the moorings, put away the gangway, and disappeared into the cockpit with Simon.

The *Lazarus* rumbled to life but at first didn't seem to want to leave the dock. Eventually, after a few choice swear words from Simon, the boat began to move. It made its way out to sea slowly, almost regretfully, as though weighed down with irrational fear.

8

Sandrine

November 1986

"How are you doing?"

The *Lazarus* was speeding across the choppy sea. Paul had just emerged from the cockpit. Sandrine was sitting on the floor of the boat, her back resting against a large bag of who knew what. She was surprised to find her stomach was holding up. Nevertheless, she carefully avoided looking out at the unsteady horizon.

"Don't judge a book by its cover," he said, nearly shouting so she could hear him over the sound of the motor. "If you fell overboard, Simon would be the first to jump in after you."

"Don't tempt me," she replied with a smile.

"Are you cold?"

"No, I'm fine, thanks. Paul, can I ask you a question?"

"Of course."

"When I turned up earlier, why did you say my grandmother was a good person?" she asked earnestly. The question had been gnawing away at her since she'd climbed aboard the *Lazarus*. She didn't doubt Paul's sincerity for a second. But that's what bothered her the most. She could tell it had been more than simply politeness, more than just a trite expression aimed at easing the pain of Suzanne's death. Sandrine was convinced that his words had come from the heart, and that he would have said the same before her grandmother's death.

A good person . . .

That didn't fit with the image she had of a woman willing to cut all ties with her family to live on an island.

"Because she was," Paul replied matter-of-factly as he sat down next to her. "I started working on the island when I was sixteen. I'm twenty-eight now. From the very first time we met, Suzanne always offered me a warm welcome. The others kept their distance and only spoke to me when they needed to give me their orders. She even admitted once that she was glad to meet an 'outsider'."

"Their orders?" inquired Sandrine, her eyebrow raised.

"Yes, Simon and I are stewards of the island. We make regular trips to and from the mainland to deliver medicine, food, and so on to its residents. We're also responsible for handling any work that needs to be done, from roof repairs to faulty fuses. We're the island handymen!"

"That sounds like a lot of work!"

"Not as much as it once was. There are only five people left on the island . . . Sorry, four now."

"Only four?" Sandrine repeated, surprised. "Just four people on the whole island?"

"Yes. Most of the time there's only Maurice, Victor, Claude, and Françoise. It's not very big, you know. You can walk all the way around it in a single day. Once every two months, a team of scientists arrives to count and identify the birds. Their visits liven the place up and give Victor a reason to use the kitchen in the guesthouse. But most of the time it's just them."

"What do they do out here?"

"They wait . . . They're waiting for their lives to be over, really. When he decided to turn the island into a nature reserve, the owner promised them they could stay until the end. He would never force them to leave. It was a generous decision on his part because the island can't be officially designated as a nature reserve until the last human has gone. In the meantime, the scientists are using the time to set up and survey the local fauna."

"But why on earth do they want to stay?" asked Sandrine more harshly than intended.

The question wasn't really addressed to Paul but to the grandmother who had remained a stranger her whole life.

"I don't know," he replied. He paused for a minute, then leaned closer. "Sandrine, do you really not know anything about this island?"

"No," she confessed.

She would have liked to add that she didn't know anything about the woman whose house she had come to visit for the first and last time either. But she was too ashamed.

"Well," he said, turning towards her, "in that case, I'll give you a quick rundown. But on one condition . . ."

"What's that?"

"You have dinner with me at the guesthouse tonight."

"It's open?" she asked, her eyes wide.

"Imagine an island with just a handful of people living on it. What would they need to keep from going mad with loneliness?"

"A place to get together. With alcohol," she replied, amused by how obvious it was.

"Precisely! And when the scientists turn up, let me tell you, they're just as glad to have a place out of the wind to have a drink together! Victor, the chef, opens it every day. He usually doesn't bother firing up the kitchen. He just serves drinks. But every time we arrive, he's got a freshly prepared meal waiting for us. I think it keeps him busy, gives him a reason to get up in the morning . . ."

"All right then," she agreed. "Indoors in the warm with a nice beer and not too many people. I think I'll survive . . . You're officially my tour guide! I'm all ears."

"Great," said Paul, moving a bit closer to her. "It all dates back to the Second World War. During the Occupation, the island was a command post for the German army. They built a blockhouse there, and accommodation for the personnel. When the war was over, they abandoned the island. The French government decided to sell it to finance their reconstruction plans, as they did with many small islands used by the Germans. That's when the current owner came into the picture. Apparently, he already had plans to preserve the island as a natural habitat for wildlife. But he didn't demolish the German buildings because he ended up having another idea when he finally visited the site: a holiday camp."

"A holiday camp?" she asked doubtfully as she pulled up the collar on her coat.

"Yes, for children who'd grown up during the war. It opened in late summer 1949. It wasn't too far from the coast and their families, but just far enough to help them forget their suffering and hardships. To launch the project, the new owner hired staff: a cook, doctors, governesses, a gardener . . . That's how the current residents found their way to the island."

"You mean my grandmother worked at the camp?"

"That's right."

Sandrine did a bit of mental arithmetic. Her grandmother had been born in 1912 according to the death certificate, so she would have been thirty-seven when the camp opened. As for Sandrine's mother, she would have been twenty when Suzanne first set foot on the island.

"So that's why she couldn't leave the island all those years," Sandrine said finally. "I had no idea—"

"It's not quite that simple," Paul interrupted.

"What do you mean?"

"The camp didn't stay open for long."

"What happened?"

"A terrible tragedy struck in late October 1949. They had planned a trip to the mainland because the staff were worried about the children, who seemed increasingly miserable. The doctors concluded that it wasn't a physical problem—just homesickness. The director decided that a day with their parents would do them a world of good. They would get all the affection they had been missing, and their parents would be able to see their children were in good health. Because in addition to being a breath of fresh air far from the ruins and chaotic reconstruction of the country, the camp also provided three balanced meals a day: the perfect environment for healing the wounds—both physical and emotional—caused by the war. The campers could play sport, go horse riding, discover the island's plants and animals, sleep in real beds, listen to the radio in a heated room, and much more. There was even a classroom. All in all, the island was a chance for each child to pick up his or her childhood right where the Germans had interrupted it. And their time away meant the parents could rebuild their homes and lives without worrying about their children for the three months they were away. But the outing didn't go to plan. As soon as they'd left the dock, the boat encountered a problem and started sinking. All of the children fell into the icy water and most of them didn't know how to swim."

"How awful!"

"Not one of them survived. The adults managed to reach the shore. Out of desperation, some of them dived back into the water to try to save the children, but it was all in vain. The current had already pulled their little bodies out to sea."

Sandrine was speechless for several long minutes. She imagined the children fighting to stay afloat in a raging sea— the same one she was travelling across now. It had been thirty-seven years since the tragedy, but she felt like she could hear their high, clear voices calling for help. She also thought about how terrible her grandmother must have felt. That sort of grief could drag anyone down into madness . . .

"I think the staff stayed to honour the children's memory. They rarely talk about it, but when you look in their eyes you can see it still weighs on them heavily."

"What happened after that?" Sandrine asked, finding it hard to speak.

"The owner decided to close the camp for good. He went back to the mainland and no one ever saw him again. He still pays a pension to the remaining residents, and he pays Simon's salary and my own every month to make sure we take good care of the last people with memories from back then. I've only ever dealt with his solicitor, Mr Béguenau, regarding my contract and occasional paperwork . . ."

"Were you there?" Sandrine asked bluntly.

"When?"

"When they found Suzanne."

"No. I live on the mainland. I found out when I came back."

"Who found her?" she asked, looking down at the deck.

"Probably one of them. Have you read Claude's report? He's the doctor on the island."

"Yes, it says it was a heart attack. What do they do with the remains?"

"They inform the family and wait for instructions. Sometimes the families want to bring the bodies back with them, but most of the deceased have asked to be buried here, in the cemetery."

"There's even a cemetery?" asked Sandrine in surprise.

"Yes," Paul replied sombrely. "A sadly symbolic place filled with tiny graves . . ."

"Paul!" shouted Simon. "Enough jibber-jabber! Come and get ready!"

The *Lazarus* had slowed, but Sandrine and Paul had been too engrossed in their conversation to notice. Now Simon's voice brought them back to the present with a jolt.

"I need to get to the bow and help guide us in," said Paul as he stood up.

Sandrine watched as the island drew nearer. She caught sight of a wooden jetty and remembered the map the solicitor had shown her. She turned towards the left-hand side of the island and saw the roofs of the small houses beyond the line of boulders and pines. To the right, on the other side of the island, there was a thick forest which, according to her grandmother's drawing, lay next to Suzanne's house. From this distance, all of it seemed ridiculously small, like a miniature model of reality. But as they got closer, the island's true dimensions became clear. Its dark, rocky cliffs glistening with sea spray grew taller as though the tectonic plates were silently shifting beneath them. The trees also seemed suddenly thicker as they stretched up towards the threatening clouds. The sea came to life as well. It had been calm and comforting for the entire crossing, but now

seemed to writhe tormentedly from the depths, making it difficult for Simon to manoeuvre the boat. Sandrine clung to the
railing.

"The currents around the island are strong and unpredict-
able," he shouted. "But don't worry—it'll be over soon!"

Sandrine thought about how rough the water must have
been for the children, how hard it would have been to avoid
the sharp rocks that jutted out of the water.

Ten minutes later, the boat had docked. Sandrine was relieved
to set foot on dry land. She stood still for several minutes,
taking deep breaths of the salty air and trying to calm the
rocking in the pit of her stomach. A narrow shingle beach lay
before her, the place "where waves go to die" as sailors would
say. Its grey pebbles were a far cry from the welcoming white
sand of a Pacific beach and the whole area was festooned with
trailing clumps of seaweed—looking like the remnants of a
monster straight out of Lovecraft.

Christ, Granny, couldn't you have died in the Seychelles?

Paul flashed a mocking smile as he came over. He didn't
seem to have been affected by the rough ride. In fact, he seemed
less steady on land than out at sea.

"I'll meet you at the guesthouse," he said as he loaded a
wooden crate onto a cart.

"I . . . Okay, but I need to go to Suzanne's to drop off my
things first."

"Not tonight, Sandrine. It'll be dark soon, and believe me,
it's not a good idea to sleep near the forest on your first night
on the island. Take advantage of your week here to get to know
the residents! They'll be delighted to meet you and tell you all
about Suzanne. There will be a room waiting for you at the
guesthouse. That is unless you'd rather sleep in a strange house
just a few steps from a haunted forest . . ."

"Haunted? I'm not ten years old, and . . . Wait, what? What
do you mean a week?"

"That's our schedule. We stay a week, fix what needs fixing,
then go back and spend a week on the mainland."

"I'm sorry? Are you telling me that I'm stuck on this island for a week?"

"Exactly. Mr Béguenau really needs to learn to explain things properly," mumbled Paul under his breath.

"Oh, bloody hell! I can't stay that long!" protested Sandrine.

"Listen, I have to unload the supplies. It'll take me an hour or two. Meet me at the guesthouse and don't worry. You'll see, time passes quickly here."

Paul made his way back to the boat. Sandrine couldn't believe it. A whole week on this rock in the middle of nowhere! Of course, it was no longer than the time off Pierre had forced her to take, but she never planned to spend all of it stuck on the island. She went through the contents of her suitcase in her head. She would have enough to make it to the end of the week, but she still couldn't swallow the idea. *Tomorrow or the day after at the latest, I'll ask Simon to take me back. I'll pay for the crossing if need be, but I can't stay here. I'll go mad!*

She followed the footpath, ignoring the first raindrops as they escaped from the clouds above.

9

Suzanne

1949

If someone had asked Suzanne to describe what childhood meant to her, she would have replied "a sense of wonder".

That was what she was seeing in the children at that moment. But she was afraid it might disappear when they approached the former blockhouse. Afraid the menacing-looking structure would frighten the campers, extinguishing their carefree attitude and even childhood itself. She feared they would forget the smell of hot chocolate, though it was growing stronger by the minute, feared they would begin to doubt, as they had during the long nights spent in dark, fragile dwellings watching the terror in their parents' eyes. And in some ways, that's exactly what happened. It was barely perceptible, but the shift was real.

As soon as they spied the large concrete building, the children slowed. None of them had ever seen a blockhouse before, but they must have heard about them. Just like they'd heard about death camps, concentration camps, Dachau and Auschwitz—all terms which had been on grown-ups' lips since the Liberation. Words their parents spoke gravely in sharp contrast with the half-smiles they produced when talking about rainbows or Christmas.

Out of habit, the children looked up to scan their surroundings. They were looking for any type of danger and for an explanation as to why these concrete walls were still standing, as if they knew nothing of the war that had just ended or were preparing for a new one.

Finally—and it took Suzanne several seconds to realize it—

the campers moved closer together and the crocodile of children tightened. Instinctively. To protect one another from a danger they had yet to identify.

Recognizing their distress, the director spoke up, standing between them and the blockhouse. "You're right," he said in a calm and reassuring voice. "This was built by the Germans. And it's terribly ugly, too! But believe me, if they knew what we'd done with it, they would *not* be pleased! Follow me and you'll see what I mean."

And that was that.

The line began moving forward again, towards the main entrance. One of the children, Louise, held tight to Suzanne's hand as the group made its way into the building whose very walls seemed to be exuding the aroma of chocolate. The long, damp corridor led to an unexpectedly large room. Françoise couldn't help but admit that the bloody Krauts knew what they were doing when it came to architecture. She repressed the urge to spit on the floor and curse them, aware that it would set a bad example for the children.

Besides, what had been was no more.

The military equipment, grey walls, and battle plans had been replaced by a long dining table under a ceiling painted with a sunny sky. On all four walls of the huge room, the sad, pale, unfinished cement, testament to a different, more destructive world, had been covered with brightly coloured murals: a field of flowers, a huge rainbow, a sea full of friendly creatures, and a mountain dotted with animals of all kinds. The children exclaimed aloud in wonder. They walked over to the walls to touch them, to make sure it wasn't a dream, that reality wasn't deceiving them. Just then, Victor, the cook, appeared out of nowhere, like a magician taking the stage. He was smiling so broadly he could have been in one of the paintings, and he was pushing a cart loaded with cups of hot chocolate.

"When I make a promise, I deliver!" announced the director as he encouraged the children to help themselves.

The group disbanded, fearless now. They reached out for

the cups eagerly, their hands no longer trembling. After that, the room went silent. Then, slowly but surely, their lips coated in a layer of chocolatey foam, they began to smile.

Once they'd finished their drinks, the director led them to another corridor and a series of open doors. "These are your rooms," he explained. "Your names are written on the doors. We'll let you get settled. When you're ready, we'll gather again in the room we've just left and present the schedule for your stay here. These rooms are yours now, so feel free to move the furniture around if you want to. Take your time and get comfortable. There will be more hot chocolate served in an hour if you like. But no obligation. There's a clock there, at the far end of the corridor. See you in a little while."

One after another, the children disappeared into their respective rooms. From the corridor, the staff could hear them laughing and calling out to one another. Because here too, the dull cement had been covered in delightful imaginary worlds: colourful clowns, green prairies, groups of children holding hands, their names painted in multicoloured letters . . .

Suzanne felt a tear roll down her cheek. *Good thing I didn't put on make-up like Françoise,* she thought with a smile.

Then she turned back the way she had come, leaving the children to their wonder.

IO

Sandrine

November 1986

Sandrine found the village of roughly twenty houses without difficulty. As she approached, she recalled what Paul had said about the Nazi base, the former employees, and the scientists who regularly visited the island. Built from solid stone, the identical buildings were simple, even austere. More like headstones than inviting homes.

She made her way to the biggest structure, which was the only one with two floors. She could see lights on inside and she assumed it must be the guesthouse. She could smell the enticing aroma of stewed meat and a thick tower of smoke rose from the chimney. She pushed through the door and was welcomed by a wave of comforting warmth that dried the droplets of cold drizzle on her coat.

Flames danced in the fireplace of the deserted room which contained a dozen tables surrounded by chairs. At the far end, a long staircase led to the floor above. At the foot of the stairs sat a small desk, which clearly marked the limit between the common areas and those reserved for guests. Sandrine rolled her suitcase over the various rugs decorating the floor and headed for the improvised reception desk. She noticed the bar with several beers on tap and the jukebox glowing silently against the wall.

"Wow," she said to herself under her breath. "I can see why this place is the centre of life on the island!" She could already see herself sipping a cold drink next to the fire and enjoying some classic jazz in the background.

She shook the bell on the desk and waited for someone to appear. Almost immediately, she heard the rumble of a male voice behind a door, and a few seconds later she was face to face with Victor. She liked him right away. He was of average height, but his big eyes made him look perpetually astonished and childlike. Sandrine noticed that he limped as he made his way towards her.

"Sandrine, I'm so glad to finally meet you! I wish it were under happier circumstances, but Suzanne didn't suffer. Claude assured us of that," he explained as he wiped his hands on his long apron.

Much to Sandrine's surprise, the cook came around the desk and took her in his arms.

"My condolences, truly. I share your pain—we all loved your grandmother very much," he said softly in her ear.

Sandrine smiled at Victor once he had released her from his embrace. She suddenly felt shy, unsure of how to respond. "Thank you," she said eventually.

"Your room is waiting for you," Victor continued. "The solicitor told me you'd be coming. But first, why don't you sit down for a minute. The crossing always makes people thirsty. Would you like a beer?"

"I'd love one, thank you," Sandrine replied gratefully.

"So, you've met Simon and Paul?"

"Yes. We chatted a bit. Well, Paul and I did," she clarified.

"Ah, Simon . . . That old bastard isn't exactly friendly, I suppose," said Victor with a chuckle. He slipped behind the counter. "But he's a good sort."

Victor pulled two pints as he watched his guest explore the room. "Memories from another life," he explained as she leaned in for a better look at the framed photographs on the wall across from the fireplace.

Sandrine found herself quickly absorbed by the pictures, most of which were black and white. Snippets of what life must have been like on the island in the early years. In one of them, a dozen people posed proudly, like a football team, their backs to a huge blockhouse. She recognized Victor thanks to his chef's garb, but she wasn't sure if another man was Simon. He was tall enough, but the young man's smile contrasted so drastically with the gruff sailor she had met earlier that it seemed unlikely. Sandrine looked for her grandmother too, but without having any clues to her appearance, she couldn't decide between the two women. One of them was rather short and was wearing a lot of make-up. The other was very thin, her eyes looking away from the camera. The poor quality of the images didn't make things any easier.

Several of the pictures showed the same people in different situations: gardening, sitting around a table in a room with brightly painted walls, playing basketball, smoking on a boulder overlooking the sea . . . *Even the island is glowing,* she thought as she studied the few colour photographs, which presumably had been taken using Kodachrome film. It felt like the holiday camp tragedy had since muted the formerly bright hues of the island. Back then, the residents' houses were decorated with pots of flowers and the sea seemed bluer. The sky was a far cry from the threatening grey that now weighed heavily upon the island.

But this dichotomy of colour wasn't what bothered her the most.

As she moved to the right, she discovered another collection of photographs. Pictures of the children. The story Paul had told her suddenly resonated inside her, like a ghost story whispered on the wind. The campers were also posed in front of the blockhouse. They all seemed to be about the same age, and their faces radiated a timid joy. They had also been photographed going about their days. On horseback, picking fruit, or throwing balls. In the last picture, the children were all seated in front of a blackboard covered in maths problems. They had their backs to the camera. A map of France hung on one of the walls next to a round clock and a row of coat pegs.

The classroom.

After that picture, the documentation stopped abruptly, the sudden emptiness mirroring the brutality of their deaths. Sandrine suddenly felt cold, as though she had stepped outside into the freezing drizzle.

"Here, this will do you good," said Victor, offering her one of the pints of beer. He placed a friendly hand on her shoulder. "Given the look on your face, I gather you've heard all about it?"

"Yes, Paul told me during the crossing," she admitted. "What a terrible thing to happen."

"Yes. It was an unbearable loss with many repercussions. But that's enough of that. Sit down and warm up. The others should be here soon."

She got settled at the table closest to the fire, beneath the framed photographs.

"The others?" she asked.

"Yes. I know at least one person who is very eager to meet you: Françoise! She and your grandmother were inseparable! She's the one with the make-up."

"So, the other woman is my grandmother?"

"Yes. Suzanne . . ."

"I didn't know she was so beautiful . . ."

"Beautiful, clever, and incredibly kind. We miss her dearly," said Victor with a sigh, gazing at the picture.

"Why have you all stayed here on the island? Why don't you go back to the mainland?" asked Sandrine after swallowing her first sip of beer.

"Because we're prisoners, my dear. Plain and simple," replied Victor enigmatically, staring at the photographs.

She waited for him to elaborate, but he had gone quiet. For the first time since they'd met, Victor stopped smiling and looked away absently, as though he had escaped from his body for a moment, his attention drawn to another time and place.

"What do you mean, 'prisoners'?" Sandrine finally asked.

"Oh, you'll have to forgive me. I'm rambling . . ." he said, coming back to life. "Seeing you here reminds me of Suzanne and . . . I'm sorry. Sometimes my old brain drifts off course . . . Enjoy your beer. I'm off to make dinner. Paul is always ravenous, and you could stand to put some meat on your bones. I'll see you in a bit."

Then he padded discreetly back to the kitchen, his footsteps surprisingly light despite his limp.

Sandrine polished off her pint in silence, watching the sunset through the windows. The wind coming off the ocean was barrelling into the branches of the pines, and if she listened closely, she could hear its eerie chant. Darkness finally engulfed the landscape. The glistening boulders turned into threatening shadows—unmoving soldiers waiting to attack. She was grateful she had listened to Paul's advice earlier. She tried to imagine herself alone in her grandmother's austere house, surrounded by the dark, anxiety-inducing natural world, sitting amid the furniture and the memories like a ghost. *And let's not forget the haunted forest,* she thought sarcastically, thinking back to Paul's words.

Just then, the doors to the guesthouse opened and an old woman stepped inside, doubled over to protect herself from the wind. A stray gust took advantage and blew in with her, leaving a smattering of tiny raindrops on the doormat.

She put down her umbrella, glanced at Sandrine, then headed straight to the jukebox. She fumbled around inside her jacket pocket, selected a song, and leaned over to put the coins in the slot. Piano music filled the room, accompanied by the first warm, crackly words of a song from the interwar years, instantly enveloping the place in nostalgia.

> *Speak to me of love,*
> *And say what I'm longing to hear,*
> *Tender words of love,*
> *Repeat them again.*

Sandrine felt a lump in her throat.
  This song . . .

She was engulfed by a strange feeling, her senses alert.

A feeling of danger that she didn't know how to interpret. It rekindled an uncomfortable sensation she knew she had felt before, though she didn't know when or where. As she stared at the new arrival, who was now making her way towards the table, an unwelcome tingling spread throughout her body. When the old woman parted her lips, which were generously covered in shiny red lipstick, Sandrine remembered now where she had felt this uneasiness: when she was leaving the farm with the swastika-painted cows, when she had seen her meticulously cleaned trainers on the porch . . .

> *By all the little stars above you,*
> *Your voice is like a fun caress,*
> *It thrills me till I must confess,*
> *I long to hear the voice that brings me,*
> *Such thrilling love and happiness.*
>
> *Parlez-moi d'amour,*
> *Redites-moi ces mots supprimés,*
> *Je vous aime . . .*

"Hello, my dear," said Françoise as she pushed a strand of grey hair away from her face. "I'm so pleased to meet you. We have a lot to talk about."

I I

Suzanne

1949

"Françoise!"

"I'm only tasting the sauce!"

"I hope your hands are clean, at least!" scolded Victor as he vigorously beat something in a saucepan.

Françoise shot Suzanne a conspiratorial glance. Her friend was smiling and leaning over the counter as she peeled the carrots, being careful not to dirty her clothes.

"Oh, my dear Victor," Françoise purred, "such skilled hands should be put to much better use, doing something other than ripping out chicken giblets and making hot chocolate . . . The war is over. The only thing that should be standing to attention is . . ."

"Françoise!" Suzanne protested with a nervous laugh.

"What? If he doesn't want to kiss me, he could at least kiss my lipstick. I could make that work . . ."

"Come on, let me work in peace," pleaded Victor. "The children will be leaving the director's class any minute now and lunch isn't going to make itself."

"See you soon," Françoise said coyly as she left the kitchen arm in arm with Suzanne. "I think he likes me," she whispered to her friend.

It had been a week since the campers had arrived. The employees had by now got used to the careful organization implemented by the director. As the head governess (a title that was almost purely honorific), Suzanne lived next to the blockhouse, at the edge of the forest. The rest of the team lived a bit further away in a small 'village' on the west side of the island. The largest of these buildings, which had accommodated additional soldiers during the war, was now used by the staff to socialize in, and in the evening after their shifts, they enjoyed having a beer here together. At night, a second team comprised of two doctors and a nanny handled any nightmares, fevers, or headaches. The teams rarely saw each together, except to hand over at the start and end of their respective shifts.

Suzanne and Françoise made their way to the children's rooms to make sure that they were tidy and that their beds were made. Teaching the children to take good care of their things was part of their job. "It's been a long time since they've had something to take care of—many of their houses were reduced to hovels during the war," the director had explained. "Our goal is to teach them how to behave like the children their parents would like them to be rather than like the children of war. They must learn discipline, how to get up at the same time every day, how to learn in a classroom, how to wash their hands before meals . . . Just as they must learn how to be children, how to be carefree. Sports, other physical activities like gardening and fort building, and even the privilege of doing nothing, will all help them learn. We will let them use their free time as they wish. A forgotten luxury."

"Do you have children, Suzanne?" asked Françoise.

"Yes, a daughter. She got married and left the region. I haven't heard from her since. Don't tell anyone though, okay? Otherwise, I'd have to leave the island. What about you?"

"Me? Hmm . . . I wouldn't know where to start with a child . . ."

"But you do very well with the campers."

"Maybe one day . . . When Victor makes up his mind," she replied with a laugh.

"What about during the war?" Suzanne asked shyly.

Françoise knew what people said about her in town. That's why she'd decided to leave the mainland for the island. She saw the job as the best way to escape the rumours. So, she was tempted not to answer. But, even though she had only known Suzanne for about ten days, she knew she could trust her. Maybe because she had never been able to trust anyone during the war. She had been forced to think about her every word and gesture to avoid attracting suspicion. *Trust is like love,* she thought. *No one can live without it for long.* "I slept with several Germans," she finally admitted. As soon as she'd spoken, a wave of relief washed over her. When others whispered it behind her back, she felt even more guilty. But admitting it freely, in her own words, lifted a weight from her shoulders she thought she would never shift.

Suzanne stopped short and looked directly at her friend. "How many?"

"Four or five," Françoise replied, looking down at her feet.

"Oh God . . . You know what they do to those women, don't you?"

"Yes. I moved on well before the Liberation. If I had stayed in my neighbourhood, I would have had my head shaved too. They weren't all bad," she said sadly. "I had to do what I could to survive."

"I know . . . I know."

"You didn't ever?"

"No," Suzanne replied in a whisper. "Never. My husband died the first year of the war. I felt lonely, you know, without anyone to rely on. But I had my daughter, so . . ."

"I was all alone, Suzie. No children, no one at all . . ."

Paired with her make-up, Françoise's melancholic expression made her look like a sad clown.

"That's all behind us now," said Suzanne, flashing her friend a smile that barely veiled the pain within. "Far behind us."

They checked the rooms one by one. The governesses didn't notice anything noteworthy, except that most of the children had hastily thrown their blankets over their beds, clearly forgetting to tuck the edges under the mattress.

But in the last room, Suzanne noticed something different.

She didn't mention it to her colleague, but the tiny detail gnawed away at her all day. In Fabian's room—the boy was about eight years old—a drawing had been added to the wall, just below the bright rainbow. A man (Suzanne guessed it was a man since there was no hair on his head) drawn in brown chalk stood on two long, stick-like legs. The torso and arms were also simple lines, so that it looked like Fabian had been playing a game of hangman. But what really caught her eye were the two words written beneath the drawing: *Der Erlkönig*.

Suzanne recognized the language but didn't know what the words meant. The few German phrases she'd learned had only been those necessary to her daily life during the Occupation.

She left the room, trying to forget the drawing and telling herself that it was probably just a child's idle scribbling. As the director had explained a week earlier, the children were allowed to do as they pleased with their rooms within reasonable limits. A drawing on the wall was hardly against the lax holiday camp rules . . .

The rest of the day passed quickly. After lunch, the staff accompanied the children during their outdoor activities. Simon, the handyman who was always smiling, took a group of four children on a two-hour horse ride around the island.

Claude, the doctor, examined all of the campers as he did at the end of each week. He talked to them, conducted the usual tests, and tended to a few light injuries—scraped knees and superficial cuts. He was pleased to conclude that all of the children seemed to be in good physical and mental health. Many of them had gained some much-needed weight, and they all seemed to feel safe and happy on the island.

Around five o'clock, Victor brought in mugs of hot chocolate, and the children immediately dropped their balls, toy guns, and bicycles as if they were on fire. Afterwards, the governesses organized quiet activities: cards, board games, and colouring. Suzanne and Françoise were proud of the warm, family atmosphere that had quickly developed in this formerly formidable place, and the doubts they had felt on the day the children arrived seemed very distant now.

"Time is relative," mumbled Suzanne as she watched the children, who were no longer afraid to run laughing through the corridors of the German blockhouse where many terrible crimes had undoubtedly been planned.

Then she travelled down into her own inner bunker, into her painful past. The week spent on the island had erased her memories of the war and restored the lost colour in her life. This safe refuge was blurring her memories, proposing another reality—a parallel reality—to the horrors she had witnessed during the Occupation. In her new refuge, the German tanks disappeared, making way for children playing ball games. The anti-air-raid sirens went quiet so that only happy, high-pitched voices broke the silence. The glaring eyes of suspicious soldiers vanished behind bright rainbows.

She wondered if the camp, which was soundly anchored in reality but also like something out of a dream, could help *her* heal too. Was she helping to make the world a better place? Or was it just an illusion?

Suzanne thought of her daughter, her other reality.

She had fallen in love with a soldier a few months before the end of the war. What Suzanne hadn't dared tell Françoise, was that this soldier was a member of the Wehrmacht, just like her friend's wartime lovers. It had been so hard for Suzanne to accept. Her daughter had sworn that he wasn't like the men who took advantage of the situation and abused the local women. She had said he was different. But Suzanne didn't believe it, so she and her daughter had parted ways. Silently. Brutally. Nothing left but a letter on the kitchen table and an empty childhood bedroom. She had abandoned her mother's love for the utopian dream of true love.

Every now and again, a letter arrived from the south of France. Monique told her mother how and what she was doing. Her handwriting had become that of a determined young woman. Her husband (*She got married without telling me!*)

wanted to have children. Monique hoped she would fall pregnant the following summer.

Suzanne penned replies filled with all the wrong sentiments. She thought that the firm tone of a parent might put a stop to her daughter's childish illusions. In the end, she had written to Monique that her happiness was too painful for her to read. She said she loved her daughter, but it would be too much for her to embrace a man who would have executed her husband if he had received the order. *Your own father, the man who bounced you on his knees and told you the stars existed just to make you smile.*

She let a month go by, hoping something would change. Eventually, though she never said or wrote as much, she realized she had probably gone too far.

But time and silence only fed the distance between them, devouring their regrets, digesting them until they were all but inaudible fragments.

There were no more letters.

A few years after the fact, the war had claimed two new victims.

12

Sandrine

Speak to me of love,
And say what I'm longing to hear ...

Sandrine listened carefully as Françoise described her grand-mother.

The old woman spoke of her kindness and her conscientious nature, and the soothing words she always had for both children and adults. She remembered the first day when they had stood on the dock waiting for the campers to arrive. She shared dozens of anecdotes: fits of giggles, evenings spent at the bar after a day with the children, drinking glasses of schnapps and then hurling the glasses against the walls in defiance of the Germans who were there before them.

"This was her favourite song," explained Françoise with a nod towards the jukebox.

"Really?"

"Yes. There was a gramophone in her house, and every morning, Lucienne Boyer's voice would greet me at the gate when I stopped by to pick Suzanne up to go to the blockhouse."

"Did she have a boyfriend here?" asked Sandrine.

"No, not that I know of. Your grandfather is the only man she ever mentioned."

"What about you?"

"I had a crush on Victor ... But believe it or not, that oddball never even kissed me! So, I moved on to Simon," she confessed with a shrug.

"Simon? The caretaker?" Sandrine asked, surprised. She couldn't help but recall the old sailor's brusque manners.

"Back then, he was a handyman. I like a man who's good with his hands," she replied with a wink.

"Did you know Suzanne had a daughter?"

"Of course. That was no secret."

"Did she ever talk about me?" Sandrine asked nervously.

"How could she not, my dear? She imagined you were beautiful and clever. She would have liked to get to know you . . . But sometimes life is complicated, and we don't always make the right decisions."

"She could have written to me," Sandrine protested.

"I know it's hard to understand, but she loved you, of that I'm sure. She just couldn't leave the island, or communicate with you . . ."

"But why?"

"Because she was scared," Françoise replied quietly, as if the topic were taboo.

"Scared?"

"Yes. Plagued with a fear you will never know," she said gravely. "And that fear, she told me much later, began one day when we were checking the children's rooms. You know, your grandmother wasn't particularly talkative. Probably because of the war. She never opened her mouth unless she really had something to say. That's why I trusted her from the first day we met."

"But what was she afraid of?"

"The Erlking."

Sandrine began to wonder if Françoise was losing her mind. She noticed that the old woman was constantly looking over her shoulder, as though she feared someone might overhear her. In reality, she and Sandrine were alone in the room. Her face also seemed to be stuck in a constant expression of wonder. Her broad smile, raised eyebrows, and high cheekbones reminded Sandrine of a clown frozen in time.

"We're chained to this place," Françoise went on. "We're all scared, though no one will admit it. Because there's a creature on this island, a creature straight out of your nightmares. But it's real. It watches us day and night. It keeps us from leaving."

All right, well this is getting out of hand, thought Sandrine, pretending to be absorbed in Françoise's story. "I'm not sure I understand," she replied finally. A strange feeling washed over her as she thought back to Victor's use of the word 'prisoner' earlier.

"People hide behind the word 'madness' when they can't or don't want to accept a strange reality. Don't make that mistake. Your grandmother was never crazy, my child. She just figured things out before the rest of us. That's why he killed her. Don't stay on this island, dear. If you do, you'll never be able to leave . . ."

"What do you mean?"

As Françoise leaned in to explain, the door burst open. Paul appeared in the doorway, his arms laden with bags of provisions.

"Victor, could you give me a hand?" he shouted.

The man appeared immediately, as if he'd been waiting in a dark corner for this moment, like an actor listening for his cue to come on stage.

"I'm coming, I'm coming . . . Hello, Françoise!" he said as he passed the women.

"Hello handsome," she replied without even looking at him. "I have to go, Sandrine. It was lovely to meet you."

Paul's presence seemed to have upset her. Françoise stood up and sighed, biting her lip (and leaving lipstick on her front teeth).

"Wait," protested Sandrine. "You have to explain . . ."

"I can't. Not here. Come over to my place tomorrow afternoon. My house is the one nearest the coast. We'll have time to talk then."

"But—"

"You shouldn't be here on this island, Sandrine," she said, putting an end to the discussion. Then she turned around and made her way back past the jukebox and out into the night

without another word. A few seconds after the door had closed
behind her, the lyrics to Suzanne's favourite song interrupted
the silence again.

> *Speak to me of love,*
> *And say what I'm longing to hear . . .*

God, what is this place? Sandrine wondered as she thought back
through the disjointed conversation. *What did she mean?* She
suddenly wanted to flee. She didn't know why, but an alarm
had been going off somewhere deep inside of her since she
had first set foot on the *Lazarus*. A strange and confusing
feeling that had only grown stronger as she'd met the island's
inhabitants.

Simon. Victor. Françoise.

She didn't entirely trust any of them. They had each in his
or her own way increased the indescribable sense of danger
she felt. Paul seemed to be the only person here who was
halfway normal. But what did she really know about him? He
lived on the mainland and came over every two weeks to deliver
supplies and carry out any work that needed doing for the
residents. He was rather handsome, but other than that, she
didn't know much.

"May I?" asked Paul. He had suddenly appeared at Sandrine's
side, as if out of thin air. She smiled awkwardly, then noticed
he was holding two beers. She hid her discomfort and pushed
a strand of hair behind her ear.

"Yes . . . Yes, of course!" she replied.

"Are you okay? You look worried," he said, a concerned
expression on his face.

"No. Everything . . . Everything's fine," she mumbled as he
pushed one of the pints towards her.

"I'm sorry. It must be hard to be here now, after Suzanne's
death," he said sympathetically.

"It's not that," Sandrine confessed.

"What is it then?"

"I just had a strange chat with Françoise . . ."

"Right, I see . . . I should have warned you," replied Paul.

"Warned me?"

"Yes. Françoise is a bit . . . Well, let's just say she may be missing a few marbles. The isolation, maybe. And Claude thinks your grandmother's death has hit her harder than she's willing to let on."

"Yes, she said as much . . . She invited me to go over to her house tomorrow afternoon to talk."

"That's a good idea! It will probably do her a lot of good to confide in someone. You see, I told you you'd be kept busy! Plus, tomorrow I'll take you to Suzanne's house. I have a spare key to every cottage."

"Thank you, Paul."

"No problem at all. So, I hope you're hungry!"

"I am! Should I expect a feast?"

Paul nodded towards the door to the kitchen, where Victor had just emerged with a large pot of stew. "Here you are: dinner for the youngsters! And I want to see empty plates afterwards!"

That night they were the guesthouse's only customers and Sandrine enjoyed Paul's company. He was easy to talk to and as the evening went on she almost forgot why she had come to the island in the first place. He told her about his life on the mainland and the feeling that he didn't belong. He said he planned to stay in this job for another year or two (implying without saying it out loud that he would stay until the last of the island's residents had passed away) and then open a tourism business. "Boat tours," he explained with a smile. "All along the coast. In the summer, there are plenty of tourists, but they all take the same big boats, which means they miss out on the most beautiful spots. I know the region like the back of my hand. There are so many other lovely areas to explore."

Sandrine was reassured by the normality of their conversation, but she was tired, and the alcohol kept her from focusing. She excused herself, thanked him for a nice evening, and went to find Victor, who was drying glasses at the bar. "Thank you for the meal. I don't think I've eaten anything that good in years!"

"My pleasure! Follow me," he said as he walked over to the reception desk and grabbed a key. "Here. It's a good room with a view of the ocean."

"Thank you again. Tomorrow I'll need to call my boss to let him know I've arrived safe and sound. Can I use your phone?"

"I haven't had a phone for years. It's not like I have tourists calling me up to book a stay. There's a phone booth near the dock. It's our only link to the outside world."

"I see. I'll go tomorrow morning then. Good night, Victor."

As she climbed the stairs with her suitcase and headed for her room, Sandrine could hear people moving around in the restaurant below. Paul was probably off to bed as well. But as soon as she put the key in the lock, the grainy words from the record echoed in her ears again . . .

> *Speak to me of love,*
> *And say what I'm longing to hear . . .*

13

Suzanne

1949

Just three days after noticing the strange drawing in Fabian's room, Suzanne found two others, with the same inscription scrawled beneath them. Fabian was a shy boy but she decided she needed to talk to him and took him aside while the children were all gathered in the canteen for their hot chocolate.

"Fabian?" she asked.

"Yes, Miss?"

"Can you tell me what it is you drew on the wall in your room beneath the rainbow?"

The boy looked down at his feet and bit his lip. It was an expression she had observed on many children's faces in the streets during the Occupation when soldiers ordered their parents to show their papers. Seeing it now made her realize she sounded too stern. Invisible wounds could reopen at the slightest provocation. She knelt down in front of Fabian and smiled.

"It's all right. You're allowed to draw on the walls in your room. You're not in trouble. It's just that I found the same drawing in Julie and Pierre's rooms, too. Did you draw them as well?"

"Yes, Miss Suzie."

"Is it a game?"

"No."

"What does *Erlkönig* mean?"

"*Earl-cur-nig*," repeated Fabian, correcting her pronunciation. "The Erlking."

"And who is this Erlking?" she asked gently.

"A bad man. My father often told me the story. All the children here know it."

"Is he some sort of boogeyman?"

"Yep," Fabian confirmed.

"There's no need to be afraid," Suzanne reassured him. "The monsters are gone now. They went back to Germany. And I'm sure this Earl-whatshisname went with them. What did this boogeyman do to upset you? You know that talking about our fears often makes them disappear. When I was little, I was afraid of the dark, too. But when I closed my eyes, the monsters vanished, like magic!"

"No!" the boy cried out suddenly, staring at her. "We can't close our eyes! Ever!"

"But why?" asked Suzanne, worried by his outburst.

"Because he comes to get us when we close our eyes. That's what he did to Julie, Pierre, and me. He makes us go to sleep and then takes us."

"Come now, Fabian. That's just your imagination playing tricks on you . . ."

She hoped her words would comfort the boy, who was clearly agitated now. Whereas before he had been standing still with a slightly lost expression on his face, now he was rubbing his hands together as though he was freezing cold and when he looked up at her, she noticed the dark circles under his eyes. She stifled the urge to ask him more questions. She didn't want to upset him further. He needed to know he was safe, that no soldier or monster was going to burst into his room shouting deafening orders.

But Fabian continued in a wavering voice. "No, Miss Suzie. He comes every night. That's why I drew him on the walls in our rooms. To remind him he's already visited us, that he should move on and leave us alone now."

Suzanne was so taken aback to see how terrified he was that she didn't know what to say. She watched Fabian drag his feet as he walked towards the large table. His two friends who had supposedly also encountered the *Erlkönig* in their dreams were sitting not far from him.

The German soldiers must have spread the story during the war to keep the children afraid. After all, what better way to achieve eternal superiority than by traumatizing an entire population from childhood? Suzanne knew, as all adults did, that our fears don't disappear when we grow up: they only become more subtle, lying in wait, easily forgotten until we momentarily close our eyes and lower our guard.

"How are you, Suzanne?" asked Claude, the doctor, appearing beside her. She had been so focused on Fabian that she hadn't noticed him until he spoke. He was wearing an elegant suit and monocle, as he did every day and the outfit gave him a distinguished look. He was showing early signs of baldness but this somehow only heightened his allure by showing off his symmetrical skull and features. Suzanne admitted to herself that she was not entirely immune to his charms.

"Oh, Claude! You scared me!" she said.

"I'm not sure how to take that," he replied with a laugh.

"No . . . It's not . . . I'm well, thanks. How are you?"

"Never better! The director is delighted with the children's health and very pleased with the work we're all doing! They were deprived of the nutrients necessary for normal growth for quite some time, you know. Another two or three years in those conditions and most of them would have experienced irreversible delays in their physical and psychological development . . . Not all of their deficiencies were corrected after the Liberation. Life was still such a struggle. It was hard to have constant access to good food."

"Indeed it was," replied Suzanne, though she doubted very much that the doctor had found the task of filling his pantry very challenging. At least not in the way that Suzanne had. He had apparently served as director of a war hospital, which was a coveted position since it was considered necessary and supported by each successive government. He had treated soldiers from both sides. Neutrality had its benefits during those troubled times.

"But thanks to our work," he continued, "the children are gaining weight and seem more energetic every day! We've probably given them a little too much hot chocolate in my opinion, but I suppose a treat now and then makes the world a better place!"

"Doctor?"

"Yes, Suzanne?"

"I've actually noticed that some of them seem tired."

"Really?"

"Yes. Do they sleep well?"

"According to the reports from the night shift, they haven't encountered any problems," Claude replied reassuringly. "Which children are you referring to?"

"Julie, Fabian and Pierre. They look exhausted."

The three children in question slumped where they sat, their heads seemingly too heavy to hold up, and their whole demeanour was in stark contrast to that of the other campers. Their complexions were also duller than usual and looked as cold as the bare, grey, exterior walls of the blockhouse.

"Probably just too much exercise," the doctor concluded. "At their age, children often wear themselves out. They don't know their limits yet. It's a healthy form of fatigue. But I'll pay particular attention to them at the next check-up, don't you worry."

"Thank you, Claude."

"You're welcome. Will you come and have a beer with us at the bar tonight?" he asked as he left.

"I can't leave Françoise alone in a place with a ready supply of men and alcohol now can I? That would be irresponsible of me!" Suzanne replied with a smile.

14

Sandrine

November 1986

Sandrine packed her bag and went down to reception. Paul had suggested they meet in front of her grandmother's house at ten o'clock. Since it was just after nine, she had plenty of time to get there. There were no signs of life in the bar. The lights were off, leaving the wan morning sun to shine through the cracks in the curtains and guide any visitors. Sandrine walked past the jukebox, its hulking presence feeling ominous in the silence.

Speak to me of love . . .

"What bullshit!" she said aloud.

She rang the bell at the reception desk, but no one appeared. Maybe Victor was still sleeping . . . She left a note on the counter and left.

It had stopped raining. That was the first thing she saw as she looked up at the nauseous sky. Then she noticed that the entire island seemed different somehow. Her surroundings were the same, but everything seemed . . . dull. The natural colours of the landscape, which were usually so welcoming, had faded as though nature itself had plunged into an eternal sleep, withering under the low, grey sky, which seemed to weigh down on the island, driving it deeper into the sea. Sandrine thought back to the photographs hanging on the walls at the guesthouse. She felt like the very landscape was travelling back through time, as if the most recent, vulgar, colour photographs had ordered the island to extinguish itself and return to the black-and-white images from the early days. The sea and the foam-capped waves formed an impenetrable expanse of dark ink that roared in the distance. The few trees she came across were bare, their austere branches reaching beseechingly towards the sky. Sandrine couldn't help but shiver—the sight of this apocalyptic panorama was making her uncomfortable. Add some exploding shells, machinegun fire, trails of blood, and clouds of gas, and it would make a perfect setting for a war film. Or a veteran's nightmare.

She again felt the urge to flee the island as soon as possible.

Sandrine walked determinedly in the direction of her grandmother's house and took the only path that led into the forest. According to the map the solicitor had provided, the house wasn't too far away.

As she got closer, the sea breeze and surrounding silence soothed her frayed nerves. She looked up, searching the sky for one of the many seabirds that supposedly lived on the island, but saw nothing. The air was as deserted as the land. Ten minutes later, she reached a house which looked identical to the ones in the village.

Paul was sitting on the porch step waiting for her. He stood up to open the gate and usher her inside. "How are you, Sandrine?" he asked. "Did you sleep well?"

"Like a baby," she lied.

It had been a rough night. In addition to the uncomfortable mattress, she had been awoken several times by a strange noise coming from outside. She had initially assumed it was the wind whipping over the rocks along the coast. But after listening for a while, she had concluded it was the wailing of a frightened animal.

"Are there cats on the island?" she asked.

"Ah yes, the famous wild cats," Paul said with a sigh. "There used to be quite a few of them. It seems someone brought a couple to the island and they reproduced. Then they had to be culled because they were a danger to the seabirds—the gulls and the eiders. They attacked their nests. The residents say there are still a few left and they mainly come out at night. But I've never seen one. It was probably a lone survivor."

"So, this is where Suzanne lived?" asked Sandrine.

"Yes."

"This is strange," she noted as she made her way round the side of the house and found nothing but a partially dried-up pond. "According to the map the solicitor gave me there should be an outbuilding here . . ."

"An outbuilding? No, there hasn't been anything here since I've been coming to the island."

Sandrine glanced at the map one last time, then slipped it into her back pocket. Paul selected a key from the bunch in his hand and unlocked the door. Once inside, they both had the same reflex and began opening the windows to let in the fresh air. Sandrine wasn't sure she could exorcise the ghosts from the house, but she could at least do something about the damp smell.

The building comprised a lounge, a small kitchen, a bathroom, and two ridiculously small bedrooms. In one of them, she could still see marks on the wall where bunkbeds must once have stood. Beds undoubtedly used by soldiers of the Third Reich. Sandrine and Paul checked all the rooms, both of them feeling slightly uncomfortable about invading Suzanne's private space. Then Paul stepped outside to smoke and let Sandrine explore the place alone for a few minutes. But no matter how many drawers or cupboards she rummaged through, nothing made her feel closer to Suzanne. She felt like she was visiting a cold, soulless model home, much like Mr Béguenau's office.

"What the hell am I doing here?!" she exclaimed as she stepped outside.

"Are you okay?"

"Yes . . . Well, no, not really. I don't belong here," she declared, on the verge of tears. "I didn't know Suzanne, who you all say was so kind, always ready with a smile. I thought that visiting this house would close the emotional distance, but

. . . I feel nothing. I'd be better off going back to the mainland and my life from before."

"I understand," Paul replied reassuringly as he exhaled a column of smoke. "Don't beat yourself up about it. Sometimes life is just . . . ill-suited."

"Ill-suited?"

"Yes, ill-suited to the living."

Sandrine sat on the steps and pondered his words. She thought of her years in Paris, when she had so often wondered what she was supposed to do with her life. She had never thought to look at it the other way around. It had never occurred to her that the capital or even her life might just be ill-suited to her.

"It's funny," she said eventually as she smiled and gazed at the horizon, "you have a gift for making me feel better."

"Really?"

"Yes. Every time I feel like I'm going under, you say a few words and I'm afloat again. I can see why my grandmother liked you. But I'm afraid I won't be able to enjoy your company much longer. I plan to go back today."

"Ah. In that case, I don't think you're going to like what I'm about to say . . ."

"Why?"

"Simon left last night," explained Paul. "Since there weren't any major repairs that required his presence, he took the *Lazarus* back to the mainland. He won't be back until next week."

"No!"

"It's my turn to keep watch over the island. Until he gets back."

"Oh please, no! Tell me you're joking!"

"I'm sorry. That's how we manage the island when things are quiet."

"I'm going to need a lot of beer to get me through," Sandrine said with a weak laugh. "And you have to promise to never leave me alone."

"I promise! Come on, I want to take you somewhere. As for

drinks, I've got a bottle of wine and a few sandwiches Victor made for me early this morning."

"All right. Where are we going?"

"To the holiday camp, on the other side of the forest."

15

Sandrine

November 1986

Paul and Sandrine walked along the steep path that led to the eastern side of the island. Just a few metres away, at the bottom of the cliffs, the sea crashed so forcefully against the rocky shoreline that they had to raise their voices to be heard. Ahead of them, the shadows of the trees drew slowly nearer, like soldiers advancing carefully through a minefield.

"Don't you think the landscape looks different today?" asked Sandrine.

"What do you mean?"

"I feel like all the primary colours have disappeared, leaving behind only shades of grey. As if a god coloured in the island with the wrong set of crayons . . ."

"Well, the sun rarely pierces through the clouds here. But the grass is green, and the sky is undoubtedly blue. I think it's just the lack of light. You're not used to it. That's all."

Sandrine realized Paul was right once they entered the forest. Everything was even duller here. The weak rays of sunlight that managed to penetrate the blanket of clouds grew even dimmer, absorbed by the dark tree branches. She kept telling herself it was morning, but the landscape and darkness fooled her senses into believing it was dusk.

"Do you visit the camp often?"

"This isn't the first time I've been, but I've never gone inside. I've always had the keys though, in case the building requires any work."

"Why now, then?"

"For you, Sandrine. To cheer you up and show you where Suzanne worked. To prove to you that your grandmother was neither crazy nor useless."

Fifteen minutes later, Sandrine was relieved when they reached a large clearing. Her eyes were immediately drawn to the concrete roof of the blockhouse and she was impressed by its overall size. She had imagined something rather small, like the examples she'd seen in history books. She knew there were larger ones elsewhere in France, like the unfinished one in Éperlecques in the north, but she hadn't expected to come across such an imposing structure on such a small island.

"Wow!" she couldn't help but say in astonishment.

"Incredible, right? They say this blockhouse was built to fire missiles at the coast. But the Germans never had time to use it. The war ended and they abandoned camp."

They walked past what must once have been a playground. A pair of birds sat motionless on the rim of an old basketball hoop. The rusted carcass reminded Sandrine more of a gallows than of a place where children had once played. The metal circle bowed towards the ground, a grieving figure staring at the grave beneath their feet. Weeds dotted the pitch, invading the once well-tended grass where children's balls used to roll unhindered.

Paul drew her attention elsewhere. At first Sandrine thought she was looking at a makeshift cemetery. Thick wooden sticks rose up towards the sky. Some of them straight, others crooked, or leaning this way or that. But she quickly realized it was a former vegetable garden. Dried roots emerged from the earth, like petrified snakes. The stakes no longer supported tomatoes or cucumbers, but given the many square wooden planters, it was clear the garden had once been sprawling and fertile.

"Maurice created this garden," explained Paul. "The way he tells it, his produce fed the whole camp. He still claims he grew the best fruit and vegetables in Normandy. If he weren't too old to get down on his hands and knees and dig, I'm sure he'd still be here every morning tending his little patch of land!"

"They abandoned it all after the shipwreck?"

"Yes. They fled this place like the plague. The day after the tragedy, they closed the blockhouse door, and not one of the former staff members has ever wanted to open it again."

"This place gives me the goosebumps," admitted Sandrine.

"You have to try to imagine it back in the day. The children laughing, the colourful orchard, the sound of balls bouncing on the ground. There were animals, too. A whole little farm! Did you see the pictures in the bar?"

"Yes, all of them."

"Then you have an idea of what it was like. Keep those images in mind. Come on, let's go and have a look inside."

The blockhouse's towering concrete façade rose up before them. Paul pulled the keys from his bag and inserted the largest of them into the lock of the imposing metal door which barred the entrance. The immediate clicking of the mechanism surprised the handyman, who hadn't expected it to work on the first try. They then heard an echo on the other side as they attempted to push it open. They tried again and again, putting their full weight into the door, before resorting to running and jumping against it. Eventually, the metal began to budge, leaving just enough room for the two amateur archaeologists to slip inside.

The first things they noticed were the darkness and the damp. The abandoned concrete walls had been exposed to the glacial wind for so long that they seemed to exhale biting gusts of wind themselves. Paul took two torches from his backpack and handed one to Sandrine. They walked quietly along the corridor, sending the light from side to side in front of them.

"This corridor is huge!" exclaimed Sandrine.

"Yes, I imagine it was designed for troops and their equipment."

"I could write an article about this place!" she said enthusiastically. The mysterious building seemed like an ideal topic.

"I'm sorry?" said Paul, confused.

"Oh, right . . . I'm a journalist. I mean . . . That's not why I'm here, but it *is* what I do for a living. Over on the mainland."

"You're a journalist? And you think you could write an article about the island and the camp?"

"Yes, I could give it a go. I'm stuck here for a week. I might as well make the most of it!"

"You can't."

"Why not?"

"No one will believe you . . ."

They continued on for several metres in the dark until they found themselves in a huge room lit by the natural light which was filtering through the slits in the walls.

"It feels like . . . It feels like the children just left . . ." mumbled Sandrine in disbelief as she walked over to the long table in the middle of the room. She didn't dare touch the glasses, cutlery, and plates still sitting there covered in dust and elaborate cobwebs. She couldn't tear her eyes away from the objects whose presence so painfully highlighted the absence of the children who had once used them. She remembered their faces from the pictures in the bar. In her mind's eye she transferred them here, placing them around the table. She imagined their laughter and smiles. She saw them drinking, eating, and talking, watched over by the kind staff. A muffled sound suddenly pulled Sandrine from her waking dream and she realized Paul had now disappeared into a neighbouring room.

"It's nothing!" he shouted. "Just an old saucepan and me being clumsy! This kitchen is absolutely huge!"

Sandrine looked around the room one more time, then made her way towards another corridor. She turned on her torch to light up the concrete tunnel. A row of open doors lay on either side. Sandrine counted ten in all. As she explored them with her light, she realized she was in the dormitory wing. She felt moved seeing their small beds and smiled sadly when she noticed forgotten soft toys still awaiting the return of their owners. The rooms were all identical: a bed, a chest of drawers, a narrow window, and walls covered in colourful murals. The vestiges of a forgotten sanctuary. Unlike the dull, tarnished island, the rainbows and other painted images here were still bright and cheerful, as though the children had managed to preserve nature's colours from the outside elements. She visited each room quickly with a lump in her throat before reaching the end of the corridor, where she discovered another heavy metal door. She turned the handle, but it was locked.

"Now *this* place gives me the creeps," said Paul, coming to join Sandrine. "I don't have the key to this door. It's not the same lock."

"This is where the children slept," mumbled Sandrine. "It's the saddest thing I've ever seen."

"I thought this would cheer you up," he said regretfully. "I should have thought a little harder before—"

"No, not at all. I'm sure Suzanne did everything she could to keep the campers entertained. Did you see the paintings on the walls? The children slept under rainbows," she said with a smile. "And did you see the little stickman drawn in each of the rooms? It looked like some sort of talisman or dreamcatcher or something. I'm sure they all slept well . . ."

"Me too," said Paul, smiling in turn.

Without another word, they started to walk back to the main room. But before she left the dormitory, Sandrine turned around one last time, wishing to pay a final tribute to the drowned children.

That's when she saw it.

At the far end.

Hanging above the sealed door.

An old clock.

Sandrine shined her torch on it.

The hands were still.

8:37.

16

Suzanne

1949

Three days later, during a gardening workshop, Suzanne grew more certain than ever that the children were suffering from a mysterious ailment. It was cool outside and a light, salty breeze played in the fruit trees and the plants weighing heavily on their stakes. While Maurice explained the importance of proper spacing between plants and the benefits of herbs, the governess discreetly studied the children's behaviour.

Julie, Fabian and Pierre were weeding a bed which would soon hold lettuces. They hadn't said a word all morning. They silently raked the soil, their heads down. Their slow movements and pale faces confirmed Suzanne's suspicions. She turned to the rest of the group. Marie caught her eye—she looked exhausted too. The little girl was busy removing bugs from the tomato plants but her features were drawn and her complexion pallid. A little further away, Jules was secretly eating the raspberries he was supposed to be harvesting. Though he was clearly delighted by his snack—and its illicit nature—Suzanne couldn't help but notice the dark circles under his eyes and the way he blinked again and again. It looked like he'd just been pulled from his bed.

"Maurice?" ventured Suzanne.

"Yes?"

"Can I leave them with you for a minute? I need to go and make sure everything is ready for lunch."

"Of course, no problem," replied Maurice. "I'll take good care of them. Hey! Jules! Stop eating all the raspberries!"

Suzanne stood up, dusted off her apron and went inside the blockhouse. She walked past the main room (where the smell of roasted chicken and vegetables made her stomach growl) and made her way to the dormitory wing. She went straight to Marie's room. After just a few seconds, she found the drawing she was looking for: the stickman was walking across the surface of a turquoise sea like the Messiah. The inscription was just below, in the waves, hidden between two crudely drawn fish.

Der Erlkönig.

Next, she headed for Jules' room. Rounded, leafy trees covered the walls, looking more like giant mushrooms than like the twisted evergreens in the forest outside. In one of them, the Erlking, drawn in dark chalk, hung from a branch.

"What is going on?" she whispered to the silent dormitory, willing the thick walls to speak.

She watched the children throughout their meal. Five of the campers were behaving perfectly normally, but she wondered how long that would last. Would the Erlking visit them in the coming days? In their nightmares? Which one of them would look utterly exhausted the next morning?

That afternoon, Suzanne decided to share her misgivings with the director, who had encouraged his team to come to him with any problems. He had set up an office in a room near the kitchen. A room where, according to him, many a Frenchman had been tortured by the German soldiers. His door was always open, and Victor proudly claimed that the delicious cooking smells coming from his kitchen were the main reason why.

Suzanne knocked on the metal door. The director invited her to come and sit down opposite him. He listened attentively with his legs crossed and a cigar hanging from his lips. Suzanne had trusted him ever since they'd first met, when, with the job advertisement still in hand, she had offered to work for him. Her daughter had vanished with her German soldier six months earlier. The pain of the separation was still visible on her face. She had spent so many nights crying and so many days hoping. But then she had moved on to resignation and a desire to escape it all. An island and a well-paid job fit the bill perfectly. The opportunity seemed like a truce in the war that was her private life.

"This holiday camp aims to heal the wounds of war," he had explained. "We'll begin with ten children. If things go well, we'll increase the number of beds. I've met with many families. All of them are enchanted with the idea."

"Why children?" asked Suzanne.

"Because children represent what is most precious to us in our lives," he replied enthusiastically. "They're both our future and our past. The equilibrium and well-being of the universe are founded on their happiness—a happiness the Nazis tried to destroy. These children and their parents made it out alive, but the adults are unable to properly care for the youngsters at the moment. We're a temporary solution."

Then the director had smiled at Suzanne and signed her contract.

"Tired?" he asked, surprised, blowing smoke towards the ceiling.

"Yes. Half of the group seems to be struggling with chronic fatigue."

"Has Claude diagnosed them?"

"No. It's just something I've noticed," admitted Suzanne.

"Do you think it's the activities? The food?"

"I don't know."

The director remained quiet for a moment, lost in his thoughts. "Maybe . . . Maybe we've taken this all a bit too fast. Maybe we didn't consider the psychological toll that being separated from their families could have on them."

"Do you think that—"

"I think you did well to come to me, Suzanne. I pat myself on the back every day for hiring you. The children love you. They call you Aunt Suzie!"

"Thank you, sir. What do you plan to do?"

"Two things," he explained as he stood up. "First, I'll ask

Claude to check on each of the children. We'll draw our conclusions from his report. If need be, we'll reduce their physical activities and ask Victor to get more vitamins into their meals. Second, we'll try and get to the root of the real problem: I think they're still craving their parents' affection. I'll prepare a surprise for them but for now, I'd rather keep it a secret. Believe me, you'll see them looking bright and happy again soon enough!"

The director's enthusiasm reassured Suzanne. She convinced herself that the Erlking was nothing more than a character from a children's story, nothing more than a monster who haunted the campers' nightmares and troubled their sleep. She hadn't mentioned the drawings on the walls to the director. She had been afraid he would be cross and they seemed like an irrelevant detail.

Two days later, the mysterious surprise arrived, brought over from the mainland by the caretaker, Simon. The director asked everyone to gather in the main room. The children and staff sat down, eager to find out what Simon had hidden in the large crate before him.

"Hello, children," said the director.

"Hello, Sir," they replied in unison.

"You've been on the island for two weeks now. Which is not such a long time, but it can feel that way when you're far from your loved ones. Your parents sent you here for one reason: because they love you. Your families are eager to have you back, but they need this time to repair everything and ready your homes. My team has informed me that some of you seem a little tired and weary. There's no need to worry. I would have felt the same if I were separated from the people I love. So, I have decided—and this is only the first surprise—that in two weeks' time, we'll all spend a day on the mainland so you can see your families."

The children couldn't contain their shouts of joy. Their drawn features were replaced with smiles. They looked at one another to make sure they had heard right. Each face radiated the same happiness to his or her neighbour, like a perfect reflection in an invisible mirror.

Suzanne was overwhelmed with joy. The director had found the perfect solution.

"And there's still another surprise," the director continued with a theatrical gesture. "I would like each of you to come up here to receive it. After that, if you have any questions, you can ask Simon. This strapping young man has many secrets—he's the one who came up with the idea," the director explained with a wink at the caretaker. "Last but not least, this gift is yours to keep. You'll take it with you when you leave the island in two months' time. So, first up is . . . Marie!"

The little girl's eyes grew wide with surprise. She stood up, both hesitant and excited, and stood in front of the director.

"Go ahead, Simon," he said.

Simon leaned over, carefully opened the crate and tenderly lifted out a sleeping kitten with his strong arms.

"Here you are, Marie. This one's for you. Give him any name you like. He's sleeping because the veterinarian gave him a sedative so he wouldn't be scared during the crossing. But he'll wake up soon, and when he does, he'll need plenty of stroking and comfort from you."

Marie clutched the animal to her chest. Nothing else existed for her at that moment.

Not the men in uniform with their twisted cross symbols.

Not the worried look on her mother's face as she went to pick up their rations.

Not the strange sounds that fell from the sky at night.

Not *Der Erlkönig*.

The kitten's purring and its soft black-and-white fur now occupied the centre of her universe.

"Pierre."

"Fabian."

"Julie."

"Sandra."

*

One after another, the campers stood before Simon, their faces radiant with expectation. Their happiness was contagious. The staff members shared in their joy when the kittens finally woke, mewling in confusion. The island's newest residents were given the silliest names: Belle, Metronome, Meow, Sausage, Socks, and so it went on. Then the director invited the children to take their new pets to their rooms to get to know each other.

"That's going to make a lot of mess to clean up," said Françoise once they were out of earshot.

"Each child is responsible for his or her own cat," replied Victor. "That includes their litter trays. The director was very clear about that. It will be an important lesson for the kids."

"Oh, my dear, dear Victor, might you have a little surprise for me hidden somewhere too?" she asked coyly.

"No time. I've got to clean the fireplace and sweep the chimney in the bar," he said with a shy smile before leaving the room with his supplies under his arm.

"Françoise, stop torturing the men of this island!" joked Suzanne, looking sternly at her friend.

"But I want a pet of my own," the other woman replied with a laugh.

"Do you know who I'm thinking about?"

"No. The doctor?"

"Tsk, no!" she countered, blushing despite herself. "Hardly!"

"Who then?" asked Françoise.

"The night team and the look on their faces when they come on duty later!"

17

Sandrine

November 1986

Paul and Sandrine sat silently on a boulder and looked out to sea. They had stopped to eat their picnic, hoping to dispel the uneasiness they had been feeling since exploring the blockhouse.

"You okay?" asked Paul as he handed her a glass of wine.

"Yeah. It's just that . . . I can't help thinking about those children. I can see them fighting for their lives in the freezing water. I can imagine the terror in their eyes. I can hear their breathing falter and then stop altogether . . ."

"I shouldn't have—"

"Stop apologizing, Paul," she scolded. "You couldn't have known what we would find inside."

Long, low clouds shaped like dark zeppelins hovered threateningly over the surface of the water. Sandrine watched as they moved slowly towards them, seemingly hesitant to get too close to the island.

Paul swallowed the last bite of his sandwich. "Is that . . . some sort of jewellery?" he asked, partly out of curiosity and partly to change the subject.

Unsure what he was talking about, Sandrine frowned uncertainly.

"On your wrist," he clarified. "The leather cuff. I've never seen a woman wear one before."

"Oh, yes, sort of," she replied vaguely.

The burning sensation returned. Long and thin. Metallic. Incandescent.

She felt the heat cut through her skin.

Think about something else, forget your suffering, drown it . . .

"It reminds me of my mother," she lied. She pulled the sleeve of her jacket down to cover it.

"Are you close?"

"We were."

"I've put my foot in my mouth again, haven't I!"

"Don't worry about it. It's nothing. Anyway, that's enough sadness for one day. Let's go and see Françoise. I'm sure her make-up is ready and waiting for us!"

They put the leftovers away in the backpack and laughed when they realized they had polished off the entire bottle of wine. They continued walking back towards the village but as they reached the edge of the twisted forest, Sandrine started to feel drowsy—undoubtedly due to the alcohol. The light and the sounds around her seemed to diminish, to the point where it took all her strength to focus and keep from falling on the dim, uneven path.

She thought she heard children crying.

She thought she heard a cat meowing.

She thought she heard a woman's voice singing, imploring the listener to speak of love, to say what she longed to hear.

For a fleeting moment, she felt like she was all alone—alone not in the decaying forest, but in a grey, concrete room behind a locked door.

Was she losing it?

Did she suffer from the same condition as her grandmother? A condition Françoise had warned her not to dismiss as madness?

Were the colours really disappearing from the island?

"I think I drank a bit too much," she said as the trees grew sparser, giving way to a green meadow interspersed with boulders. Suzanne's house appeared up ahead to their right. "Where's the phone booth?" she asked as they passed the empty dock.

"Up the path that way," replied Paul, "behind one of the houses. It's not easy to find."

"I need to call my boss later," she explained. "To let him

know I'm okay. And to suggest an article, maybe. A traveller's log of sorts . . ."

"Are you sure you want to write about this place?" Paul asked dubiously.

"There's enough mystery here to intrigue any reader," Sandrine replied enthusiastically. "It'll be a nice change from talking about cows . . ."

"That's Françoise's house over there," he said, pointing. Then he stopped, as if frozen to the spot.

"What's wrong?" asked Sandrine.

Paul wasn't sure. But he had just seen Claude the doctor rush into the house. Then Maurice came out of the same door, hunched over from his many years spent working the land. When the retired gardener spotted Paul and Sandrine, he trotted over to them.

"What is it, Maurice?" asked Paul. "You shouldn't run. It's not good for— "

The old man was still several yards away, but Sandrine could already hear his laboured breathing. She could see the fear in his eyes, too.

"Hurry," he said. "Something's happened."

Françoise lay on the floor. She was clearly already dead. Her make-up eerily underscored the paleness of her skin, as though the bright colours were mocking the corpse beneath. Claude was kneeling next to the body, his stethoscope around his neck. His hand trembled as he closed Françoise's eyes and crossed himself. Paul, Victor, and Maurice, who were all standing behind him, followed suit.

"Heart attack," declared the doctor.

There was a long silence as each of them thought back, shifting through their memories. Sandrine watched, not daring to move. She realized what all of the island's inhabitants must be wondering: when would it be their turn? When would old age carry them off to be reunited with Suzanne and Françoise?

She turned her attention towards Françoise's body. The first and last conversation she had had with her grandmother's friend came back to her. *We're chained to this place. We're all scared, though no one will admit it. Because there's a creature on this island, a creature straight out of your nightmares. But it's real. It watches us day and night. It keeps us from leaving.*

Sandrine noticed a detail that had escaped her at first: Françoise's neck was positioned at an unnatural angle, as though her head were trying to escape her body. "Claude," she began. "Her neck . . .?"

"Yes," he agreed, looking over. "She must have broken it when she fell. I think she must have been standing there when it happened. There's some blood and hair on the corner of the table. She couldn't stop herself from falling and hit her head in the process."

"What do we do now?" asked Sandrine.

"We have to call the mainland and get Simon to come back with the police."

"I'll do it," offered Victor, on the brink of tears. "I'll do it." Then he stepped outside, hanging his head, unable to hold back his sobs any longer.

"Let's not stay here," said Claude after covering the body with his tweed jacket. "We can't do anything more for her now. She's at peace."

"I wouldn't turn down a drink," said Maurice, his eyes moist and his already craggy face scrunched up in pain. He swiped a tear from his cheek with a sturdy hand as though it were a determined mosquito, his anger and exasperation palpable. Sandrine could tell the old man needed more than just a drink.

"Come on, let's go to the bar," said Paul, taking his arm.

No one spoke as they walked there. Despite the cold wind that whipped at her face and the slight headache she had from the wine, Sandrine studied their surroundings attentively. She noticed low stone walls, trees leaning towards the ground as if they were trying to return to their original seed state, and tall grasses dancing feverishly in the gusty sea air. She looked past the missing colours and had to admit the place had its charms.

It had an austere appeal that contrasted sharply with the arrogant lights and constant din of the capital. It reminded her of a book she had read once. *Wuthering Heights.* She also remembered reading somewhere that the wind could drive you mad. Some people thought the wind carried with it voices from beyond the grave and a few were so convinced of this that they would wander the countryside trying to soothe the errant souls. Had she heard one of those voices in her room the night before? Had it been a feral cat or just the wind? Would Françoise's madness whisper through the trees in the forest now? Would she come to explain her fear?

You're being an idiot. Can't you see the island is just trying to win you over? It wants to keep you here. Have you forgotten what Françoise said?

You shouldn't be here on this island, Sandrine . . .

The funeral procession reached the bar and they all sat down. Paul served them each a whisky, leaving the bottle on the table so they could help themselves to a second glass.

"Poor Françoise," said Claude in a whisper as he loosened his tie.

"May she rest in peace," added Maurice, gulping down his drink.

"Does she have any family we should inform?" asked Sandrine.

"No," replied the gardener. "None of us have any family to inform. Your grandmother was the only one. But she kept that hidden from the director."

"Why?"

"That was one of the conditions for joining the staff on the island. The director wanted employees who wouldn't quit after a few weeks because they missed their families. Suzanne told him she had no one but her husband, and he had died at the beginning of the war."

Sandrine was lost in thought for a moment. Was that why she never got in touch all those years? Was she afraid the director would find out? She was sure they were all concealing things from her. Ever since she had set foot on the *Lazarus*. The residents kept things short, using words that were as dull and sanitized as the colours outside. She decided to shake things up. They might think she was impolite or disrespectful, but Sandrine couldn't take the insinuations or the way they worshipped the island and its secrets anymore. She wanted to know what was behind the mysterious warnings Françoise and Victor had given her. She needed to understand why they were afraid.

Just as she was about to ask her questions, the door to the guesthouse flung open to reveal Victor who was as white as a ghost. "The . . . the . . . the phone booth," he stammered. "It . . . It's been vandalized!"

"What do you mean?" asked Paul in astonishment.

"Destroyed. Totally and utterly destroyed. We're completely cut off from the mainland now . . ."

Sandrine read on their faces then the primitive, childlike terror of people who know they are doomed . . .

18

Suzanne

1949

From then on, the atmosphere at the camp was one of almost monastic calm.

The children spent most of their time taking care of their kittens in their rooms or in the dining hall, ignoring the balls and horses outside. Claude noticed some improvement, but still recommended a daily walk along the coast for at least an hour, if only to get some fresh air in their lungs.

As for Suzanne, she didn't notice any further signs of fatigue in the days following the cats' arrival. She was also relieved not to see any new *Erlkönig* drawings on the walls of the children's bedrooms. She was able to convince herself that the difficult period they had experienced due to the lack of contact with their families—as the director had so quickly realized—was behind them.

Now they were back to working to *make the world a better place*, albeit with slightly less physical activity involved. The campers' smiles shone brightly again, like in the early days. The kittens also seemed happy and explored their new home with insatiable curiosity. Victor complained to himself under his breath whenever he found them trying to get into the kitchen, but the cats eventually won him over, as they had with the rest of the team. The cook even ended up placing tiny bowls of hot chocolate on the floor in front of the door to the kitchen, which the kittens were banned from entering. The compromise seemed to satisfy Belle, Turd, Snowball and the others, who quickly learned to mew for their bowls, forgetting they had ever considered entering the kitchen to help themselves.

The incident took place on a Wednesday, just three days before the planned trip to the mainland.

A high-pitched scream, lonely and anguished, echoed down the dormitory corridor.

A scream incompatible with the lazy afternoon atmosphere they had cultivated while *making the world a better place*.

Like a door slamming in an empty house.

Françoise and Suzanne, who had been busy cleaning the dining room, hurried to uncover the source of the blood-curdling scream. They found Emilie, a small nine-year-old girl, standing outside her room with her face in her hands, trying to muffle her sobs.

"Emilie, was that you screaming? What's going on?"

"It's Fabian . . . He . . . He killed Giggles . . ."

"He did *what*?"

Suzanne stepped into the bedroom and found Fabian sitting on Emilie's bed, his feet dangling over the side. The kitten's unmoving body lay on the floor.

"Françoise, take Emilie to the kitchen and get her a cup of hot chocolate while I talk to Fabian," she suggested.

Françoise nodded and picked the girl up to console her. "Come on, princess, it will all be okay."

Fabian remained silent, staring at an invisible spot on the wall. Suzanne sat next to him and glanced down dolefully at the lifeless body.

"Fabian, did you kill Emilie's cat?" she asked. "Why would you do such a thing?" She didn't expect an answer, really. He undoubtedly regretted his actions and was too ashamed to speak. But, to her great surprise, the boy pointed to the drawings on the wall. Suzanne studied the green meadow with its multihued flowers. Daisies, hyacinths, azaleas—a kaleidoscope of cheerful primary colours. At the top of the field, she noticed the Erlking shooting up out of the grass like a scarecrow. She was certain he hadn't been there the day before when she'd inspected the dormitory.

"It's the only way to escape *him*," explained Fabian. "We have to kill the cats . . ."

"You mean to escape your nightmares? You think you have to kill the kittens to be free of your nightmares?"

"They're not nightmares. He's real. I killed Biscuit two days ago and the Erlking hasn't come back. I broke his neck. He didn't suffer. My dad taught me how to do it when he used to hunt rabbits."

"You killed *your* kitten, too? But, Fabian . . ."

"I didn't want him to hurt Emilie," the boy explained earnestly as he stood up and finally looked at Suzanne.

His gaze was feverish, and the whites of his eyes were tinged with red from the swollen capillaries. *My God, how long has it been since this kid slept?* Suzanne wondered in horror.

"I like Emilie a lot," he continued, ignoring the tears streaming down his cheeks. "And when I saw her this morning, I knew she hadn't slept. So, I drew him up there on the hill, so he would see it and leave her alone."

"But . . ."

"I know you don't believe me," said Fabian. "Only those who have seen him can understand."

"But why Giggles and Biscuit?"

The boy took Suzanne's hands in his and looked deep into her eyes, as though searching for her soul. "We have to kill the cats," he articulated slowly. "It's the only way to get the *Erlkönig* to leave us alone."

"I'll take another shot, please."

"Suzie, are you sure that—" Victor protested.

"Yes, I'm sure," she replied, cutting him off.

The cook filled her glass with schnapps, then put the bottle away. They both sat with their elbows on the counter. Behind them, loaves of bread rose cosily in the warm oven, cloaking them in a reassuringly homely aroma. Ten minutes earlier,

Suzanne had stormed into the kitchen and demanded a drink. When he saw the troubled look on her face, Victor had got out the bottle of pear eau-de-vie.

"What's going on?" he asked. "You're white as a sheet."

"Two of the kittens are dead," she replied.

"What?"

"Giggles and Biscuit. Fabian killed them."

"*Killed* them? But why would he do that?" Victor asked in a shocked voice.

"Because, according to him, a monster comes to hurt the children at night."

"I don't understand," he confessed. "Maybe you should talk to Claude or the director."

"Claude knows. Fabian is in his office now. He's given him a sedative so he can rest. Have you noticed anything strange about the children lately?"

Victor studied Suzanne for a moment. Maybe the shift in the children's mood he'd noticed was actually real and hadn't just been in his head after all? But was it serious enough to alert the rest of the staff? "Not since the kittens arrived," he replied, only half convinced by his own words.

"And before that?"

Before . . . Victor thought to himself. *Before what? When I noticed that the kids weren't so eager to drink their hot chocolate? When their smiles faded like wilting flowers? When I convinced myself it was all my imagination?*

"Well," he finally said aloud, "it's true they seemed a bit listless. And some of them were a little pale. They weren't eating very well either. I noticed that when I cleared their plates after meals."

Suzanne thought for a while before she spoke. She remembered the day the children had arrived. Their guarded faces, darting eyes, and tangible fear when they had walked through the forest to a camp they knew nothing about. But then there had been smiles. Now the kids seemed to be experiencing the same process in reverse. It was as if time itself was ticking backwards. As if this invisible monster had dragged the children off without their consent.

"Victor, does the Erlking mean anything to you?"

"Never heard of him!"

Suzanne decided to have a chat with each of the children with an *Erlkönig* drawing in their room. She didn't want to take it to the director until she knew more. She came up with several excuses to have a few minutes alone with the campers. Each of them told her an almost identical story: the nightmares, the exhaustion, and the drawings. What surprised Suzanne the most was that all of the children were aware of the legend of the Erlking. They all swore he was the creature who visited them at night. Another detail came to light when she asked them to tell her about their dreams. Despite their muddled explanations, they all described the same thing: a clock floating in the air like a kite trapped in the wind.

When Suzanne went to find Françoise and ask after Emilie, she found her friend sitting outside on a stone wall watching the children play with their kittens in the special enclosure designed by Maurice. It resembled a huge fenced-in chicken coop with a big tree in the middle, which the cats tried to climb as their owners encouraged them.

"How is she?" asked Suzanne.

"Not great. I promised her Simon would bring her a new cat. Why did Fabian do it?" Françoise wondered aloud.

"I still don't know," Suzanne lied as she accepted the cigarette her colleague held out to her.

"Suzanne?"

"Yes?"

"What's going on?"

"What do you mean?"

"I don't know. I just feel like . . . something's off. The children are different too, I've noticed. Maybe it's that they miss their families. But, honestly, I think it's something else."

"Do you remember the contract you signed to work here?"

"Of course, Suzie."

"Did you read it before signing?"

"Of course!" exclaimed Françoise. "It seemed too good to be true, so I was cautious."

"And you didn't find anything . . . strange in it?"

"Besides the fact that we had to have no family to work here?"

"Yes, that and . . ."

"And the promise to never leave the island without the director's authorization, even if the camp were to close?"

"Pretty binding for an otherwise straightforward job, don't you think?" said Suzanne, her eyebrow raised.

"A very well-paid job!" her friend pointed out. "Complete with free lodgings, a bar that is always fully stocked with alcohol, and a life free of rumours . . . But yes, it is asking a lot . . ."

"And what about the night team?"

"What about them?"

"We never see them, except when we hand over. We know nothing about them," said Suzanne.

"Of course we don't! When we're working, they're sleeping and vice versa. It's a bit complicated to grab a drink together and chat," replied Françoise, unperturbed.

"Two doctors," Suzanne mused aloud. "Two doctors are on duty while the children are sleeping . . . In the daytime, there's only Claude."

"True, that's a bit strange. The director sleeps on site too though don't forget. Maybe he has an illness that needs monitoring . . ."

"Have you ever heard of the Erlking?" asked Suzanne, abruptly changing the subject.

"The poem by Goethe? Of course! I . . . Um . . . I knew a German, a musician . . . He loved that poem."

"What's it about?"

"In short, an evil being who lives in the woods and kills any children who have the misfortune to come too near. Why? Did you run into him on your way to work this morning?" joked Françoise as she stubbed out her cigarette on a rock.

But when she turned back to her friend, the look on Suzanne's face made her smile disappear. "What is going on, Suzanne?" she asked seriously. "You know you can tell me anything."

"I don't know, Françoise. I don't know. But I'm scared."

19

Sandrine

November 1986

"We've no other choice then . . ."

All of the residents nodded in silence.

Sandrine watched them but didn't understand. Why were they all so calm? And what did that mean?

Victor stood up, walked over to the bar and started casually preparing more drinks, as though someone had just ordered a round. Sandrine searched Paul's eyes for an answer, but he stared fixedly down at the table.

"What do you mean 'We've no other choice'?" she finally asked Claude.

"It means many things, my dear."

"What is going *on*? We have to find a way to reach the mainland! Christ, what if Victor or any of you has a heart attack! You have to leave this island. We all have to leave this island, whether the children's ghosts forgive you or not. We have to leave!"

Sandrine couldn't take it anymore. Her nerves felt raw and exposed. She decided it was time to bring up her discussion with Françoise from the night before. "What are you all afraid of?" she asked. "Yesterday Françoise told me you were all afraid of . . . a creature . . . The Erlking, yes, that's what she said. She told me that *he* killed Suzanne. What if . . . What if there's a murderer on the island? What if these deaths are actually murders?!"

They all looked at her as if she were mad, with a combination of morbid curiosity and fear in their eyes. "They're suicides," announced Maurice, speaking up for the first time since they'd left Françoise's house.

"Yes, suicides. Pure and simple," confirmed the doctor.

The three men nodded with certainty and relief, like a jury confirming a sentence.

"I . . . I don't understand . . ."

"You see," Claude continued, "this island is special. It's our refuge, the only place we feel safe. Like any refuge, if too many people come here to hide, it fails and becomes useless. It's a precarious balance, I must admit, but that's the way it is. And we have to protect it."

"You mean that you killed them to . . . stay safe?" asked Sandrine, horrified.

"No, of course not. We haven't killed anyone. Françoise and Suzanne took their own lives . . . To keep you safe, to make sure you can leave this island and be free again."

"What? You're nuts! So *I* can be free again? What are you talking about?"

The coffee machine behind the bar suddenly let out a loud whistle, making Sandrine jump. She glanced angrily at Victor, who ignored her and continued frothing the milk.

Claude waited patiently for the whistling to stop before he went on. "Haven't you noticed anything strange since you arrived?"

"Is this a joke? Anything strange? How about *everything* strange! *You* are strange! Paul is strange!"

"You'll need to calm down if you want to make it out of here. Think back to when you visited Mr Béguenau's office," Claude said firmly.

"The cross-eyed solicitor? His immaculate desk? The broken clock?"

"What time did it read?"

"What?"

"What time did the clock read?" asked Claude. "Where were the hands?"

Sandrine replayed the meeting with the solicitor in her mind.

She couldn't for the life of her think what these tiny details had to do with anything and it angered her further. *If this is a joke, you evil bastards, I swear you'll pay for it! The article I write about you will earn you a one-way ticket to the nearest psych ward . . .*

"8:37!" she exclaimed when the memory suddenly resurfaced.

"Exactly, 8:37. Doesn't that remind you of anything?"

Sandrine sifted through her recent memories and came to a terrifying realization. "In the blockhouse," she mumbled. "The clock over the locked door . . . It also read 8:37. What does this—"

Sandrine stopped mid-sentence.

Another detail had suddenly resurfaced in her memory.

Another clock . . .

She stood up without thinking, as if manoeuvred by invisible strings, a puppet manipulated by the inescapable hands of fate. Claude, Maurice, and Paul observed her steadily without moving. They watched as she walked over to the fireplace and looked at each framed photograph in turn.

There.

The school picture.

Showing the children from the back of the classroom.

The map of France on the wall . . .

And the clock . . .

8:37.

She began to shake as her nerves gave out. She clenched her fists, drove her nails into her palms and closed her eyes so tightly that her eyelids began to sting. The scars under her cuff bracelet burned fiercely.

Victor joined the others carrying a tray filled with cups of hot chocolate. He sat down, handed a cup to each of them and poured Sandrine another whisky.

"What happens at 8:37?" she asked, turning back towards the four men.

"Come and sit down, my child, and we'll explain."

20

Suzanne

1949

Things started to get out of hand two days later.

Suzanne couldn't sleep any more. Every time she closed her eyes, she thought she could hear a plaintive, guttural noise coming from the forest just outside her house. Most of the time, she got up, turned on the gramophone and sat in the lounge. She would put on her favourite record and sing with Lucienne Boyer as she pushed the curtains aside to keep an eye on her surroundings.

Speak to me of love . . .

But the tears always ended up flowing down her cheeks as she sang.

Tears of fear and regret.

Why had she accepted this job? Why had she given up hope of ever seeing her daughter again? She was certain now that only madness awaited her on this island.

Her isolation would end in madness.

It was as inevitable as the storm which thundered in the distance as it edged ever closer.

As unshakeable and determined as the German bombers in the jet-black skies over Paris.

But Suzanne was a survivor. She had lived through too much to give in now.

Since talking to the children, she had thought long and hard. She was now convinced that the clock the children mentioned was the one hanging above the door at the end of the dormitory corridor. Especially since the only other clock in the blockhouse was in the kitchen.

What's more, no one on staff actually knew what was behind the sealed door. The director had forbidden them from trying to open it, claiming that that part of the blockhouse hadn't yet had a safety inspection.

Suzanne had no idea what she would find beyond that door.

But she became convinced that behind it lay the answers to many of her questions.

That's where she would find what she needed to reassure the children about the Erlking and the floating clock.

So she came up with a plan.

But for this to work, she was going to need Françoise's help.

"You want me to do *what*?"

Françoise hadn't meant to shout, but her friend's request was so unexpected that it had caught her off guard. They were smoking as they walked together along the cliffs during their morning break.

"Just a few minutes, long enough for me to go to his office and get the key," explained Suzanne.

"But don't you think it's . . . dangerous? You could lose your job. All over a few nightmares!"

A powerful wave slammed into the rock wall below and sprayed the two women, who were too distracted to notice the fine droplets settling on their skin.

"Listen, I know it's hard to understand, but Victor has noticed it too. And what Fabian did is clear proof that something is not right. Plus . . ."

"What, what else is there?" Françoise asked as she puffed worriedly on her cigarette.

"The drawings. I checked this morning. They're in every room now. The children have all been 'visited'."

"What if it's all just a misunderstanding? I don't know . . . Maybe it's just someone from the night staff who goes into their rooms to make sure they're sleeping or turn out any forgotten lights . . ."

"Maybe! But I have to find out. It'll only take ten minutes. I'll get the key, open the door, look around, and then put it back. Ten minutes," promised Suzanne.

"During which I have to keep the director occupied . . ."

"Exactly."

"You're not asking me to . . ."

"Oh God, no! Keep him busy however you like. I don't know. Tell him . . . there's an intruder! Tell him you saw a man in the forest, a man watching you smoke. That's serious enough to get him to leave his office."

"But Suzie . . ."

"Please! After this I promise I won't bother you with their nightmares anymore."

"Why don't you wait until he's teaching? Then you'd have over an hour," suggested Françoise without much conviction. Her friend's determination seemed to have already crushed all other possibilities.

"He always locks his door when he's leaving his office for that long. He has to be called away suddenly, so he doesn't give it any thought," argued Suzanne.

"I'm warning you, if we lose our jobs, you'll be swimming back to the mainland!"

The two women agreed to put their plan into action after lunch. In the meantime, they went about their daily tasks in heavy silence.

Around two thirty, the director was sitting in his office quietly savouring a cigar as he went over the final details of the outing to the mainland. Suddenly, a scream coming from the kitchen caused him to jump out of his chair. But before he could leave the room, Françoise burst in and stopped in front of him. "There's someone on the island!" she wailed. "I saw him! He had a rifle!"

"What?"

"Come quickly!"

"Are you sure? No one is allowed to dock here . . ."

"I saw him! Oh God, I was so scared . . ."

It seemed Françoise had missed her calling in life. Her talents as an actress left no room for doubt. The director hurried out of his office, forgetting to lock the door, and even leaving his still smoking cigar in the ashtray. As soon as he was gone, Suzanne slipped inside to get the key.

She quickly made her way down the corridor. As she did so, the children looked out of their rooms, and Suzanne was certain she could read gratitude as well as curiosity on their faces. When she reached the door at the end, they all stepped out into the corridor as if to encourage her or share a final message.

Sandrine slid the huge key into the lock.

She stepped inside the forbidden wing, feeling around for a light switch and fighting the urge to vomit as she became aware of the overpowering smell of cleaning products that filled the air around her. Her right hand finally found a light switch and the neon bulbs hissed with discontent before eventually flooding the space with harsh light. She walked to the end of the corridor and discovered a room as big as the dining hall. But here, there were no cheerful murals on the grey walls. No welcoming table at its centre. Just three beds on wheels.

"Hospital beds," whispered Suzanne.

She walked around the room examining the medical equipment which was carefully stored away in metal drawers. Syringes, intravenous drips, a refrigerator stocked with jars of blood, packets of gauze, a wide range of pills, a sterilizer, morphine, an electrocardiogram, and more.

Suzanne walked over to a strange electrical machine hooked up to a mass of tangled cables that reminded her of jellyfish tentacles. She read the metal label on the front: *electroencephalogram*.

My God, what is this? What are they doing to the children?

Suzanne shivered. She took a step back, realizing it was time to go.

She had to get out of there.

Return the key.

Demand an explanation.

She turned out the lights and the white curtains between the beds disappeared like ghosts into the darkness. Suzanne closed the metal door and locked it, then turned around.

That's when she saw him, standing perfectly still at the other end of the corridor.

The director.

Or rather, as she now knew, the *Erlkönig*.

"Come with me, Suzanne. I think we both have some explaining to do."

21

Sandrine

November 1986

"Why did my grandmother bring me to this island?"

"To help you escape."

"That doesn't make any sense," protested Sandrine.

"Not yet, but you'll understand soon enough."

"When? At 8:37? Today? Tomorrow? A year from now?"

"Time is relative, Sandrine."

"I know, I've heard that before. Is the Erlking real then?"

"Yes," replied Claude.

"And the children from the camp saw him? And you all did, too?"

"Exactly. That's why they died," explained Maurice.

"You realize we're talking about a creature from a poem coming to life, right? Claude, you're a doctor, you're supposed to be governed by logic . . ."

"Call him the *Erlkönig*, the boogeyman, the devil, or the SS soldier. The name doesn't matter. *He* is the reason the children wanted to flee, and now *he's* the reason you must escape."

Sandrine felt sick. Her migraine was growing more intense by the minute, as though it was feeding on her confusion. She tried in vain to convince herself they were all mad, but Françoise's warning echoed through her mind: *People hide behind the word "madness" when they can't or don't want to accept a strange reality. Don't make that mistake.*

"Okay, fine . . . Let's say you're right," she conceded to save time. "How do I get away? The *Lazarus* is on the mainland

and Simon is probably dancing to sea shanties after a few too many glasses of rum!"

"Simon is dead. We're the only ones left," said Claude.

"Dead? How?"

"You don't have much time, Sandrine. Look at the clock," urged Victor.

She did so almost involuntarily. Their words, though insane, were strangely comforting. Part of her wanted to refute them, but another part of her accepted them unquestioningly. Sandrine read the time on the clock. "7:35."

"Just over an hour left," said Maurice.

"But how can I get off the island if Simon is dead?"

"You have to leave us behind, Sandrine. Forget about us," Paul said weakly. "Like you forgot about Suzanne. Just remember the sound of our voices."

As if in answer, the jukebox came to life without anyone going near it and began its gentle litany of words.

Speak to me of love . . .

Suzanne.

It was her favourite record.

Why do I feel like I listened to it with her?

No images resurface. Just smells and sensations.

A freshly baked apple pie . . .

A rough hand stroking my cheek . . .

A silhouette moving towards the gramophone to start the song again . . .

Could it be?

When Sandrine opened her eyes, a metal key sat on the table. She had no idea which of the four men had placed it in front of her. When she looked up at them, she was struck by their pallid complexions.

"What's wrong? What's going on?" she asked.

Maurice collapsed first. His chair made a muffled thump as it hit the carpet.

And say what I'm longing to hear . . .

Then Claude passed out. Just before his head slammed into the table, she thought she saw him smile at her.

Victor used his final seconds to voice one last piece of advice before his breathing stopped. "Hurry."

"Let us go, Sandrine. That's it. It's the only way," Paul said, struggling to finish his sentences.

"I don't understand . . ."

"Isolating yourself here won't protect you, it will just cause you more suffering. Flee now, hurry . . . Forget about us . . ."

"Paul . . . I'm sorry . . ."

"If you come across the feral cat, you must kill it, Sandrine. It's the only way to escape the Erlking for good . . ."

Paul's head began its trajectory towards the table once the muscles in his neck had gone slack. Sandrine had just enough time to intercept it and place it down gently on the wooden surface.

She stood there for several minutes, tears streaming down her face as she took in the bodies of the island's inhabitants one last time. Poisoned hot chocolate dripped off the side of the table and onto the carpet like blood gushing from an open wound.

The jukebox finished its song and fell silent as Sandrine picked up the key and ran to the blockhouse.

22

Suzanne

1949

"Experiments," the director said casually, as if speaking about nothing more sinister than a routine medical check-up. He relit his cigar and watched Suzanne's face.

"Experiments? On the children?"

"Precisely. We're neither the first nor the last to conduct such experiments. The Germans had the Lebensborn programme. And we think the Americans had something similar."

"Are you suggesting that the French government has asked you to—"

"No, no, let's not get carried away! That said, I am thoroughly convinced that our results will attract the attention of our politicians."

"You can't be serious! This is horrific!"

"Come now," the director said reassuringly. "The experiments aren't painful. I'm not a monster! I simply study their behaviour. I'm collecting data and monitoring their heartrate when confronted with certain stimuli. I use the most sophisticated equipment available. Did you see the electroencephalogram?"

"Yes."

"It allows me to measure their brainwaves! To quantify their fear, joy, stress, and fatigue! Thanks to that marvel, we can turn emotions into concrete data that we can plot and study!"

"But isn't it dangerous for them?" asked Suzanne, still worried.

"Not at all. Most of the time, they're asleep. If we need them to participate, we wake them up gently and explain what we need them to do. They all go along with it without the slightest objection."

"Do their parents know?"

"Of course! They all signed a release form," replied the director. "I understand you have questions, but you should have come to me directly to spare us this whole misunderstanding."

"Why don't the children remember any of it?" she asked.

He stared at her for a moment, his lips pursed. *This woman won't give up,* he thought to himself as he puffed on his cigar. *Nothing I can say will satisfy her . . . It's a good thing I took certain precautions . . .*

"As I said," he finally continued aloud, "they're asleep." He smiled to mask his exasperation.

"They should wake up when you take them from their beds."

"Ah, nothing gets past you. I knew you were bright. That's why I hired you. Out of respect for your work, I'll share my secret: it's all about making the world a better place."

"Making the world a better place?"

"Yes, don't you remember the advert? *Menier Chocolate: making the world a better place!*"

"No, I'm afraid I don't recall," replied Suzanne.

"Have you ever heard of Pervitin? It's a drug. During the war, the Germans gave it to their soldiers. And guess how they administered it to them? They put it in their hot chocolate. Clever, wasn't it? I use the same technique here: just before bed, we make them hot chocolate and the doctors add a little sedative to the milk. The children love it, as you've seen."

"You . . . You're drugging them?"

"Suzanne, it's nothing serious, I assure you! I know from experience that the children are healthy. It's really just monitoring, that's all."

"So you're the *Erlkönig.*"

"Do they really call me that? I'm both honoured and slightly shocked. I'm not a monster, as you well know. But Goethe was a genius, it's true . . ."

"I don't believe you."

This time, the director failed to hide his annoyance. He methodically stubbed out his cigar in the ashtray, using the pause in the conversation to underscore the importance of what he would say next. "Do you remember the contract you signed, Suzanne?" he asked sternly.

"Yes."

"In addition to the fact that you are prohibited from ever leaving the island without my consent, you also committed to never revealing any details about the camp to anyone else."

"I thought that clause was to keep us from talking to the competition, not to keep experiments I feel are dangerous to the children's health a secret," she countered, determined not to leave the office until the director had promised to immediately suspend his "experiments".

"Did your daughter tell you she's had a baby girl?"

Suzanne opened her mouth, but no sound came out. She stared at the director, a blend of disgust and anger on her face. "How . . . How did you—"

"I'm a meticulous man. We performed a background check on all of our employees in case we needed leverage at some point. Just in case . . ."

"You *are* a monster!"

"What do you think the police would say if they found a former collaborator hiding out on this island? I'm referring to . . . horizontal collaboration, of course, if you catch my drift."

"Françoise has nothing to do with this!" replied Suzanne fiercely.

"True, but it is strange that she's the only one to have seen a supposed intruder at the precise moment when you were sneaking into the laboratory."

Suzanne could hardly breathe. Questions whizzed through her mind. Had he really just threatened them? Had her daughter really given birth without letting her know? She suddenly felt incredibly alone. Not just geographically or physically, but emotionally.

Speak to me of love.

She wanted to take refuge in her house and destroy the gramophone so she would never have to hear that song, that enchantment, again. She had to get away. Far away from this monster. As far away as she could get.

"Why the children?" she asked, delving deeper into the horror despite her better instincts.

"Haven't you figured it out? I would have thought their use of the term *Erlkönig* would have clued you in. They're all children born to French women and German SS soldiers. Half-bloods. It's my duty to study them to see if the destructive genes they inherited from their fathers will be problematic for the reconstruction of our nation. Listen, I'll make you a deal."

"A deal?"

"I promise to stop the experiments, and you promise to keep quiet. We've collected enough data already."

"And my daughter?"

"If you agree, she never needs to know. The experiments stop, you get back to work, and Françoise keeps her hair and her dignity. Making the world a better place."

"You're never going to let me leave this place, are you?"

"The baby's name is Sandrine. She's a beautiful, healthy little girl. Let's make sure she stays that way."

The director waited for Suzanne to leave, then lit another cigar. He'd lied to her, of course. He'd omitted certain details about the experiments that the curious governess would never have accepted. Speaking of which, despite his thinly veiled threats, he still wasn't certain she would keep their discussion to herself. What if Suzanne talked? Were the tears he had seen on her cheeks before she left tears of revolt or resignation? The director was filled with doubts. Was this a risk worth taking?

And she wasn't the only problem.

The children.

They had alerted her.

With their fatigue.

Their nightmares.

Their fuzzy memories.

They could repeat all of it to their parents.

"The subjects have been compromised," he whispered to himself through the cloud of thick smoke. "They're useless to me now. Dangerous. I must find a solution."

23

Sandrine

November 1986

Sandrine ran as fast as she could through the forest as the lid of dark clouds slowly descended until they seemed to brush the tops of the tallest trees. The raindrops felt like tiny frozen arrows burrowing into her skin, but she didn't slow down until she reached the treeline. She stopped to take a deep breath and turned her tormented face skyward. Then she took one more step and finally the roof of the blockhouse came into view.

As she passed what was left of the old sports pitch, Sandrine caught sight of a female figure standing on the cliff edge. She domed her left hand over her eyes to block out the rain and make sure she hadn't mistaken a twisted boulder for a person. But she had been right the first time: a woman was standing stock still looking out to sea.

Sandrine cautiously made her way towards the mysterious figure. She tried to call out to the stranger, but the wind was so strong and the crashing waves so loud, that there seemed to be little point. She thought about placing her hand on the woman's shoulder, but decided against it, afraid the surprise might lead to disaster with the edge of the cliff looming less than a metre away. Once she reached the woman, Sandrine stood to one side and approached her from the right.

"Madam?" she shouted at the top of her lungs.

She was unable to say another word. Nor move another muscle. What she was seeing was impossible.

And yet, there was Suzanne, contemplating the water.

She stared at her grandmother, who remained perfectly still, standing very upright, her eyes unmoving while her hair danced in the wind like the frayed pieces of a ripped dress.

Sandrine looked towards the sea, trying to spot whatever was holding Suzanne's attention, but all she could make out was the rough surf. She turned back to her grandmother's ashen complexion and waited for a sign, anything that might explain why she had found herself in the presence of this woman who had to be a pure product of her imagination.

"I have to go now," she said. "You're not real. I don't know why I'm seeing you, but you're not real. Maybe I'm losing my mind, but I don't have time to think about you right now . . . I have to seek refuge elsewhere . . ."

She turned away from Suzanne and towards the blockhouse, but as she did so, her grandmother gestured with her chin towards the sea, urging her to look out at the water.

That's when Sandrine saw them.

Among the freezing, choppy waves.

The boat was sinking at an astounding rate. Half of the hull was already underwater.

The children struggled in the waves; they were trying their best to keep their heads above water and shouted incomprehensibly, surrounded by fear and death. Wearing bright-orange life vests, the only two adults on board jumped into the water and made their way straight to the rocks, ignoring the flailing campers. Once they were safe, they climbed up a corniche to reach the firm ground of the island. They walked past Sandrine without seeing her, as though she too were a ghost, and disappeared into the forest.

Sandrine could still hear them all. The wind and the waves had gone quiet and the tree branches had stopped rubbing together. As if the island itself had paused to watch the spectacle. She heard their cries as they grew weaker. The crunch of skulls impaled on pointed rocks. Macabre gurgling. The slap of palms trying to push off the surface of the water as if it were solid matter. The final cries full of rage and resignation. The lapping sound created by their sinking bodies.

And then nothing.

No more boat.

No more children.

Suzanne, too, had disappeared.

Only Sandrine remained.

So that's what happened . . . The children were murdered . . . That's the secret of this island . . .

She fell on her knees in the muddy earth and pounded her fists into the ground.

"Sacrificed to preserve the island . . . To save this bloody island!" she shouted, cursing the bit of rock surrounded by ocean on which she now found herself.

She stayed there crying for the children a few minutes longer, her fists clenched in anger. Then she opened her right hand. The key was still there.

It took all of her strength to stand up and run to the blockhouse. She made her way down the corridor and through the dining hall where the children had been happy once. She cried harder as she walked past the doors to the victims' bedrooms.

Sandrine was shaking so badly that it took her several attempts to insert the key into the lock. She didn't dare look up at the clock overhead.

She finally opened the forbidden door.

And stepped inside.

THE SECOND BEACON
The Erlking

Du liebes Kind, komm, geh' mit mir !
Gar schöne Spiele spiel ich mit dir .

Goethe, "Erlkönig"

Thou lovely child, come, go with me!
Delightful games I'll play now with thee.

Goethe, "The Erlking"

I

November 1986

The phone woke him at 7:40.

Too early. Two hours before his usual wake-up time. Damian groaned and stretched, waiting for the ringing to stop. But as soon as it did, it started again, seemingly more determined than before.

"God dammit," he grumbled as he stood up. "Can't even have a lie-in on my day off . . ."

He made his way to the lounge, said good morning to the framed picture of his daughter (the only one in the flat: Melanie stood proudly in front of the gates to her middle school in new red trainers with pink laces), and picked up the receiver.

"Hello, boss?"

Shit, thought Damian when he recognized his colleague's voice. *No going back to bed this time . . .*

"Yes, Antoine?"

"Boss, we've got a problem down at the station."

"A big enough problem to drag me out of bed on my day off?"

"I think so, boss," Antoine replied gravely.

"What is it?"

"We found a young woman on the beach."

"So? Probably just got lost after a night of partying too hard . . . Is there anything else?"

"Well, she's not making sense."

"Just keep her at the station until she sobers up."

"It's not that simple, boss. She claims she came from an

island off the coast. And there's not a drop of alcohol in her blood."

"What?" Damian said worriedly, suddenly picking up on Antoine's serious tone.

"It would be better if you could come in. It's hard to explain on the phone."

"Christ, what do you mean?"

"She . . . She's covered in blood and keeps saying children have been murdered."

"Blood?"

"Yes, a lot of it."

"Where is she?"

"At the hospital. She's in shock. The doctors sedated her so she can rest."

"Who found her?" Damian asked, fully awake now.

"A jogger. He's at the station giving his statement. He's the one who called the emergency services. Boss, I'm sorry, but I really don't know what to do . . ."

"All right. Where are you?"

"At the hospital with her."

"Okay. Stay there in case she wakes up. And fax me the hospital admission file asap. I'm on my way to the station to talk to the jogger."

"Boss?"

"Yeah?"

"I'm sorry about your day off."

Damian hung up and stood stock still next to the phone for a minute. A woman covered in blood? An island? Murdered children? He could hardly believe what he'd just heard. Villers-sur-Mer was a tiny seaside town with barely two thousand inhabitants, all of whom were completely devoid of criminal ambitions. In the three years he'd worked there, the only illegal activities brought to his attention had been a few noisy late-night dips in the sea and one stolen postbox. In fact, the town was so quiet that the station was facing permanent closure so that the powers that be could "concentrate law enforcement officers in priority areas".

The detective took a quick shower, threw on a pair of jeans and a sweatshirt (it was his day off after all) and made a call to check on his daughter. No tragedy could ever come between him and this ritual. At the beginning of every month, he called a phone hundreds of miles away and an eager voice would always reply on the other end, as if the expected call was just as important to both parties.

"Hello?"

"Patrice?"

"Hey, Damian."

"Any news?"

"No, still nothing."

"That's okay. Soon, maybe."

And that was it.

The exact same exchange they had been having every month for three years. Sentences reduced to the bare minimum but that somehow also managed to communicate their fundamental meaning—the ultimate concentration of hope and disillusionment in the smallest number of words possible.

Fifteen minutes later, Damian parked in front of the police station. He said hello to the receptionist and collected the jogger's statement before making his way to his desk, where the witness was seated.

"Thank you for waiting for me," began Damian.

"Of course. My boss thought it was a joke when I told him I was at the police station. He doesn't like it when we're late."

"We'll contact him to confirm your story," Damian reassured him as he read the written statement, which the man had signed an hour earlier. "Tell me exactly how you found this woman on the beach."

"Well, like I told your colleague, I go for a run every Monday morning. To get the weekend's excesses out of my system if you know what I mean. I'd finished my run so I was just jogging along slowly on the beach, cooling down, and that's when I saw her."

"What first drew your attention to her?"

"Oh, you know, at that time of the morning in November, there aren't a whole lot of people out for a stroll . . . And, well, I noticed how she was walking—she was all over the place, like a drunk who's had one too many beers. I went over to her to make sure she was okay, and that's when I noticed her clothes were drenched. I didn't realize it was blood right away."

"What did you think when you realized what it was?"

"That she must be hurt. I was scared for her. You know, I felt like I was in that horror film . . . Oh, shit, what's the title? Help me out here. At the end a woman's walking down the road and her dress is covered in blood . . ."

"Doesn't ring a bell," replied Damian, who wasn't much of a film aficionado.

"Oh, come on . . . It's on the tip of my tongue . . . Wait a minute . . . *Carrie!*"

"Never seen it. So, what did you do then?"

"I asked her if she was hurt. But she didn't really answer. She just kept repeating the same words over and over again. It didn't make any sense . . . The island, the children, the pearl king . . ."

"The pearl king?"

"Yes," said the jogger with a nod. "That's what it sounded like to me. I told her to stay there and I ran to a café which had just opened. The owner let me use his phone to call the emergency services. When I came back, she was sitting on the sand, still mumbling the same words again and again. That's it."

"You did the right thing."

"Is she . . . Is she okay?" asked the man.

"She's sedated. She needs to rest, but you've been a huge help," Damian reassured him.

"Christ, I never would have thought I'd see something like that in Villers!"

"Me neither," mumbled the detective.

Damian spent the rest of the morning combing through recent missing persons reports from the region. None of them matched the hospital information, which Antoine had just faxed over. Next, he called all of the psychiatric institutions in the area to make sure no female patients were missing. But again came up empty-handed. When he put the name on the hospital forms—Sandrine Vaudrier—into the police department's electronic phone directory, a dozen addresses and phone numbers came up, most of them with the Paris area code. He called each of them, but every time a woman picked up and confirmed her identity.

As a last resort, he called the tax office in Caen, since Sandrine Vaudrier could have declined to have her contact information published in the phone book. But nothing turned up there either.

The detective then changed tack and called the coast guard to see if there had been any boating accidents out at sea during the night, but here too, he drew a blank. In November, few people were willing to brave the cold and the erratic currents to visit the coastal islands. It seemed this woman had simply emerged from the waves, mysteriously rising out of the sea like Venus Anadyomene.

Around two o'clock that afternoon, Damian finally got a call from the hospital.

Sandrine had woken up.

2

"Hello?"

"Patrice?"

"Hey, Damian."

"Any news?"

"No, still nothing."

"That's okay. Soon, maybe."

Patrice Fleurier, superintendent of the Saint-Amand-Montrond police force, sat quietly for a few minutes. Every time his former colleague called, it left the bitter taste of injustice in his mouth. They had worked together for a dozen or so years and had quickly become close friends despite the fact that the two young policemen seemed to be opposites in every respect. Patrice was a stocky, thick-necked solid-looking man, who spoke so quickly that it was hard to get a word in edgeways. Damian had given him the nickname Bucephalus—an allusion to Alexander the Great's famous horse. As for Damian, he was rather more phlegmatic. His long, thin frame always gave the impression that he was moving slowly, and this was only exacerbated when the two men stood side by side. He rarely spoke, and when he did, he got right to the point. Not a single superfluous syllable ever crossed his lips. Patrice had at first thought of calling him the Sharpshooter, but it was such a good nickname that it would have overshadowed his own. In the end, he settled on the Astronaut, because Damian's unhurried strides reminded him of the footage he'd seen of the first man on the moon.

When they were off duty, Bucephalus and the Astronaut generally spent their evenings in the local bars. They had toured all of the region's wine festivals—Sancerre, Menetou-Salon, Châteaumeillant, and more—in the hope that they would both get a feel for the local culture (every time they were called to a crime scene, the victim opened a bottle before beginning his or her statement) and meet a beautiful woman who would seduce them without a drop of sauvignon or gamay in sight.

Not long after he moved to the region, Damian met Linda. Bucephalus watched over the young couple with pride. They had met partly thanks to him. His constant, enthusiastic persuasion tactics had finally convinced the shy Linda to make the first move on Damian, who had been sitting a few metres away on a café terrace on the Place Carrée.

Two years later, they got married on a bright summer's day. For the first time since Damian had known him, Patrice, whom he'd chosen as his best man, stammered during his speech. His words seemed to hesitate before leaving his mouth, as if weighed down by a misfortune no one could ever have imagined at the time. He said it was the emotion of it all, including the joy of seeing Linda's belly looking round enough for him to hope he'd soon be a godfather.

A few months later, Melanie was born.

A few years later, Melanie disappeared.

On a foggy, grey winter's night.

On her way home from middle school at the start of her first term.

Around six o'clock that evening, Linda started to worry when Melanie didn't come home. She called all her friends, but none of them had seen her since home time. Damian was in Paris for a week-long training course. When she still hadn't heard anything at eight o'clock, she called Patrice. He immediately sent out a patrol and had several teams talk to the last people who had seen Melanie. Damian came home that night and walked the streets himself.

A week later, Melanie was still missing.

The police organized searches of the surrounding fields and

forests and most of the town volunteered to help. Specialist teams dredged the Saint-Amandois Canal as well as the Cher and Marmande rivers.

They even searched the part of the town's sewer system between the stone bridge and the old cemetery, too, because the local teenagers often hid at the entrance to the tunnel drinking, especially in the summer when the cool water of the Marmande helped chill the beers they had stolen from their parents' garages.

They found nothing in the ruins of Montrond Fortress.

So, after two months of fruitless searches and zero leads, hypotheses fuelled by centuries-old traditions began to surface.

People spoke of witchcraft.

Of black magic.

Of werewolves and other dark creatures.

Of *birettes*—men and women who sell their souls to the devil and wander the night dressed in white sheaths.

Of satanic cults and the blood of virgins.

Of a cemetery that had been disturbed to build the new town centre—la Place Carrée—and of ghosts on a quest for revenge.

The seers, of which there were many in the Berry region, got involved.

One of them led the police to Mers-sur-Indre, home of the devil's pool described by George Sand. But instead of a body, all they found were stagnant water and a few tadpoles surprised by the sudden attention.

In the end, neither supernatural powers nor rational police-work managed to locate Melanie.

She became a mystery in a mysterious region.

The investigation ran out of steam as the police tried to untangle a host of convoluted statements and false leads. They began looking in neighbouring local areas, but never searched beyond the confines of the region. The local media outlets tried to maintain public interest by regularly publishing articles featuring large photographs of Melanie, but eventually the posters in the windows of the high street shops became illegible, bleached by the sun, and no one objected or replaced them. The case was filed away and forgotten only two years after Melanie walked through the gates of her middle school for the last time. Memories of her faded, just as fleeting and lonely as a will-o'-the-wisp in a Berry graveyard.

Bucephalus watched as the Astronaut struggled to find enough oxygen to breathe. He realized that, paradoxically, his friend needed to get as far away from earth as possible to avoid suffocating. Damian requested a transfer. His wife felt he was turning his back on her and on their daughter's memory. He left the region and the forgotten posters in the streets.

He arrived in Villers-sur-Mer alone.

He kept hoping, kept calling Patrice.

But over the years, his faith turned into a ritual devoid of illusions.

Melanie was dead, he was sure of that. Her body had probably been hidden somewhere inaccessible. This painful realization was his refuge from madness. He had built walls of resignation around his daughter's memory, and now emerged only to call his former colleague at the start of each month.

Then he slunk back inside to keep from sinking into depression.

3

When Damian arrived at the hospital, a single thought was playing on repeat in his mind: *This can't be for real. Not here.*

Antoine welcomed him as soon as he stepped into the lobby with his usual, "Hi, boss!"

When Damian had asked why he called him that, Antoine had replied that it "sounded cool", mentioning a film that Damian inevitably hadn't seen. A film that took place in a small seaside town in the United States. A town like Villers. The next day, the detective had ventured to the municipal library to rent *Jaws* and see for himself. Damian had been forced to admit that it did have a certain ring to it. So he had let his colleague carry on, proudly allowing a small slice of Hollywood into their daily lives.

"Is she awake?" asked Damian as he followed Antoine to the lifts.

"Yes, boss."

"Have you spoken to her?"

"No, not since the beach. The psychiatrist wanted to meet with the person in charge of the investigation first."

"The psychiatrist?"

"Yes. She wants to see you before we talk to the victim."

"Why?" the detective asked, surprised.

"She's the only person who's spoken to her since the nurses finished all their physical tests. It seems they talked for quite a while, and when she left, they administered a sedative. The psychiatrist must have information to share with us, since she insisted on seeing you."

The two men made their way to the third floor, where a receptionist told them to wait for the specialist.

"What does she look like?" asked Damian, staring at the linoleum floor.

"The victim?"

"No, the psychiatrist. Is she an old woman with glasses?"

"No, quite the contrary. She's young and rather pretty. She looks like she recently graduated. She must not be from around here. I've never seen her before."

Damian remembered the only psychiatrist he had been unfortunate enough to know. Her waxy complexion and short, stiff, grey hair reminded him of a statue brought out in extremis from a museum storeroom. The so-called specialist had only mumbled incomprehensibly, offering him advice devoid of compassion and stale truisms memorized years earlier. She reeked of scepticism and the clear urge to terminate their interaction as quickly as possible.

Less than five minutes later, a young woman in a white coat came over. Antoine's description had been remarkably accurate. With her blonde hair pulled back in a ponytail, she offered the men a youthful smile and invited them to follow her.

"My office is this way," she explained, gesturing towards a corridor just past the reception desk. "Oh, I'm sorry," she said, turning around to hold out her right hand. "I'm Dr Veronique Burel. I'm one of the psychiatrists on staff here at the hospital."

After introducing themselves, the police officers sat down and watched guiltily as Dr Burel's shapely figure stepped around to the other side of the desk.

"I wanted to speak to you before you visit Ms Vaudrier," she said. "If that's even her real name, of course." The way she got straight to the point was proof she was used to working under pressure, omitting all superfluous information. "I was able to speak to her this morning, just after she was admitted," she went on. "It would be an understatement to say her story is incoherent."

"I'm glad I'm not the only one who thinks as much," Antoine interjected. He had heard the victim tell her improbable tale on the beach.

"So, she's lying," guessed Damian.

"I'm afraid it's not that simple, detective," countered Dr Burel.

It never is, thought Damian, remembering how he had stopped going to see his psychiatrist after shouting at her that none of her nonsense could ever bring Melanie back and slamming the door of her office shut behind him.

"The victim seems be suffering from acute stress, dissociative amnesia and partial memory loss, which all have one thing in common: they all stem from a past trauma."

"So, you think she could have been assaulted?" interrupted Antoine again.

"Yes, that's the impression I get. Here are the results of the blood tests conducted on her clothes," said the doctor as she slid a file towards the two men. "I've only just received them. The blood isn't hers. And she doesn't have any visible injuries, except for some cuts on the inside of her left wrist."

"Could she have been . . . raped?" Damian asked, clearly troubled by the thought.

"They've taken some samples, but I don't have the results yet."

"If she wasn't attacked and there is no evidence of sexual assault, how can you be so sure she's suffering from the conditions you mentioned?"

"Post-traumatic stress disorder, to be precise," rectified Dr Burel. "It's a common enough condition and easily identifiable, detective. Talking to her and observing her behaviour were enough."

"I trust your judgment," said Damian, "but I would like to question the victim so that I can draw my own conclusions as well. If she has someone else's blood all over her, there may be someone hurt out there somewhere, and my priority is to find them, since Ms Vaudrier is now out of harm's way."

"I understand, but *my* priority is to find out why all this woman remembers is her trip to a mysterious island. And I am almost certain that the answers to all of our questions will come from there, especially given that for now we have no other leads. I'm sure you'll be as intrigued by her statements as I am."

Veronique Burel opened a drawer and pulled out a tape recorder, which she placed in front of the policemen.

"You recorded her?" Damian asked, surprised.

"I did," she replied as she slid a cassette into the recorder. "With her permission, of course. It's a common practice in my field. Sometimes new details come to the fore on the second or third listen. I think you should hear what she says before I tell you a bit more about post-traumatic stress disorder. May I just check that you are in charge of this investigation? Because I can only share this recording with whoever is in charge."

Antoine glanced inquisitively at Damian. As a detective, Damian reported directly to the superintendent, who, when apprised of the situation, had simply asked him to wrap things up quickly. The superintendent hadn't mentioned Antoine at all.

Antoine immediately recognized the hesitation in his boss's eyes and stood up to leave. There was no need to risk angering the superintendent or compromising the case over a procedural error. In fact, he was almost relieved to escape the room. He had seen the victim on the beach. The blood. Her distress. Her fearfulness. As though a threatening shadow was hiding somewhere beneath the sand, waiting patiently to swallow her whole. His mission had been to collect her and get her safely to the hospital. But deep down, he would have preferred to hide away at the station and pretend it was a normal day. A day without Carrie White, a mysterious king, or murdered children.

The psychiatrist waited until he'd shut the door behind him, then pressed play.

Damian listened as Sandrine began to tell her story in a fragile, trembling voice.

4

When the psychiatrist turned off the tape recorder, Damian sat quietly for a moment. He stared at the machine, hoping for answers—as though a rational explanation might magically pop out of it, like a rabbit from a top hat. He knew the region well enough to know that no island had hosted a "holiday camp" like the one Sandrine had mentioned.

There had been a concentration camp on Aurigny Island and an orphanage on Jersey, but her descriptions didn't match any real place. What was more, no children's bodies had ever washed up on the local beaches. If a dozen corpses had suddenly emerged from the waves one day, there would be police reports and press articles in the local archives. And what about the legend of the Erlking? What did that have to do with anything? It was a poem any middle school student was likely to learn. Sandrine must have included it in her tale to make it more surreal and add a mythological dimension to her story.

"I know what you're thinking," Dr Burel said, breaking the silence. "You think she's crazy."

"I do, you're right," Damian admitted as he straightened in his chair. "It's the only explanation that makes any sense!"

"I'm guessing you've already called all of the psychiatric hospitals in the region?" she asked, a mischievous look in her eyes.

"I have," he replied with a nod.

"But none of them are missing a patient?"

"Not one. But madness isn't always locked away," countered the detective, who disliked the doctor's haughty tone. "Do you have any other information that could be helpful to the investigation? It's my belief that her statements are fabrications of a sick mind, but I still have to investigate them. And time is of the essence."

"Will you verify her identity?"

"I already have," he replied proudly.

"Any boating accidents?"

"Not for weeks," he said, getting into the swing of this game of questions-and-answers.

"Was there ever such a holiday camp?"

"I'm certain there wasn't."

"Are you going to look into the Goethe poem and the song lyrics she quotes?"

When Dr Burel mentioned the melody from Sandrine's story, a strange sensation came over Damian. He swallowed hard. Then, realizing the psychiatrist might read something into the gesture, he swallowed again, trying to pretend it was a meaningless reflex. Dr Burel watched him in silence, her professional mask firmly in place.

"Yes, of course," Damian said finally as he stood up to leave. "Thank you for sharing this tape with me. Now I'm going to need to ask this woman a few questions myself to get a concrete answer to the only question that really interests me: where that blood came from. And I fully intend—"

"She won't talk to you," interrupted the psychiatrist firmly.

"I'm sorry?"

"You can try, but with your preconceptions and your old-fashioned rationalism, she won't say a word," she retorted defiantly. "You see, her brain is like this tape recorder. It recorded a story and will simply repeat it again and again without shedding any further light on its meaning or veracity. You'll be stuck listening to the same song over and over again, like a scratched record. This woman has been traumatized. She's neither crazy nor a pathological liar. If you want to know where the blood came from, you'll have to trust me."

"Trust you!" the detective barked. He suddenly regretted

wearing jeans and a sweatshirt instead of a suit for his meeting with this arrogant woman.

"If I'm right, Sandrine has been tortured, most likely by a man," she insisted, clearly growing weary of the conversation. "The only way to get her to talk is to reassure her, to make her feel safe. And there's no way a man can do that right now. You'd remind her of whoever hurt her."

"Maybe she's just toying with us. I only want to ask her this: whose blood was it and where is that person now? After that, I'll leave you to your theories."

"Here, I made a copy of the recording," she said dryly as she held out a plastic box. Once he'd taken it, she gestured towards the door. "Go ahead and interrogate the victim. If you need my help, you know where to find me. Good luck."

Damian found Antoine leaning against a vending machine in the corridor. When he caught sight of the furious look on his boss's face, Antoine didn't dare finish his coffee and fell in step behind Damian without a word. When they reached room thirty-eight, a doctor let them in, advising them not to draw out the conversation. The patient was awake, but exhausted. The priority was to stabilize her condition by letting her rest as much as possible and avoiding all sources of stress. Damian feigned agreement as he signed the log and stepped into the room, determined to prove to Dr Burel that his methods were just as effective as hers.

Sandrine's eyes were open. Her pale, unmoving body reminded Damian of the work of an anonymous Flemish artist that had caught his eye once at the Fine Arts Museum in Rouen, and specifically a painting entitled *Young Woman on her Deathbed*.

The cold November light trickled in through the shutters, and the morose atmosphere immediately quelled the detective's enthusiasm.

He had expected to come face to face with a drooling madwoman, her features contorted and her hair tangled, but instead he discovered a pretty, fragile-looking woman whose gaze inspired nothing but kindness and gentleness. If there had ever been blood on her skin, the nurses had washed it away. Her dark-brown hair cascaded over her shoulders and her naturally pink lips curled into a slight smile when she realized the two men were there.

But Damian reminded himself that madness is often disguised under a veil of normality. He remembered that the witches of the Berry region weren't always old women with hooked noses, that sometimes they were beautiful strangers full of deceitful charm. And that in Goethe's poem, which his daughter had studied when she was ten years old, just before she disappeared, the Erlking himself enchanted children with sweet promises.

"Ms Vaudrier," Damian began, "can you hear me?"

She nodded.

"I'm Detective Bouchard and this is my colleague. Would it be all right if we asked you a few questions?"

She nodded again.

"Could you please tell us what happened?" he asked.

Sandrine stared at him.

Her eyes, which had appeared relaxed just seconds before (thanks to the sedatives Damian assumed) suddenly went dark. Her pupils dilated in response to some unseen emotion and her hands, which had been lying still at her sides, came together as if clutching an invisible object. Worry lines appeared on her face and she began to glance wildly from one man to the other, like a boat rocking in the waves.

"Don't worry," said Damian quickly, concerned by this sudden metamorphosis. "We're here to help. You're perfectly safe . . ."

The detective noticed the bandage on the inside of her left wrist. The hospital admissions report had mentioned the deep, uneven cuts. The dressing had bright-red stains on it now, which meant the wounds had reopened recently, like poorly healed stigmata.

★

"Don't worry . . ."

But it was too late.

Sandrine began her tale as Damian and Antoine looked on in astonishment. Her fear was palpable. Captivated by the feverish stream of words and hypnotized by her haunted face, neither one of them dared to interrupt her.

"Keep your mind busy . . .
   Recite your poem, for example . . .
   It'll make things easier . . .
   Tomorrow, when your teacher has you stand up in front of
the class, you'll have me to thank . . .
   Come here . . .
   Come closer . . .
   It'll make things easier . . ."

The next morning, Damian got up before his alarm went off.

He had spent much of the night listening to the tape and jotting down anything that seemed important to him. The words on the recording were identical to what he had heard Sandrine say in her room, as if she had memorized her lines for a performance. And she never revealed where the blood on her clothes had come from.

After that, Damian had contacted all of the hospitals in the region to see if they had admitted a seriously wounded patient suffering from severe blood loss, but none of them had.

Around three o'clock in the morning, he decided to go to bed, with Sandrine's voice still blowing through his head like a stubborn, inescapable wind.

He had dreamed of an island hidden in the fog. He strode across the wet grass, the smell of chlorophyll wafting in his nostrils. He touched the lichen-covered boulders as he passed, listening as an invisible animal yowled over the sound of the waves. A vast forest rose up across from him before suddenly disappearing. And then a woman cloaked in blood appeared out of thin air, like Niobe turned to stone, alone and unmoving amid the rocks and wild grasses. Her scarlet dress danced in the sea breeze like the flag of a ghost ship. Sandrine waited for him to reach her before mumbling an incantation in a hushed voice: *Who rides forth to-night, through storms so wild?*

Damian woke up in a sweat with the first line of Goethe's poem still echoing through the silent room. It took him a few seconds to realize he was at home in his flat and not out wandering on a damp, mysterious island. He cursed the night-mare and gave up on sleep altogether. Thirty minutes later, as the first rays of sunshine came over the horizon, he was in the car on his way to the station.

Damian shut himself in his office with a cup of hot coffee and spent the morning making calls. He left another message with the tax office in Caen and also managed to find out that there was no solicitor's office near the port in Villers-sur-Mer. Indeed there was no registered solicitor anywhere by the name of Mr Béguenau. And he could find no trace of anyone by the name of Suzanne Vaudrier, living or dead.

He talked to people at several different tourist offices throughout the region and spent a whole hour in discussion with the information desk at the navy headquarters in Caen, but no one could think of an island anything like the one Sandrine had described. And none of the ports along the coast had a boat called *Lazarus* in their records.

As he checked out the various potential clues in Sandrine's story, he crossed them out furiously on the list he had written the night before. Before long, there were only two leads left, and Damian swore out loud when he realized he was trying to find someone with nothing to go on but an old song from the twenties and a German poem.

That's not enough to justify asking the coast guard to search the islands one by one, hoping to find an old holiday camp and the bodies of a few residents, he thought bitterly.

It seemed obvious that though it had been told with discon-certing conviction, the whole story was a lie.

But where did the blood come from, for Christ's sake?

The tests had concluded that it was human blood.

Somewhere between one and two litres according to the experts.

And it didn't match Sandrine's blood type.

What happened?

*

Damian reluctantly admitted to himself that the case he had hoped to solve quickly was at a dead end.

A song and a poem.

Without thinking, he whispered the lyrics under his breath. *Speak to me of love, and say what I'm longing to hear . . .*

Everyone knew that song. It had been a symbol of rebirth and joy in a country that had survived a world war and didn't yet suspect another would soon follow, and it had become an integral part of France's cultural heritage and collective memory, sung by lovers and parents alike.

So why did Damian feel like this detail didn't fit with the rest of the story? Why did this anachronism bother him so much? Why had he felt so shaken when he had heard it in the psychiatrist's office?

Around one o'clock, he finally admitted he needed help with the case and decided to visit Dr Burel. *A change of scenery will do me good,* he thought, trying to convince himself as he grabbed his suit jacket. The four walls of his small office hadn't brought him any clarity, and the phone was unlikely to ring during his lunch hour. Maybe the psychiatrist would have new information from another talk with the victim.

"Detective! What a surprise! I thought you would have wrapped things up by now!" said Veronique Burel from behind her desk where she sat poring over a file, though she didn't look surprised to see him in the slightest.

"All right, no need to rub it in," replied Damian. "I wonder which psychological problem causes sarcasm," he joked. "Have you tried therapy?"

"Yes, of course. It's due to an acute allergy to people who think they know everything . . . Ever experienced anything like that?" she asked with a chuckle.

"It does ring a bell . . . But I'm not here to debate our respective shortcomings. I need some advice."

"Ah, I gather your session with Sandrine didn't quite go to plan then?" she said with a smile.

"No. I felt like I was listening to a recording . . ."

"I did warn you."

"Dr Burel . . ."

"Veronique," she insisted, by way of a peace offering.

"Okay. Veronique, is this woman crazy?"

"In some ways, yes. Madness is relative. You might think she's crazy, but for me she's perfectly sane."

"She's sane?" Damian asked, his voice raised in disbelief.

"The Erlking, the murdered children, the island dwellers so desperate they were willing to commit suicide one after another . . . It all means something, whether you believe it or not. Real madness lacks structure. That's not the case here. My job is to figure out what it means, or, in other words, to learn to understand her 'madness'. Have you had lunch?" she asked as she stood up.

Damian suddenly realized he hadn't. In fact, he hadn't had dinner the night before either. He had been running on nothing but caffeine for the past twenty-four hours. The psychiatrist unbuttoned her white coat and hung it on the rack near the window, then grabbed her handbag.

"Not yet," Damian replied.

"Perfect. Neither have I. I know a nice restaurant where we can talk more about our common acquaintance."

Five minutes later, they were sitting on a bench in the hospital garden enjoying sandwiches from the cafeteria. Dark clouds loomed on the horizon, threatening an imminent downpour.

"We do agree on one thing," admitted Veronique as she swallowed a mouthful. "Sandrine's story is pure fiction."

"In my line of work, people tend to lie when they're guilty," Damian noted as he watched several families stroll past. Some of them had a person in a cast with them, while others had no visible illnesses. One man struggled to push an old woman in a wheelchair. Another leaned sadly over a child's shoulder. They both seemed so pained that Damian couldn't figure out which one of them was the patient.

"Well, in mine, it's most often victims who lie. Did you notice anything when you spoke to her?"

An ambulance siren rang out in the distance. Damian waited solemnly for the vehicle to park in front of the building and silence its cry. The entire park seemed to go quiet as it awaited the arrival of a new tragedy.

"She . . . She was frightened. Terribly frightened," he finally replied. "The look in her eyes, her hands, her pursed lips . . . Her story felt like an incantation. It felt like she was trying to ward off the devil."

"Have you ever tried to ward him off, detective?"

The question caught Damian by surprise. He stared at the psychiatrist for a moment, wondering if she knew. A detective with a tragic past arrives in a small town, but the rumours cling to him from hundreds of miles away . . . It was more than plausible.

He thought back to the searches in the woods.

To the divers combing the murky waters but coming up empty-handed.

To the endless nights hoping the phone would free him from this state of not knowing.

To the horned devil hiding in the fog and his evil laugh, which echoed in Damian's ears the day he left without having found Melanie.

"No, never," he lied. He took a sip of his drink.

"No one ever succeeds. Sandrine thinks she's keeping him at bay by telling the story of the island. But it's an illusion, a refuge."

"A refuge?"

"Remember yesterday when I told you about post-traumatic stress disorder? When people are subjected to intense stress, their minds build up walls to protect them."

"What sort of stress?"

"The worst kind. Rape, physical or psychological abuse,

constant fear, isolation . . . In these cases, the brain disconnects the emotional circuit to protect the victim. It's a complex process, so I'll spare you the technical details, but the brain can produce hormones that function much like hard drugs to anaesthetize our emotions."

"What do you mean exactly?"

"Imagine yourself in a stressful situation: your brain secretes enough adrenaline and cortisol to produce an adequate response. In this scenario, the hormones are far from dangerous. But if the stress is extreme enough, the dose of hormones secreted could become lethal for both your brain and your heart. You could literally die of stress. So, what does the brain do to keep us alive?"

"It disconnects?" suggested Damian.

"Precisely. It disconnects our emotional circuit—the one that secretes adrenaline and cortisol—and anaesthetizes it by producing morphine- and ketamine-like substances. That way, the victim experiences the violence in a kind of trance, protected by an emotional void that protects them. That's the famous wall I was telling you about."

"But I don't see how that applies to Sandrine."

"She has all of the symptoms of PTSD," affirmed Veronique, as she had the day before.

"And no evidence of rape?"

"The tests that came in this morning didn't seem to detect anything like that."

"So you're basing this theory on nothing but the fact that this woman has told us an unbelievable story?"

"The wall I mentioned protects the victim as the violence is happening. It's a neurological response to a short-term experience of extreme stress."

"That much I understand," said Damian.

"But afterwards," continued Dr Burel, "when the victim has escaped the perpetrator, they're often left with PTSD symptoms: anxiety, trouble sleeping, repeating the same story over and over, avoidance behaviours, etc."

"You're losing me again . . ."

"Sorry. To get back to Sandrine, I'm certain that her symptoms are due to PTSD."

"But what about the island? The children? The Erlking?"

"Imagine that you want to forget about something in your past. You want to completely erase it without leaving a gap in your memories. How would you fill the hole?"

Damian hid his discomfort by pretending to think, but as soon as Veronique finished her sentence, a throaty laugh that reeked of sulphur echoed through his mind.

Go on, you worthless excuse of a father, answer the lady. What would you do to erase the way you abandoned her, to forget how you left your daughter to dance with the devil? Eh? Thank you in any case, I had a good time with her . . .

"I . . . I would make something up," mumbled Damian.

"Exactly. That's what I call a 'refuge': a parallel memory that replaces reality to put a stop to the victim's suffering. An illusion created by the brain to stay alive, much like the wall I mentioned earlier. In short, it's a place for the victim to hide from the truth, like children hide from monsters under the covers—real or imagined."

"So, this story . . . You think it's her refuge?"

"Yes," she confirmed. "That's why she keeps repeating it. To forget what she really experienced. It's a sophisticated lie which she isn't aware she's telling, one her brain has spun to hide the truth. For Sandrine, the island, the Erlking, the last residents, and the children—they all exist. And it's likely that this imaginary narrative is dotted with details from reality, like beacons, to remind her why the lie is so necessary."

"So, how do we untangle the truth from the lie? How do we find out what really happened to 'Sandrine'?" Damian asked, clearly frustrated.

"I only see one way, detective. We're going to have to take shelter in her refuge. We have no other choice."

" . . . but her treatment could take weeks, months, years even. The only way to speed things up is to reassure Sandrine, to make her feel safe enough to come out of hiding. And the only way to do that is to prove to her that the perpetrator can no longer hurt her. You see the problem? She has the answers to all our questions but won't share them with us unless we can help her feel secure enough to open the door and step outside," concluded Dr Burel.

Damian returned to the station to type up his report. He would have liked to see Sandrine and ask her all his questions, but he knew she would simply repeat her story from the day before: the children, the island, and the Erlking. And Veronique had also convinced him that rest was the first step to healing an intense trauma. Though he had no idea exactly what had happened to Sandrine, he couldn't deny she was obviously exhausted. He thought back to her pallid skin and slow, weak movements. Whoever the real Erlking was, Damian was certain a few more days with him would have killed Sandrine.

He drafted a summary of his conversation with the psychiatrist, attaching photocopies of all the test results, the hospital admission form, and a photo of Sandrine. He listed the various phone calls he had made, noting the few answers he had obtained, and placed the file on the superintendent's desk to await his return from Caen the next day. Damian also left the recording Veronique had made. He couldn't help but imagine his boss's face when he was confronted with all of this information. His initial reflex would be to dismiss it all, as Damian had done: *Impossible. Not here, not in our little town. This woman's crazy.*

But madness is relative, he said to himself with a smile, recalling his discussion with Dr Burel.

Back at his desk, he got to work on a public appeal asking any witnesses to come forward. If no one reported Sandrine missing within forty-eight hours, he would have to get the press and local radio stations involved as well. And every police station in the area would hand out posters for local businesses to display on their premises.

Sandrine Vaudrier.

Who are you really? wondered Damian. A wave of fatigue from his sleepless night washed over him. *What made you seek refuge in a false identity?*

The phone rang, making the detective jump. Without realizing it, he had slipped into a half-sleep.

"Detective Bouchard," he mumbled.

"Hello detective. My name's Chantal and I work at the tax office in Caen. I'm returning your call from earlier today."

"Yes, of course. Thank you. What do you have for me?"

"You asked me to check our logs for the names of several taxpayers, and I've just found an address for one of them."

Damian could hardly believe it. His first proper lead. *Sandrine Vaudrier, Sandrine Vaudrier,* he prayed silently. *Please let it be her so we can wrap this up . . .*

"Who have you got?"

"Frank Wernst. Here's the address . . ."

Damian noted down the information, thanked Chantal and rushed out of his office.

"Where's Antoine?" he asked the receptionist.

"He must be outside smoking. I've been wanting to ask you, when the station closes, do you think you could recommend me for a transfer to—"

"Not now!" barked the detective as he left the building.

*

Frank Wernst.

The farmer whose cows had been painted with swastikas.

Could this be one of the beacons Veronique had mentioned? Damian found Antoine leaning against the wall, a cigarette clamped between his lips.

"What's up, boss?"

"Come on. I'll explain on the way."

"Where are we going?" asked Antoine.

"To ward off the devil."

8

Sandrine was finding it difficult to stay awake. She felt groggy from the drugs they were giving her and couldn't quite recall how she had ended up in the hospital bed. She remembered the ambulance and a woman who had come to talk to her, as well as a visit from two men.

Then other memories emerged, little by little.

She remembered the island.

Had she really escaped?

Sandrine closed her eyes for a minute and tried to concentrate.

What had happened? How had she ended up on that beach?

She searched her mind for an answer, trying in vain to penetrate the thick fog of her amnesia. She then attempted to sit up, but even that was too much for her. Every muscle in her body was stiff and the slightest effort brought unbearable pain.

She stared at the ceiling and thought back to the last scene she could remember: the bar, the islanders passing out one by one, running through the woods towards the holiday camp, seeing her grandmother, the children drowning . . .

And then Paul's final warning.

When this name resurfaced in her mind, Sandrine wanted to cry with rage. Why had he abandoned her like that? Why hadn't he helped her escape? They could have been together on the mainland, far from the Erlking, Suzanne, and all that suffering!

But she had no explanation for that either. Just an empty feeling in the pit of her stomach as she recalled his final words:

If you come across the feral cat, you must kill it, Sandrine. It's the only way to escape the Erlking for good . . .

What had he meant?

She felt a migraine building deep in her skull. Like the shy beginnings of a destructive storm rumbling in the distance. And yet, her biggest concern was the man she had spoken to the day before, accompanied by his colleague in police uniform. Sandrine had noticed the scepticism in his eyes as she had told them her story.

He hadn't believed her. Of that she was sure.

And she didn't doubt for a second that he would try to uncover the truth.

What would happen if he tried to reach the island himself?

Didn't he understand that the Erlking would be waiting for him?

9

The farm slowly came into view as the police van struggled to avoid the potholes littering the gravel track, which was more like a narrow ravine between two fields than a proper road.

The police van pitched this way and that as a herd of cows looked on impassively. It started to rain as they finally parked and got out.

"Thank God the suspension held up," exclaimed Antoine as he gave the car a once-over. "Are you sure this is the right place, boss?"

"It's the address they gave me," replied Damian as he studied the letterbox. "And it's the right name: Frank Wernst."

"I hope this bloke has something to say . . ." Antoine said with a sigh as a raindrop slid down his forehead.

"Me too, or we're back to square one."

They walked past the main building and explored the property. The rain was really starting to come down now, and the smell of wet grass, cow manure, and damp earth filled the air. They discovered a barn as well as a muddy farmyard containing some farming equipment, a four-by-four, a cattle truck, a stack of several hay bales, and a few chickens wandering around. Damian scanned the surrounding fields for the owner but saw no one. A light fog rose on the horizon, swallowing the surrounding hedges like a monster gobbling up tasty morsels in a single bite.

"This place looks deserted, boss," said Antoine. "Do you really think he's here?"

"I don't know. But the cows definitely don't have any swastikas painted on them," Damian replied as he watched the animals grazing peacefully next to a small lake.

"Yet another invention," complained Antoine.

Antoine didn't believe Sandrine's story either. In fact, he couldn't care less who the blood belonged to, or if the Erlking was real. What concerned him was the unsettling atmosphere the young woman had brought with her from her island, an invisible virus that had started to spread through Villers-sur-Mer and take hold of the quiet seaside town. What's more, he appeared to be the only one who had noticed. The jogger, the doctors, the psychiatrist, and now Damian—all of them were obsessed with this story. Antoine wanted nothing to do with it. He just wished everything would go back to normal, so he could spend his days checking parking meters rather than investigating strange clues provided by a madwoman.

"Let's go and look inside," suggested Damian. "That way we'll know for sure. And at least we'll be in the dry."

They went back the way they had come and approached the long, narrow, main building. It was entirely built of stone and its roof reached towards the sky in an impressive pyramid. A few roof tiles looked slightly loose, but the building had clearly weathered so many storms that it could easily survive whatever came its way for another century or so. The roof stopped the rain in its tracks, sending it careening chaotically along the rusty gutters and down to the ochre-coloured ground beneath, where it gathered in large puddles.

Damian knocked on the wooden door. There was no answer, but a small movement caught his eye. The door had been left ajar and now swung open slightly. Antoine shot his boss a wary look. Alarm bells started going off in Damian's head. He was about to knock again, then froze.

"Is that . . . blood?" stammered Antoine.

Damian stood perfectly still as he stared at the stains on the door frame. Blood stains. Dark, wide marks. "Get on the radio now. Request an ambulance asap," he ordered. Damian waited until Antoine was in the car before pushing the door open with his foot. "Mr Wernst, are you there? It's the police."

Still no answer.

The detective took out his gun and pulled a small torch from his jacket pocket. He then stepped into the house, following the blood stains on the floor. It was suspiciously dark and silent inside, the stillness disturbed only by the pounding of the rain on the roof.

The entrance hall led to a spacious lounge, but the lights didn't come on when he tried them. He scanned the space with his torch, revealing a bleak room packed with mismatched furniture. Several rolls of fly paper hung from the exposed ceiling beams. Some of them were dotted with dozens of black corpses while others, which must have been hung more recently, had only trapped a few specimens. Damian walked past a large, empty fireplace, then made his way down a corridor covered with faded panelling, doing his best to ignore the acrid, unfamiliar fustiness of the place.

This part of the house was completely dark, without a single window to let in the spectral light of the stormy sky outside. Damian could barely make out the blood stains now. He was forced to kneel down several times to make sure he was still on the right track. As he went deeper into the house, he fought a growing feeling of disgust. The rooms felt eerily devoid of life, fresh air, and reassuring light, and the shutters were closed, making it feel like a mausoleum inside. He could feel the thick dust dislodged by each footstep and frowned in revulsion when the torchlight revealed the cracked, yellowing walls were covered in mould.

"Bloody hell, the farmyard was cleaner than this hellhole!" he mumbled under his breath.

The corridor opened out onto a basic kitchen which reeked of spoiled meat and cleaning products. The smells made Damian nauseous. He inspected the room, ignoring the half-eaten meal sitting on the table surrounded by a swarm of flies, and made his way towards a closed door set back into an alcove. Bloody handprints covered the handle and the doorframe. But what really alerted his attention was the padlock. It gaped open, hanging from one of its hinges like a sinister chimpanzee dangling from a branch.

"Jesus, this house is creepy . . ." Antoine said, appearing suddenly at Damian's side.

"Christ! Are you trying to give me a heart attack?"

"Sorry, boss. I didn't mean to scare you . . ."

"I hope you didn't touch anything at least?" grumbled Damian.

"No. Backup are on their way," Antoine informed him. "They wondered what the hell we were doing out here in the middle of nowhere . . ."

"Okay, great. The blood trail appears to lead to this door and . . ."

"Don't you think we should wait for the others, boss?"

At least part of Damian agreed with him. No policeman from Villers-sur-Mer had ever been in this position before. No other police report of theirs had ever contained mentions of blood trails, creepy houses, or calls for backup. And he had never, not once in his entire career, needed to take out his gun to search a place, afraid of what he might find.

He stood silently in front of the door for a moment.

He remembered the fear that had burned in his chest as he walked through the woods looking for his daughter. That intimate, revolting feeling which felt like the devil's breath on his neck . . . Was that the putrid smell that filled this house?

"There might be someone wounded behind here. We can't wait," he said finally as he opened the stained door.

A long wooden staircase descended into the darkness.

The detective aimed his torch down the steps, but it wasn't powerful enough to reach the bottom.

"Mr Wernst? We're coming down into the cellar. If you're hurt, don't move. An ambulance is on its way!"

Silence.

"Antoine, I need you to stay here," he ordered, turning back to look at his colleague. "Wait for my signal before coming down."

"Boss, are you sure that—"

"Cover me."

"There's a nasty smell coming from down there. We should—"

"That was an order. If backup arrive, send them in."

"Okay, boss," Antoine replied reluctantly.

He watched as Damian disappeared down the stairs.

"You okay, boss?"

But Damian didn't answer.

He had reached the cellar.

The smell was stronger now.

At first, he couldn't bring himself to look around the dark room.

Just like you almost couldn't bring yourself to search the sewers . . . It takes a dead body to make death real . . . Admit it, you bastard! You didn't want to find what I'd left behind . . . But I left her in pretty good shape, all things considered . . .

But when he finally lifted his torch, the first thing he saw was a mattress on the ground covered with a woollen blanket.

Next, he looked to the right and the torch beam fell on a metal, clawfoot bathtub. He stepped closer until he could make out a strange shape inside, floating in a dark liquid.

My God . . .

Damian realized this was the source of the repulsive smell. At first he thought what he could see was hair, and by extension wondered if he would find several heads along with it. His hand shook as he slowly shone the torch on the bathtub.

That's not hair . . .

The bathtub was full of dead bodies.

"Cats," he whispered, his face twisting in disgust.

Sickened by the scene, he turned away. He was about to

climb back up the stairs when a second detail struck him. The image only lasted a second, maybe less. But when he had turned his back on the bathtub, his torch had fleetingly revealed something else.

Damian tightened his grip on his gun and turned back around to face the room. The wooden step on which he had placed his right foot creaked, as if urging him not to move. The detective could hear the devil's mocking laugh in his ear and stifled it as he shone the light on the floor.

Congratulations, you piece of shit. You don't run away like a coward any more . . . Maybe you've grown some balls since abandoning your family . . .

Antoine was smoking under the willow tree outside and watching out for the ambulance when he heard a noise in the house. Before he could reach the front door, Damian had rushed out to be sick on the waterlogged ground.

"Are you okay, boss?"

Damian tried to speak but a second spasm made him double over to expel more clear bile. "You were right," he finally managed to say as he forced himself to stand upright. "We should have waited for backup."

The rain didn't let up for hours. It was still pouring when the ambulance arrived, and when two additional police vans pulled up half an hour after that.

"It'll take us at least two full days to search this place!" exclaimed the superintendent, gesturing at the farm and its outbuildings as he looked around.

Damian had called him as soon as his nausea had abated. Fourier had left Caen early and driven straight to the station to collect the file the detective had compiled for him before heading out to the crime scene.

For those who didn't know the superintendent, appearances could be deceiving. He was a stout man with a round, kindly face, but he was terribly impulsive and quick to anger—a trait all of his officers had experienced first-hand at one time or another. Not to mention the fact that his characteristic bad temperedness had been further exacerbated by the announcement that his station would soon be closing. Ever since, he had barked orders at his team even more ferociously than usual.

"How did we end up with this bloody mess? Here in Normandy, just half an hour away from Villers? Has the woman talked yet?" he growled, gesticulating wildly.

"Not about anything other than the island. Did you listen to the recording?" asked Damian.

"Yes, in the car. Do you think the blood in the cellar will match the blood from her clothes?"

"It seems likely. We'll know soon enough."

"Station men at the turnoff. I don't want any journalists

turning up here claiming they're just after some fresh milk. Set up a proper roadblock! And get me the generators I asked for! It'll be dark soon!"

The search team secured a tarpaulin over the generators in the farmyard to protect them from the rain. Once the powerful spotlights were plugged in and switched on one after another, they bathed the house in sterile, white light, exposing the sepulchral intimacy of the tomb inside.

The first police officers on the scene were under strict orders to take pictures and not disturb anything. The medics waited for the superintendent to give the order before placing the corpse in a black body bag and taking it back to town for autopsy.

"This was in his back pocket," said one of the medics, handing Damian a wallet.

Damian used a tissue to open it. "Frank Wernst," he sighed as he studied the driver's license. Now the only real name from Sandrine's story belonged to a dead body.

"No television, no telephone. A few books about the Second World War, some framed medals, twenty-year-old newspapers . . . Christ, it's like this house was in a time warp, stuck in the past," said one of the officers. "And that horror show in the cellar, that scene is positively *medieval.*"

The cellar.

A bathtub full of dead animals.

A tattered mattress on the floor stained with blood and God only knew what other bodily fluids.

A rusty iron chain with what looked like a handcuff at one end.

A dead body with its skull bashed in. Brains spilling out all over the grey cement.

The detective felt sick again as he watched the officers come and go. Those who went down into the cellar returned looking grave and not even the superintendent could hide his astonishment. He stood perfectly still under the rain for a few minutes, as if trying to wash away the nightmarish scene.

An hour later, he ordered Damian and Antoine to go home and get some sleep, so they could be back at the station first thing in the morning. They left the brightly lit farmhouse and the investigators' palpable incomprehension behind as they got into the car.

Damian started the van without a word, then turned on the windscreen wipers, hoping to sweep aside more than just the raindrops on the glass.

"Why cats?" asked Antoine twenty minutes later. He had been staring out at the horizon through the passenger window.

"No idea," muttered Damian. "Sandrine mentions them in her story."

"And Wernst? Was it that bad?" Antoine hadn't had the courage to go down and see for himself. Watching his boss vomit under the willow tree had been enough to dissuade him.

"Here, take a look," said the detective, pulling a polaroid from his jacket pocket. He'd requested it from the police photographer before he left.

"Oh, Christ," Antoine swore as he handed the picture back to Damian.

"That about sums it up."

"You think she did that to him?"

"We don't know yet. But if the blood matches what we found on her clothes, we'll have to figure out how a woman her size could have shattered the skull of an adult male farmer. And why."

Damian put the photograph away. Frank Wernst's crushed head stayed with both men for a minute. From the picture you could tell the perpetrator would have had to hit him incredibly hard to cave in the skull like that, shattering the prefrontal bone like papier mâché and completely deforming the top of the face as whatever weapon was used pushed the orbits aside and made its way to the brain. A stone covered in blood, hair, and bits of skin had been found near the body.

"And after that she just wandered through the fields until she reached the beach? This whole thing is completely nuts!"

"There's more."

"What?" asked Antoine.

"A chain."

"A chain?"

"Yeah, bolted to the wall, with a metal handcuff at one end. And you saw the padlock on the cellar door yourself . . ."

"What are you thinking, boss?"

"Maybe Sandrine isn't crazy after all . . ."

The next morning, Damian and Antoine were in the superintendent's office at eight thirty sharp, as promised. None of them looked well rested.

"The blood is a match," the superintendent confirmed, to the point as always. "Forensics can't get to the scene until tomorrow. They're understaffed and handling another case that's been deemed more important. It's as if our station already doesn't exist . . . So, for now, the only thing we know for sure is that Sandrine was there. We also found *her* blood inside the metal handcuff chained to the wall. The simplest explanation is that she was kidnapped and held against her will. But that hypothesis means nothing without a confession. We have to get her to talk."

"We've tried," replied Damian. "She just recited the same story she gave the psychiatrist."

"Well, try harder!" ordered the superintendent, slamming his fist down on the desk for emphasis. "This station is on the verge of closure because some bureaucrat somewhere threw together a bunch of statistics and decided that we're not needed. Solving this crime could turn things around for us. Do you understand what I'm saying?"

"Yes, sir," they mumbled as they left his office.

Damian and Antoine stepped outside the building, as they often did when they wanted to talk freely and didn't want to be overheard or interrupted. They had been working together for almost three years. Damian had liked Antoine and his lack of ambition right away. It meant he was always willing to lend a helping hand, without asking for anything in return. It was a rare quality, especially in a station where everyone was vying for promotion and trying to impress their supervisor.

"Handle any new cases that come in," ordered Damian as he lit a cigarette.

"What? But you're going to need me," protested Antoine.

"I need you here. Someone has to stay at the station and manage the team. You're my eyes and ears. If there's any news, I'll call you."

"All right," agreed Antoine. "Do you think she'll talk?"

"I'm certain she will."

"Really? Did you have an epiphany last night?" he joked.

"Not really, no."

"So why are you so optimistic?"

"Because I think I've found the key to her refuge."

Dr Burel happened to be at the hospital reception desk when Damian walked in through the revolving doors. Given the look of grave determination on his face, she knew something terrible had happened even before he opened his mouth.

"Detective?"

"We need to talk."

"No hello? What's going on?" she asked as she signed the form a nurse held out.

"Not here. Your office?"

"Lead the way!"

Veronique shut the door and sat down across from Damian. The detective placed a large manilla envelope down on her desk.

"What's this?"

"You said the best way to get Sandrine to talk would be to reassure her, right?"

"Yes, she'll continue hiding in her imaginary world as long as she feels she's in danger. To get her to leave the island, we have to prove to her that the Erlking can no longer hurt her."

"So, if I had proof that her attacker can no longer harm her, would that be enough?" he asked.

"You found him?"

"It's possible," replied Damian. "Without the victim's testimony, all I can say at this point is that it's possible."

"If this man is the one who hurt her, the change in her should be visible. Her refuge will crack and then collapse because she won't need it anymore. But the process could take days, weeks, or even years. Unless . . ."

"Unless what?"

"Unless your proof is irrefutable. That could speed things up."

"Do you think this will do?" asked Damian as he pulled out a close-up of the photograph of the dead body and placed it on the doctor's desk alongside the envelope. A yellow Post-it covered the victim's face. Only the large puddle of blood alluded to the violence hidden beneath the paper square. Veronique expressed neither disgust nor fascination. Her expression remained neutral, professional. She was clearly more than the novice he had imagined the first time they had met. She took a moment to reflect on what it would mean for Sandrine.

"Who is this?"

"Frank Wernst."

"The farmer from the beginning of her story?" asked Dr Burel, clearly surprised.

"Yes. I guess he was a 'beacon' in her memories."

"Have you found any other beacons?"

"Not yet. But I still have a lot to get through."

"My God," whispered Veronique as she sat back in her chair. "This isn't good . . ."

"What do you mean?"

"Time is often an important beacon in a refuge. It can be used in a concrete way, but it can also be deceptive . . . For example, Sandrine's story begins in 1949. I think we can both agree that she can't have been alive then since she appears to be in her early thirties?"

"Right," Damian replied with a nod.

"So, 1949 isn't a real date. It represents the passage of time. She herself said again and again that *time is relative*."

"So, you think . . ."

"I think she wasn't just held prisoner for weeks or months. I think it was much longer than that. Years, most likely. That's why her story begins so long ago. And if this man is who Sandrine is trying to escape, the fact that he's present almost from the beginning of the story tells us he has also been a presence in her life for a long time . . ."

"I only searched recent missing persons reports," mumbled Damian, realizing his mistake.

"Well, you'll need to look at older ones."

"Most of the files disappear over time," he replied. "If Sandrine was kidnapped when she was about fifteen, the case would most likely have been filed as a runaway. When no body is found, people tend to blame everything on teenage angst."

"Then I can't bear to think how many children must disappear if even the police don't search for them properly," Veronique lamented.

"Can we get her to talk?"

"What? Now?"

Damian pulled another photograph from the envelope and showed her the mattress and the chain bolted to the wall. The scene required no explanation. "You were right," said Damian. "From the beginning. The blood found inside the handcuff matches Sandrine's blood type. And if your theory is correct, this must have gone on for years."

"I . . . We'll need to prepare her for this. Given her condition, we have to be careful. You'll need to sign a release."

"Of course," agreed the detective.

"And you'll need to let me do the talking," she added.

"No problem. You're the therapist."

"I'll prepare a sedative," explained Dr Burel. "Emerging from her traumatic amnesia and opening the door to her refuge will likely be very painful for her, maybe even destructive. Her reaction might not be what you're hoping for. A nurse will be there just in case. We can't take any risks."

"I won't interfere," promised Damian. "I just want her to know she has nothing to fear any more. I'll take notes on any details she reveals that could be useful for the investigation."

"All right, then. You can wait here while I get everything ready."

★

Veronique came back half an hour later. Damian could hear the concern in her voice. She knew very well that Sandrine might react violently to the psychological shock of being confronted with the reality she was hiding from. The young woman was comfortably settled in the refuge she had built, and in a few minutes, Dr Burel and Damian were going to rip her from her reassuring haven and make her face the raw truth. As she recovered her memories, the victim would likely experience the events again, and relive them, submitting her brain to the trauma it had consciously worked to shut out.

They would have to be careful. Veronique warned Damian that the drugs would help soften the blow, but they would have to stop the interview if anything suggested the patient was in danger. The detective agreed immediately, placing his trust in her professional judgement.

It could take months to treat Sandrine's condition. But the superintendent had been very clear. Damian was trapped. Sandrine needed time to heal. And time was something their police station didn't have. He gave Veronique a list of subjects to bring up with Sandrine: *the war, Suzanne, the children, the cats, the poem, the song, 8:37, hot chocolate.* He had jotted them down hastily, seemingly banal topics which wouldn't mean very much to anyone else who happened to glance at the list, but they were all potential leads, any one of them the potential thread which, when pulled, would untangle the secret to the whole mystery.

Veronique read the list, then informed Damian that Sandrine was awake and that she had received a dose of sedatives and betablockers to mitigate her biological reaction to stress. Her dulled consciousness would reduce the intensity of any trauma she might experience.

"We need her testimony to use in court," explained Damian as he walked with Dr Burel towards Sandrine's room. "I'm not thrilled about having to rush the victim either."

"I know," replied the doctor, her jaw clenched. "I know."

*

When they stepped into the room, a nurse was already present. She was adding water to a vase of flowers she had picked herself in the garden. Veronique told her she couldn't stay, since this was an ongoing investigation and Sandrine's condition didn't require constant visual monitoring. The nurse nodded and sat down in a chair just outside the door, ready to intervene if necessary. The psychiatrist placed her tape recorder on the Formica table and smiled at her patient. Sandrine smiled back, but her reaction was muted and less spontaneous—due to the drugs, no doubt. She turned her attention to Damian, who had placed his chair behind Dr Burel's. The detective tried in vain to decipher her expression. She stared at him as if he were a wall, a safe place to rest her weary mind. Her eyes were vacant. He smiled anxiously, thinking about everything Sandrine had been through. Everything he was about to make her go through again. The brown envelope he held in his hands grew heavy with remorse.

"How are you today, Sandrine?" Dr Burel asked gently, placing her hand on hers.

Sandrine nodded.

"If you'll allow it, we'd like to have a chat with you. I'll record our conversation, like last time. Would that be okay?"

"Yes," Sandrine replied, her voice barely audible.

The psychiatrist switched on the tape recorder.

"Detective Bouchard here is responsible for finding the person who hurt you. He'd like to stay during our conversation. Is that all right with you?"

Sandrine turned towards Damian again. She studied him for a moment, then gave him a small smile, as if she'd only just realized he was there. "I know you," she said, beaming now.

"Yes, we spoke yesterday," he replied.

"No, from long before." Her faded eyes suddenly shone. Damian felt uncomfortable to see this unexpected change in her.

"I . . . I don't think so," he countered politely. He was fully aware that anything he said could influence this whole process.

"I guess I'm mistaken then," agreed Sandrine, turning her attention back to the psychiatrist. "He can stay. I like him."

Veronique thanked her, managing to mask her concern at this exchange between them. She decided to bring Sandrine back to the reason for their visit. "I'd like to talk to you about the Erlking," she began.

"He killed the children."

"I know, Sandrine. You mentioned that before. The boat sank."

"He drowned them," she said, raising her voice slightly. "They were too drugged to swim."

"The Erlking was a man, wasn't he?"

"Yes, a strong man."

"Did he hurt you as well?"

"Not on the island. He left me alone on the island."

"Where did he hurt you?"

"In the bunker . . . No, somewhere else. I don't remember . . ."

Veronique wasn't surprised by Sandrine's muddled answers. The simple fact that Sandrine had mentioned another place which she couldn't fully recall was an indication that her memory was trying to reconnect to reality.

"Did he hurt you a lot?"

"Yes," she said, lowering her gaze.

"Would you be relieved to learn that the man is gone?"

Sandrine looked up at the psychiatrist, clearly confused. Her mouth was open, but not a single sound came out. Tears streamed down her cheeks. "They call to me every night . . . They want me to free them from the murky waters," she said finally.

"The children?"

"Yes . . . I wish they would be quiet . . . Just for one night . . ."

"If we caught the Erlking," continued Veronique, "would the children leave you alone?"

"Yes, that's why they're always screaming. Because he's there. Because they're afraid."

"Sandrine, how would you feel if I could prove to you that the Erlking is gone forever?" asked Dr Burel.

"Relieved."

"Do you remember Mr Wernst?"

"Yes, I went to his farm to write an article about his cows."

"The ones that had been spray-painted with swastikas?"

"Yes."

"How did you feel when you left the farm?"

"Afraid. It felt like I couldn't really leave. It felt as though an invisible chain was keeping me prisoner . . ."

"But you did leave, didn't you?"

"Yes. To go . . . to the island," Sandrine replied hesitantly.

"Do you want to continue this discussion?" asked Dr Burel. She had noticed the shift in her tone.

"Yes, I want to be able to sleep soundly at night."

"Detective Bouchard thinks he has found the Erlking. Would it be all right for him to show you a picture?"

"Yes."

Veronique sat silently for a moment, trying to determine what Sandrine really wanted. Sometimes victims refused to hear a word about their attackers. Any mention of them could undermine their recovery. No one could blame them for wanting to forget. The patient's well-being had to be the priority.

"Wonderful," she finally said. "You're going to look at this photograph. Afterwards, you don't have to talk about it if you don't want to. I'll just have one last question for you. If you want to end our discussion then, we will. We can come back to talk to you another day. You're under no obligation to push yourself, okay?"

"I understand."

Damian walked slowly towards the bed. Sandrine watched him curiously, her eyes unblinking. The psychiatrist had proceeded carefully, cultivating trust between them. With her short questions, she had slowly but surely introduced the idea that the

Erlking might be no more, preparing the victim for what she was about to see.

Veronique had told Damian that showing her the photograph would be the pivotal moment. When she saw Wernst's dead body, the emotional anaesthesia the refuge provided might suddenly give way, causing all of her repressed feelings and pain to surface. That's why the nurse was waiting outside the door with a dose of powerful sedative in her pocket. If Sandrine reacted this way, they would have to end their conversation and begin a long, drawn-out treatment to which he would not be a party. So the detective was well aware of the stakes.

Sandrine sat perfectly still in her bed. Damian suddenly wanted to flee the room and let the poor woman recover from a trauma he couldn't even begin to imagine. He felt the guilt and shame of an executioner taking the victim rather than the culprit to the gallows. The potential closure of the Villers police station and the superintendent's orders seemed insignificant beside Sandrine's gentle eyes and lost innocence. He carefully removed the photograph from the envelope and handed it to Veronique. She placed it on the blanket covering Sandrine's lap, then asked in a neutral voice, "Is this the Erlking who hurt you so badly?"

Sandrine stared at the picture for a long time. She didn't even realize she was sobbing until a tear landed on the photograph.

Confusing memories resurfaced, recollections as fleeting and ephemeral as rays of sunshine on a cloudy day. She wanted to scream, to rip the image to shreds, but her fatigue dulled her anger. So, she cried instead, evacuating the feelings through tears, expelling them from her body and letting them slide down her cheeks. Voices spoke to her, coming from an invisible place, telling her to leave them behind, urging her to forget the children. Paul, Victor, Maurice, Françoise, Simon, Claude, Suzanne . . .

Let us go, Sandrine. That's it. It's the only way . . .

Isolating yourself here won't protect you, it will just cause you more suffering. Flee now, hurry . . . Forget about us . . .

Then a louder, more threatening voice mounted a final assault on her senses:

"Keep your mind busy . . .

Recite your poem, for example . . .

It'll make things easier . . .

Tomorrow, when your teacher has you stand up in front of the class,

you'll have me to thank . . .

Come here . . .

Come closer . . .

It'll make things easier . . ."

Sandrine realized it was time to open the door and leave the island.

She decided to tell the truth that had suddenly emerged, unleashed from the depths of her memory.

Veronique and Damian watched Sandrine apprehensively, study-ing her reaction. The psychiatrist feared the trauma caused by the act of remembering might cause the patient to become violent, either towards others or herself.

Much to her surprise, that didn't happen.

Sandrine cried. For several long minutes. Her pain, distress, and fatigue channelled into her sobs. She took the hand Dr Burel held out, even drawing her close for a hug. Damian swallowed hard, trying to fight back his own tears. He thought about the chain in the cellar. The worn mattress. The repulsive grey cement. The smell of damp and mould. Wernst's heavy body. And the fields that surrounded that cursed place for as far as the eye could see.

He thought of the devil disguised as the Erlking.

He thought of all his disguises.

Old legends.

Ancient poems.

Deserted forests and rivers with no answers.

Rooms with no one to dream in them.

Bouquets tied to the front gate of a middle school in tribute.

The list was long. Too long.

The two women broke apart without a word. Sandrine's sobs dwindled and then disappeared, like a candle flame deprived of oxygen. She sat up straight in her bed and looked at the photograph one last time.

"Yes, that's him. *Der Erlkönig*," she said eventually.

Veronique was taken aback by Sandrine's declaration. She was no novice, but the resilience of the human brain continued to astound her, even after years in the field. There were still many unanswered questions, but she felt it was time to let Sandrine rest. Though she was no longer crying, the doctor was certain Sandrine's entire world had just been upended. The drugs could only do so much. When they cleared Sandrine's system, the revelation of her kidnapper's death would tap away at her mind and free more suppressed memories. She would need Dr Burel's help to keep hold of her sanity.

"Sandrine?" asked the doctor.

"Yes," she replied weakly.

"We're going to let you rest now. A nurse will come in to administer something to help you sleep. You have been very brave."

"No," protested Sandrine. "Don't leave."

"I'll come to see you when you wake up. We'll talk more then."

"No, stay. I want to get this over with. Let me tell you the truth," she insisted.

"Are you sure? You're very tired. You can take a few days if you need."

No, it can't wait. I understand the meaning behind the islanders' last words now . . . "You have to leave us behind, Sandrine. Forget about us."

That's what I have to do. I have to leave them behind on the island and forget about them. I have to tell the real story, the one hidden behind the door to my refuge.

Will this detective believe me now? He's doubted me since the beginning. Will a cellar seem more real to him than an old Nazi military base or children's bodies carried off by the currents?

I'm leaving now, my friends. You protected me. You, the ocean, Suzanne . . . You all protected me from the Erlking.

But the time has come. There's no turning back. I have to tell the truth.

Even if it hurts.

Even if I have to forget you altogether.

*

Several minutes went by before Sandrine spoke again. She seemed to be engaged in an internal debate, which neither Veronique nor Damian wanted to interrupt. Her eyes went vacant again and her lips mumbled words intended for an imaginary audience.

Or ghosts.

Or pieces of herself.

Then, suddenly, Sandrine went still. She looked at Dr Burel and the detective in turn, her features drawn, her gaze timid, oscillating between the real world and somewhere else as she tried to figure out how to begin.

"I was on my way home. It was dark and cold. I was sixteen . . ."

14

I was sixteen.

I had just come out of the school gates. I had a German test at eight o'clock the next morning. My best friend, Marie, asked me if I had memorized the poem. Then she waved as she climbed onto the school bus to go home.

That's the last time I ever saw her.

I started walking. I knew the route by heart and could have done it with my eyes closed if I'd wanted to. Every day I took the same street and bumped into the same people. Françoise, whose bakery filled the neighbourhood with the smell of fresh bread. Victor, the butcher whose blood-stained apron had frightened me as a child. And Claude, the friendly bookseller, who smiled at me every morning, his eyes bright with knowledge. I knew each of them. Their habits and obsessions. The cigarettes left smoking outside the door because a customer had surprised one of them, their grumbling when the weather was bad, their greetings, which hadn't changed a bit over the years . . . "Reading is the key to knowledge, Sandrine!" "You need to eat more meat, darling, you're looking pale!" "Can you smell the croissants fresh out of the oven, Sandrine? How's your boyfriend, Paul?"

That night they all happened to be inside, presumably taking care of the bookkeeping or tidying up, when I walked past a man leaning against the wall. I was so absorbed in making sure I knew my poem by heart that I didn't notice him at first.

I kept walking towards home. I realized he was following me when I went into a narrow alleyway and heard his footsteps echo behind me. I wanted to turn around, but there was no time. A thick arm suddenly grabbed me and a hand was clamped over my mouth.

That's all I remember from the kidnapping.

I woke up in a dark room. I didn't understand where I was. My head hurt and I couldn't see anything around me. I tried to stand up and was horrified to discover that my left wrist had been chained to the wall. I pulled as hard as I could, trying to break free, but it was no use.

So, I cried. And screamed.

But no one replied.

I told myself the police would find me.

That I would soon be free.

That it was just a nightmare.

The night came and went.

The next morning, I was still chained up. I had snuggled down on the mattress despite its rancid smell. Daylight slowly chased away the shadows. Seeing a long wooden staircase leading up to a door above, I realized I was in a cellar.

I could see the sky through a tiny rectangular window. Blades of grass obscured my view, but they were too sparse to completely block out the sunlight.

There was a bathtub, too. I stood up. My chain was long enough for me to reach the tap. I drank. Long, deep sips, with my eyes closed. I was sure that when I opened my eyes again, I would be back home in my bathroom, and that when I looked up, I would see my reflection in the familiar mirror.

But all I saw was a peeling grey wall. The damp had eaten away at the paint leaving the foundations exposed.

A wave of panic washed over me.

I spent hours screaming, crying, begging, and pulling on that chain. The handcuff stung my wrist.

Then I waited, huddled into a ball to protect what hope I had left.

*

The sun had just set when I heard a door open. Fluorescent lights immediately crackled to life above my head, bathing the room in their white glare. A man came down the stairs. He placed the tray he was carrying at the foot of the staircase and sat down.

"Are you hungry?" he asked.

"Let me go!"

"That's not what I asked."

"The police will find you, you bastard!"

So, the man went back up, ignoring my insults.

He came back much later. Although I hadn't paid much attention to him during his first visit, now even his physique was intimidating. He was not much taller than me, but violence emanated from his muscular frame. His cold, blue eyes froze the blood in my veins. He scratched his chin with a hand so heavy and thick it could have suffocated me with astounding ease. I had never encountered such a brute. His tangled beard and unbrushed hair made him look like an animal—a predator. And I was his prey.

While he was gone, he had left the lights on, so I could stare forlornly at the sandwich he had placed just beyond my reach.

"Are you hungry?" he asked again.

"Yes."

"You won't do anything stupid if I feed you, will you?"

"No."

"First, drink this hot chocolate. I made it for you."

"All right."

He came closer and held out a large mug. It seemed terribly fragile in his rough hands. There was an advertising slogan on it: *Menier Chocolate: making the world a better place!* I dipped my lips in the warm, sweet liquid and almost drank it all in a single gulp. It was delicious. I hadn't eaten anything in twenty-four hours.

Everything around me went blurry. My surroundings, the man's words, even my presence in the cellar . . .

He told me to lie down. Then I felt his hands on my clothes. I wanted to push him off, but I couldn't. My eyes kept closing against my will. I felt like I was underwater, unable to see, hear, or move naturally. Then I felt cold. I turned my head and saw my clothes on the floor. I didn't remember taking them off. The man came so close that I could feel his breath on my forehead. I cried. I think I cried.

Then he whispered something in my ear:

"Keep your mind busy . . .
Recite your poem, for example . . .
It'll make things easier . . .
Tomorrow, when your teacher has you stand up in front of the class,
you'll have me to thank . . .
Come here . . .
Come closer . . .
It'll make things easier . . ."

And I did as I was told.
Wer reitet so spät durch Nacht und Wind . . .

I recited my poem. I took refuge in it. I imagined myself standing up in front of the class. I had to do my best: I wanted to get a good mark. I repeated it in my head as the man took off his trousers.

It felt like my body was being ripped apart. The pain was indescribable.

Weeks passed, then months.

The ritual was always the same.

8:37 p.m. He came down the stairs.

I had to drink the hot chocolate, and then he lay on top of my body and penetrated me.

Afterwards, I slowly emerged from my lethargy. Sometimes it took hours. Hours spent wandering between reality and an imaginary world, telling myself that it hadn't really happened, that I missed my mother and my friends so much that I was delirious.

The pain was real, though. Too real to be a lie.

Sometimes my captor would disappear for a few days. I don't know where he went, but before he left, he always brought down a tray loaded with several sandwiches, carefully wrapped in plastic. He would tell me that he wouldn't be able to come and see me for a while, so I had to ration my provisions. He would bring me a gift, *if I was good* . . .

Every time, I was surprisingly angry as he climbed back up the stairs.

But not at him.

At myself.

Because when he closed the door behind him, I was overwhelmed by an inexplicable sadness. It was hard to admit and accept. But that man became the only human contact—as revolting as it was—I was allowed. The only voice I ever heard.

The first time he went away, I sat staring at the door for hours. I should have been thrilled, tried to break the chain, find a way to escape, or call for help . . . Instead, I just sat there waiting for him to come back, checking the clock on the wall, and hoping that I'd hear his steps on the stairs at the usual time. I was like a dog waiting for my master to return.

I slapped and scratched myself, disgusted to feel such sadness at his absence. The feeling was much more suffocating than the four walls of my prison. I called myself a whore, a madwoman, an idiot. But even during this hypocritical rage, I couldn't help but glance at the clock and pray that he wouldn't abandon me like my father had done, years earlier, by simply shutting the door behind him, never to return. Without an explanation or even a glance in my direction.

8:37 p.m.

There were no steps on the stairs that night.

I was alone.

Presumably forgotten by my loved ones since I had never heard a police siren wail anywhere near my cell. Had they even reported me missing? Maybe I had done something to deserve it . . . I hadn't been the model daughter my mother had hoped for. Full of teenage angst, maybe I had talked back to my teachers once too often. Didn't I deserve it? Wasn't my presence here, in a dirty cellar, abandoned by my captor, the result of my bad habit of disappointing everyone who knew me? Maybe no one had even noticed I was gone?

What if they had all forgotten me, put me to the back of their minds like the vague memory of an uneventful winter?

The first gift he brought me was a book about the Second World War. The pages were wrinkled, and the cover was damaged, but I treasured it. At last I would have somewhere to escape to—even battlefields, bombed out cities and mass graves were preferable to the four walls of the cellar. I read the whole thing in a day, only stopping to go to the toilet, which was a crude hole dug in the cement with a plastic tube cut in half lengthways that disappeared into the wall to ferry my waste outside.

Other books joined my collection after each of his trips: *The Stranger, Wuthering Heights,* a collection of Goethe's poems (a birthday present), *Journey to the End of the Night,* and more. Now every time he left for a few days, he came back with a book.

One night, when he asked me if I would like to read a particular author, I dared to make a request of my own. It took me a while to spit it out. But I could sense that, even though he drugged me and raped me on a regular basis, he did want to make my situation more comfortable. The sandwiches I'd received at the beginning had made way for homecooked meals. They had been simple at first, and I regularly ate the same soups over and over again, but after a while he began bringing me a variety of proper dishes, meat and fish . . . Though breakfast and lunch weren't always guaranteed, he never failed to show up in the evening.

8:37 p.m.

The door would open, and the smell of stew would waft down to me, mixed with the sweet aroma of hot chocolate, which he brought me without fail.

He grew slightly gentler, less controlling.

He was letting his guard down. I thanked him with my silence.

He probably thought I was falling in love with him. That famous syndrome, what's it called again? I spoke more calmly, banishing the bitterness from my voice, but the latent threats were still there, carefully hidden.

So, as a test, I asked for something else: newspapers.

He trained his blue eyes on me without saying a word. I didn't know if my request had been accepted or refused. He disappeared back up the stairs before I could properly gage his reaction.

I had lost all sense of time. I didn't know anymore how many months I had spent chained to the wall. I had tried to keep track by tracing lines on the cement with a rock. At first, I used tally marks, clustered in groups of five, each line representing one day.

But when he noticed, he erased them. He scolded me, telling me I didn't understand, that time was relative, that it could drive a person crazy . . . So I changed my technique to keep from worrying him. I drew stickmen on the walls and told him it was just a game to help me pass the time. The caricatures were my imaginary friends, and more and more appeared over the weeks to come.

Two lines for the legs, two for the arms, one for the body. Five lines, five days. And a circle for the head. Like a dying sun. Like the bright star I could only imagine from the light filtering through the tiny window, without ever being able to see it directly.

But when my collection of imaginary friends got so large that there was hardly any empty space to draw a new one, he decided to get rid of them all. He scrubbed the walls as I looked on in dismay, trying feverishly to count all of the hanged men before they disappeared. I had barely reached a hundred before the grey cement was as empty and useless as a clock without hands.

The next day (to make it up to me?) he came down the stairs with a pile of newspapers. I forced my lips not to smile, feigning anger and resentment. But deep down, I was impatient to start reading the news from the outside world, to open my window a crack and learn about what was going on in that faraway place to which I no longer belonged. He put them down in front of me and left without a word. Once he'd closed the door, I grabbed the first one off the top of the pile and looked for the date. A few seconds later, I angrily threw the newspapers across the room.

They were all from 1961.

Old papers that had turned yellow from the damp. A portal to the past instead of the hope I needed to survive in the present.

I fell into a nervous rage. I shouted, pounded my fists on

the walls, pulled on the chain with all my might, praying for my wrist to snap off, and cursed my stupidity. How had I been so naive as to believe for a second that I had any power over him? How could I have forgotten that for him I was just a piece of meat to screw, just a chained-up dog he could do with as he pleased? Afterwards I sat there sobbing, my back against the newly bare wall, occasionally glancing up at the clock opposite me.

That night, at 8:37 p.m., the fluorescent lights stayed on, but nothing happened. He simply brought me a plate of food and went back upstairs without even looking at me.

That was the final lesson of the day: his presence had to be earned.

My behaviour had left him disinterested, which could have been a good thing, of course. No hot chocolate, no touching, no penetration and no feeling of disgust afterwards.

But I was also certain that if I was of no further use to him, he would get rid of me . . .

The days passed. He no longer had to force my legs apart. They now seemed to open for him of their own accord. A reflex. My foggy brain recited my poem automatically and he no longer had to suggest it. And little by little, the faces of my classmates disappeared. I tried to concentrate, tried to visualize their features, but the drugs and the passage of time had turned them into blurry shadows. When he left, I would eat, still feeling groggy, then spend a long time soaking in the bathtub. I thought about killing myself. I had read somewhere that you don't need much water to drown. But I never worked up the courage. Maybe it was a survival instinct, but I think it was just weakness.

I know what you're thinking: when did she build her island refuge?

I'm getting to that.

Before I could go, I needed a reason.

The violence and isolation were reasons enough, of course. But over time, I'm ashamed to admit, I'd got used to it. My initial revolt had been replaced with resignation, as if my brain were whispering, "It's all right. Just a bad patch to get through. You'll survive. Close your eyes and recite your poem." I felt like I was watching as it all happened. When he raped me, my conscience escaped my body to wander freely through a forest peopled with mythological creatures. But one night, the cruel reality of my situation became all too obvious.

As soon as he started coming down the stairs, I realized he wasn't his usual self. He was unsteady on his feet. As he leaned over me, I looked for the hot chocolate, but there was none. His breath reeked of alcohol.

He slapped me, shouted that no poem could ever save me, and rammed himself inside me with a rage I had never seen before. This time, I was unable to escape. I was trapped in my body when he turned me over and entered a part of me that no one had ever touched before. It was like the first night all over again. But worse.

I didn't eat for days afterwards. I wrapped the chain around my neck but couldn't pull it tight enough. I feared the moment when the hands of the clock would reach the appointed hour now more than ever before.

That's when I met Sandrine.

That's when she saved me.

Sandrine was on page twelve.

I first met her in the travel section of an old newspaper. I read it by chance, searching for something to escape my boredom. But once I started, I identified with her immediately. She presented herself as this strong, independent woman. She had graduated from a prestigious school of journalism and was sharing her impressions as she toured the world.

Sandrine Vaudrier.

I liked her right away. I was also jealous of her.

She enjoyed a freedom I couldn't even begin to imagine. I dived into her articles with the same fervour I had felt for the books I had read over and over again. I carefully removed the articles and hid them under my mattress in case my kidnapper, whose violent episodes were becoming increasingly frequent, decided to deprive me of reading material.

Thanks to Sandrine, I began dreaming again. I hadn't dreamed in years.

I don't know if my discovery had a visible impact on my mood, but my captor seemed to notice something had changed. He rewarded me for it, in his own way. He probably thought I had accepted my fate, that I had finally realized he didn't want to hurt me, that it was just the way things were, and that it was better not to resist. He stopped drinking—or at least when he came down he no longer reeked of booze—and kept bringing me old newspapers and homecooked meals.

Then one morning, something unusual happened.

He came down to deliver my breakfast, then went back up. But, instead of closing the door as he usually did, he left it ajar.

I craned my neck to see what was beyond the door, but in vain. A few minutes later, a cat padded down the stairs. The confidence with which he crossed the threshold into the cellar, which had harboured only two living creatures for so long, was disconcerting. His tabby stripes undulated like waves as he walked. I closed my eyes, certain I was imagining him, but when I opened them again, he was even closer. He gracefully jumped off the bottom step and disappeared into a dark corner of the cellar to get comfortable.

The next day, my abductor left the door open again, and Paul (since I didn't know what he was called, I decided to name him after my boyfriend from my previous life) appeared once more. This time he approached me cautiously, his pupils dilated and senses on high alert. I didn't dare move. I was afraid even the slightest motion would make my chain jangle and scare him away. The cat continued towards me, glancing fearfully in my direction. Eventually, he gently touched his cheek to my calf, then rubbed against my knee and began to purr discreetly, creating a bubble of normality for us to enjoy.

That's how Sandrine and Paul became my first friends. The first sparks of light in the darkness. They structured my days for months. I would spend the mornings stroking Paul and the afternoons reading about Sandrine's adventures. In the evening, an old poem helped me escape reality.

My whole life was now organized around these habits. The hours seemed less long and time started to accelerate, carrying me away from my childhood.

My captor took care of me. He cut my hair, regularly brought me soap and tampons, and occasionally freed me from the chain so I could walk around the room and stretch my legs. He was always watching though. One wrong move and he was ready to strike.

Since he knew the cat had been spending more and more time with me, he left a bowl of cat food next to the bathtub. Sometimes he even brought Paul down himself. The cat would purr contentedly in his arms before jumping down onto the mattress to rub against me. Seeing my abductor act with such kindness made me doubt his depravity. He would whisper comforting words to the cat, stroke him gently with a smile, and watch with delight as Paul frolicked around the cellar.

Seasons came and went.

New books appeared.

My moods alternated between periods of deep depression and resignation.

I let the days pass, no longer trying to hold on. I hadn't given up on the idea of escape, but I had more and more questions about the world I would find outside. Paul visited daily and sometimes even slept with me at night. I talked to him and imagined how he might reply. I told him stories and recited my poem. I told him my name was Sandrine, that I was a journalist, and that I would love to take him along with me on my next trip.

Then, one morning, another cat appeared in the cellar. A black-and-white female with a round belly. She came down the stairs, followed by Paul, and found a hiding place under the stairs. A few hours later, the tiny cries of kittens filled the room, and the man came down with a huge smile on his face. He said I'd be less lonely from then on.

I named each of the babies. There were ten of them in total, from two different litters. They all wandered freely between the cellar and the outside world—the door was left open at night too by this point. My former classmates now visited me disguised as animals. I pursued the conversations we had had as children, conversing earnestly with the tiny balls of fluff which tumbled around me. I assured Marie, a white kitten with a single black spot on her nose, that I could recite my poem flawlessly, and she told me all about her time at university. Pierre, Fabian, Julie, Marie . . . They all came back to keep me company.

They all wanted to hear the tales of my amazing travels.

17

From then on, my captor became less intrusive. He continued to visit me to satisfy his urges, but not as frequently as before. He regularly came down to the cellar just to stroke the cats. Afterwards, he would disappear back up the stairs and I wouldn't see him again until the next day.

As for me, I spent my time taking care of them. I read them passages from my books, and told them how my grandmother, Suzanne, had lived through the war. I explained that I wished I had known her better, that I wanted to ask her so many questions. I erased her death by inventing a life for her, far from my reality, but isolated, just as I was, on a secret island. I told them she never would have let the Erlking come near them. I imagined that one day I would be sent to her island for a story and together we would make time stable again. The kittens asked me questions, and I answered in great detail. I created a story in which we were all prisoners of the Erlking, but I reassured them that none of us would fall for his tricks, because Suzanne would protect us and ultimately set us free.

At night, I sang my mother's favourite song as a lullaby to put them to sleep.

> *Speak to me of love,*
> *And say what I'm longing to hear ...*

An old song to combat an old poem.

I almost forgot I was being held prisoner. Not only because I had friends to talk to and spend my time with now, but also because I was actually inhabiting the stories I told. The grey walls of my cell disappeared, making way for wild grasses and boulders as far as the eye could see. The ocean roared, filling my mind with its briny smell. The cats turned into classmates with whom I played ball, went horse riding, and drew colourful pictures on the cellar walls. The room became a former block-house from a book I had read about the Second World War. The landscape outside resembled the wild moors described by the Brontë sisters. And I became the heroine of my own travel column.

I could have passed the time like that for years without thinking of escape. In fact, the mere thought of leaving my friends behind was unbearable. But that wasn't the only reason the situation felt less dire than before.

He played a key role in the charade.

The man I called the Erlking now rarely tormented me. His visits became more and more erratic, before stopping altogether. I didn't know why. But one thing was certain: his absence no longer affected me as it had in the beginning.

I had other people to keep me company.

One morning, however, a simple piece of stone made the possibility of escape very real. One of the cats, a grey female named Emilie, had got herself stuck exploring the narrow space between the bathtub and the wall. I could hear her mewing for my help. I pulled my chain to breaking point so that I could free her, then scolded her so she wouldn't do it again.

That's when I saw it.

Over the years, a slow leak had eroded the mortar between the stones. I'm not sure exactly when this particular stone had come loose, but when I held it in my hand, I was surprised by its impressive weight. It was heavy, with a pointed end, like a large flint. I put it back in its place. I was so afraid he might find it that I was shaking. I sat back down on the mattress, my mind whirling with the new possibilities that rock had just opened up.

I had a weapon.

Now all I had to do was get angry enough to use it.

Unfortunately, a hideous turn of events the very next day meant I didn't have to wait long for that opportunity to present itself.

18

A voice woke me up. I slowly emerged from my lethargy, gently pushed aside the kittens that had cuddled up to me during the night and sat up to listen better. My heart started to race. I concentrated hard, trying to work out if the conversation I could hear was coming from the open door. The words were too muffled to be coming from inside the house, but now I was certain of it: two people were talking not far away.

Out of the corner of my eye, I spied a sudden movement. I could see legs outside the tiny cellar window. Someone was standing there. A tall, thin stranger who looked nothing like my captor.

I didn't hesitate.

I stood up, got as close to the window as I could, dragging my chain behind me, and screamed louder than I would have ever thought possible. The cats fled at the sound of my bird-like screeching, startled by my sudden transformation. My throat burned as tears of anger and hope blurred my vision, but nothing could stop me now. I could suddenly feel the searing pain of that unwanted invasion of my body night after night. I could taste the bitter hot chocolate laced with sedatives, and feel the aching open wounds from my metal handcuff . . . I channelled all of my hatred into those screams. My hatred of him and of myself, and of all those years during which I had simply accepted my fate. I jumped for joy when the legs disappeared from view. Soon the stranger would come and save me. He would call the police and that bastard Erlking would rot in hell . . .

But the knight in shining armour never appeared.

Instead, my torturer rushed down the stairs and barrelled into me. He raised his heavy hand and hit me so hard I fell to the ground. It took me a few seconds to regain consciousness. The taste of blood filled my mouth and a high-pitched whistling echoed through my brain.

"You dirty whore, you'll pay for that! After everything I've done for you! Believe me, you'll regret this!"

I heard him climb back up the stairs. I couldn't think any more. My head throbbed. I lay on the floor for hours. I no longer had the desire to do anything. I didn't have the energy to get up, to seek revenge. Not even to live. The only thing I wanted was to seek refuge on the island, to cry in Suzanne's soft arms and have fun with my friends.

So, I closed my eyes. I imagined I was on a boat, sat next to my boyfriend. I prayed for time to be more reliable, prayed to avoid my certain death, to escape aboard the *Lazarus*.

But all my prayers couldn't change Goethe's poem and its gruesome ending. The Erlking came back that evening carrying a tray. He was visibly tense and didn't speak a word.

8:37 p.m.

Was he going to rape me in some new and even more humiliating way? Was he going to torture me to make me regret what I had done?

He placed a number of bowls on the ground spaced out around the cellar and went over to the bathtub. I watched him from the corner of my eye as he put in the plug and turned on the tap. Steamy water filled the bath as the first cats streamed down the steps, attracted by the smell of food. Some of them came over to me to be stroked before heading to their bowls to devour their dinner. The man made his way back to the stairs and sat down on the first step. He stared at me darkly. He had a look in his eye I had never seen before, not even at his most depraved.

Once the bath was full, he turned off the tap and took Paul in his arms. He stroked him for a long time, until the cat fell into a deep, peaceful sleep. I thought that he was about to go back upstairs. That he was simply going to let me stew in my fear and maybe return later to seal my fate.

But instead, he walked over to the bathtub and plunged Paul into the water. Paul, the first cat to bring me comfort in this waking nightmare. I was terrified, unable to make any sound at all, petrified with fear and horror. He held him under for what felt like an eternity. When he finally let go, Paul's body floated to the surface like a stuffed toy forgotten on a bed. Then the Erlking turned his attention to the other cats, who all seemed terribly sleepy and unaware of the danger they faced. I shouted to wake them up. I stood with difficulty but he slapped me hard, and I went down again, my body slamming into the mattress.

One by one, that monster drowned them all.

I tried to stop him and crawled towards the bathtub intending to fish them out. I screamed that I was going to take them to the island, that everything would be like before. I told them they shouldn't have drunk the chocolate—chocolate was supposed to be sweet, was supposed to make the world a better place, not leave a bitter, synthetic taste in your mouth . . .

But it was too late.

They were all dead.

The man stood next to me. He was eerily still. "I told you you'd regret it. It's your fault they're dead. You did this."

I don't know how I managed it.

I don't even remember picking up the stone from behind the bathtub. All I know is that he turned his back to me, and I seized the opportunity. I hit him once. His scalp was bathed in blood. He stared at me, an uncomprehending look in his eyes. Before he could gather his thoughts or even move, I slammed the stone into the top of his forehead. Once. Twice. He collapsed on the floor, but I kept hitting him. I couldn't stop. His skull cracked with each impact, covering my clothes, my face, and the cement with its contents. When it was over, I sat down next to him for a long time.

Then I rifled through his trouser pockets and found his keys.

I freed myself and staggered towards the stairs.

A pair of immaculate white trainers sat on the porch. I put them on and stood there unmoving, taking in the grey landscape.

I had been right. No one was waiting for me outside. Nothing but fields as far as I could see. No signs of a friendly presence or any reason to hope.

I wasn't ready to confront this new silence and solitude. I had no idea what the world beyond the hedges and the willow tree was like. I truly wondered if my rightful place in the world wasn't the one I had just left behind, the one I had just destroyed by killing a man.

I didn't know if I could survive out here.

So, I went to the island.

19

Sandrine's voice dwindled to a whisper as she finished her story.

Veronique and Damian remained silent. Partly out of respect for her memories and the horror they contained, but also because they felt like they had been with her, trapped inside those cellar walls.

The young woman stared down at the blanket on her hospital bed, as her fingers fiddled with its threads. She struggled to keep her eyes open as she began to slip helplessly into a drug-induced sleep.

The detective wanted to intervene, but the psychiatrist placed her hand on his forearm to stop him.

"Thank you for talking to us, Sandrine," she said, bringing their visit to a close. "You were very brave to confront that man the first time, and then to relive those tragic moments again. We'll let you rest and we'll come back tomorrow to talk more if you agree. I want to help you. It will take some time, but I'm certain we can get you through this. Does that sound all right?"

Sandrine simply nodded, as though all her strength had left her the moment she had finished her story.

"Good, very good. We'll leave you alone now. You've taken an important step. I'm very hopeful about the future," concluded Veronique as she picked up her tape recorder and smiled kindly at Sandrine. The rules of her profession prevented her from getting too involved, but she was finding it hard to ignore her feelings. She wanted to take Sandrine in her arms again, comfort her, and tell her she had done the right thing killing that bastard . . . But she had to make do with a smile instead.

They left the room, and only started breathing freely again once they were in the corridor. The nurse who had been waiting just outside the door stood up when she saw them.

"Give her sedatives for the next twenty-four hours," said Veronique. "I'll leave the details at the nurse's station."

"Yes, doctor."

"Check on her regularly and . . . do keep bringing her flowers. That was a good idea."

"Of course," agreed the nurse with a nod.

Damian waited a few minutes before speaking. His humanity had been shaken by the victim's revelations, but he was still intensely focused on the investigation. "I would have liked to ask her a few questions," he said as they left the hospital.

"Yes, I know. But it wasn't the right time."

"She didn't even tell us her name . . ."

"You don't realize how much it must have taken out of her to tell us her story! Her brain protected her in a host of different ways during her imprisonment, and now we've forced her to leave her refuge. We both have so many questions to ask, you for the investigation, and me to help her heal. But we can't ask them all today. I think you have enough to close the case as it is, don't you?"

"Unfortunately not. I need a signed statement and . . . a name," Damian pointed out as he pulled a cigarette from his pack.

"Her biographical memory—the part of her memory that constitutes her identity—was almost undoubtedly disconnected as well. Not completely, just enough to allow her to enter her refuge. She had to forget who she really was because being Sandrine Vaudrier helped her survive and escape to places outside the cellar. We have shown her she no longer has anything to fear. When she fully accepts that, her body will awaken all of the parts of her brain it had to put to sleep during her captivity: her memories and emotions. Given how quickly she told her story, I don't think it will take long. I will probably be able to ask her for her name tomorrow when she wakes up and we begin her treatment.

Damian listened attentively. He smiled at the psychiatrist who he had at first mistaken for an inexperienced graduate. The way she had let the victim narrate her memories without interruption, giving her subtle non-verbal encouragement, and protecting her from his cold and impatient questioning was clear proof that she was an accomplished professional he could trust. "You did well in there. I mean . . . with Sandrine."

"A compliment!" she exclaimed, raising her hands in surprise. "Might I steal a cigarette to celebrate this momentous occasion?"

"Yes, of course. Here. What do you think about her story from a psychiatric point of view?"

"Good try, detective."

"What do you mean?"

"Sandrine has agreed to be my patient. As such—"

"You're bound by doctor–patient confidentiality."

"Exactly. What do *you* think?"

"I'm sorry, but this is an ongoing investigation," he teased.

"Very funny. One thing's for sure: the bricks Sandrine used to construct her refuge coincide with her experiences in the real world. It will take me a while to analyse them and find all the links, but you already have the victim, the perpetrator, and the motive. I'll make a copy of the recording for you."

"Thank you. Can I ask you one more question?"

"Go ahead."

"Do victims always open up so easily?"

"Do you really think it was easy for her in there?" the doctor asked, surprised.

"She only hesitated for a moment. She seemed determined," replied the detective.

"Every victim reacts differently. The hardest part in cases like this one isn't telling the truth, but accepting it," she explained. "Tomorrow, or sometime soon, Sandrine will realize that many years of her life were stolen from her, and that killing her captor won't bring them back. And believe me, when that moment comes, she won't find any solace in meds or the knowledge that she sought revenge."

20

Damian waited in the lobby while Dr Burel made a copy of the recording. He thought of Sandrine as a teenager, trapped in the cellar, chained to the wall for years. He imagined her despair, distress, and incomprehension. And that massive body on top of hers. He was relieved to drive out of the hospital car park and flee the dangerous comparisons between Sandrine's story and what might have happened to his own daughter, which had started to invade his thoughts.

When he reached the station, he went straight to his office. In the corridor, he ran into his colleagues who were all busy stacking boxes against a wall. "What's going on?" he asked.

"We're getting rid of old files," replied Antoine. "We're sending them to the archives in Caen. Chief's orders."

"Already?"

"Yeah. It seems the decision to shut us down is final. So we might as well get to work. What's happening with your case? Any developments?"

"Yes. I'm going to go and type up my report now before someone packs my typewriter!"

Damian sat down at his desk, lost in his thoughts.

The case is basically solved. Soon the psychiatrist will be able to give us her name. The mystery of the island won't have lasted long, except in the victim's head. She'll be spending months or even years putting the pieces of her past back together.

He lit a cigarette as he opened the file he'd compiled the day before. The agents who had photographed the scene had slipped an envelope of pictures inside. He spread them out on his desk. Then he pulled the cassette tape from his jacket pocket, hesitant to listen to the revelations it contained yet again. He didn't want to dive back into the story yet, but he had to summarize the latest information for his boss. He opened a drawer and took out his tape recorder. He listened to Sandrine in the background as he typed his report.

I was on my way home. It was cold and dark. I was sixteen . . .
Sixteen.

For the moment, with neither a name nor a date of birth, it was hard to know exactly how many years had passed between the kidnapping and her escape. But according to the medical team, Sandrine appeared to be between twenty-five and thirty years of age. That meant she had been imprisoned for a duration of anywhere between nine and fourteen years . . .

He noted in his report that the victim's identity would be shared with them as soon as the psychiatrist got the information. Once they had it, they could close the case. Finding the young woman's family would be the final step to putting this mystery, which had washed up so unexpectedly on the shores of Villers-sur-Mer, behind them. The sleepy town would be able to go back to its usual boredom.

When he had finished, he stopped the tape and lit another cigarette. For the first time since he'd met the mysterious Sandrine, he relaxed as he thought about what would become of him after the station closed. Everyone would be transferred to one of the major stations in the region, but Damian still hadn't been told where he was going. All he wanted was to find himself somewhere quiet, where he would never need to explore anyone else's 'refuge'.

He gathered up all of the documents in the file and was just putting the photographs back into the envelope when one of them caught his eye. It had been taken in the cellar, just a few hours after the gruesome discovery. It featured the wall to the right of the stairs, located opposite the mattress and the bathtub. The photographer had knelt down to take a picture of what would have been the victim's viewpoint from the makeshift bed.

"Sandrine must have spent hours, days, and weeks staring at that wall," said Damian to himself with a sigh. "How many times did she make the wall collapse in her dreams? How much hope did she use up on wishing away that impenetrable concrete?"

In the photograph, Damian could guess at the position of the tiny window because a weak halo from the spotlights outside glowed on the far right of the image.

He looked at the picture for a long time. He didn't want to admit it, but part of him was still surprised that Sandrine had given up the truth so easily. He didn't understand the intimate workings of the human brain, but he had expected more resistance on her part. There was another detail that intrigued him, too. It had felt like Sandrine had been reciting a text, like a bad actress hurrying through her lines. If there hadn't been tears at the end, it would have been easy to think that the episode narrated in the hospital room had little to do with the person telling it.

He thought back to Dr Burel's remarks. She had said it was normal, that it would take time, that her brain hadn't assimilated all of the information yet, that the drugs would make her seem absent and detached . . .

But, as he glanced one last time at the picture of the wall, the hairs on the back of Damian's neck stood up. He sat perfectly still, trying to figure out what had set off the alarm bells in his head. After a few seconds, he began to focus his attention on a detail he hadn't noticed at first.

Well, well, well, whispered a voice that reeked of sulphur.

Damian rewound the tape to find the passages that interested him.

8:37 p.m. Time is relative.

He went through all of the pictures of the cellar again but didn't find what he was looking for in any of them.

*

So, you worthless excuse of a father, what will you do now? Eh?
Will you turn your back on her again? Run away to some other
part of France so you don't have to confront me? Or will you dance
with me this time?

Damian jumped up, grabbed the file, took the cassette from
the tape player, and reached for his car keys.

"Leaving so soon?" asked Antoine, his arms laden with boxes.

"I have to check on something at the farm. If anyone asks,
I won't be long. Is there still a team out there?"

"I don't think so. Everyone went home because of the rain.
The super said we should wait for it to die down before going
back. He's still hoping that forensics will be able to help out."

"All right. Antoine?"

"Yeah?"

"If he asks where I am, you have no idea, okay?"

"Whatever you say, boss!"

The detective turned down the bumpy road without a second
thought for the car's suspension this time. The windscreen
wipers struggled to push away the pounding rain, and he had
to concentrate to keep from driving into the ditch on the side
of the road.

Sandrine's voice blared out of the car's speakers. *I ran as*
fast as I could through the forest as the lid of dark clouds slowly
descended until they seemed to brush the tops of the tallest trees.
The raindrops felt like tiny frozen arrows burrowing into my skin,
but I didn't slow down until I reached the treeline.

He arrived at the farm, parked near the willow, and sat in
the car for a moment, studying his surroundings.

So that's what happened . . . The children were murdered . . .
That's the secret of this island . . . I fell on my knees in the muddy
earth and pounded my fists into the ground. "Sacrificed to preserve
the island . . . To save this bloody island!" I shouted, cursing the bit
of rock surrounded by ocean on which I now found myself. I stayed
there crying for the children a few minutes longer, my fists clenched

in anger. Then I opened my right hand. The key was still there.

Damian cut the ignition and ran to the front door, paying no heed to the mud squelching beneath his feet and ignoring the branches of the willow which cracked like whips in the wind. When he reached the porch, he tore through the police tape, pulled the file from inside his jacket, and slipped inside.

The detective didn't waste any time—he went straight to the cellar. The stench of damp and rotting flesh seemed even stronger than before.

When he reached the stairs, Damian turned on his torch and descended step by step, as respectfully as if he were entering a tomb. He held the photograph of the bare wall before him like a compass.

He sat down on the mattress to find the exact spot where the picture had been taken. He didn't dare touch the heavy chain which lay next to him. He closed his eyes and thought back to Sandrine's story.

8:37 p.m.

There were no steps on the stairs that night.

I was alone.

Presumably forgotten by my loved ones since I had never heard a police siren wail anywhere near my cell.

8:37 p.m.

The door would open, and the smell of stew would waft down to me, mixed with the sweet aroma of hot chocolate, which he brought me without fail.

8:37 p.m.

Time is relative.

I had barely reached a hundred before the grey cement was as empty and useless as a clock without hands.

Damian stood up and shone his torch on the wall opposite, looking for a mark of any kind.

But there was nothing.

He ran his hand over the surface, stopping at anything that jutted out, but found nothing conclusive. He took a big step back to stare at the wall again. He still couldn't see anything, no holes from a missing nail, nor even a faint circle of dust which could have accumulated over time.

Damian finally admitted to himself what had been troubling him, and the putrid smell inside the cellar grew stronger, as though encouraged by this impossible truth.

Ha, ha, ha, you rotten father . . . Now the real fun begins . . . I told you . . . Time is your enemy. Ask Melanie what she thinks. She had all the time in the world to dance with me . . .

"8:37 p.m.," mumbled the detective as he pushed the devil's voice from his mind. "But there was never a clock down here . . ."

THE THIRD BEACON
The Children

Mein Sohn, was birgst du so bang dein Gesicht?
                            Goethe, "Erlkönig"

My son, why cover thy face thus in fear?
                            Goethe, "Erlking"

I

Sandrine watched out of the corner of her eye as the psychiatrist and the detective left her room.

When the door had closed behind them, she contemplated the raindrops as they slid down her window—something she remembered doing often in the cellar. Watching through the tiny basement window as the rain fell, she would imagine herself outside, sticking out her tongue to taste it, shivering when the cool water found its way down the back of her neck and between her shoulder blades.

As a child she had always loved to play in the late autumn showers. Rainy weather made her feel more alive than the indolent warmth of the summer sun, which put her to sleep and left her feeling lethargic and useless as she lay on a beach or on the riverbank. The few times her mother had taken her to the local pool, Sandrine had spent every minute swimming lengths and trying to beat her own record for holding her breath underwater while her mother, who rarely went in at all, perfected her tan on one of the deckchairs.

"You must have got that from your father, this constant need to be in the water like a fish," her mother would say disdainfully. She was always justifying the invisible rift between them, which grew deeper and wider with each passing day until it was an unpassable obstacle that Sandrine found much more daunting than the concrete walls of the cellar where she had been imprisoned for nearly fifteen years.

"Your father."

Every time she made a mistake, every time she brought home a disappointing mark, every time she misbehaved, there was only one explanation: her father. Sandrine's mother turned him into a token excuse, pulling him out of her hat every time she failed to understand why her child hated maths, why she couldn't eat without dirtying her clothes, or why she preferred swimming to basking in the sun. If her mother had seen her chained up on the tattered mattress, she probably would have said her daughter had always liked to put on a show. That her need to perform had been inherited from her father, a strange, manipulative man for whom she had played the adoring fan for far too long before he finally walked out on them.

Sandrine tried to fight the urge to sleep, but closed her eyes nonetheless. *Just to help me think*, she convinced herself.

She knew she didn't have much time.

Soon, the detective would begin asking questions. She was sure of it. Though she was convinced she hadn't betrayed herself, she had seen a strange light in his expression, a light powered by doubt, but also by something else—a hunger for the truth perhaps.

She wondered where that spark had come from. What ordeals had he survived? What dark experience had slowly suffocated his inner fire until nothing was left but the incandescent embers behind his eyes?

Sandrine fell into darkness for a moment. She was exhausted from her escape and the drugs administered by the doctors, which prevented her from thinking clearly. She opened her eyes and was startled by the brightness of her hospital room. She could feel a migraine brewing at the back of her head. But she was reluctant to close her eyes again. She knew that if she let go, she would find herself back in the cellar, back in the torturous hands of her abductor.

Of course, there was also the other part of the truth, the part she had omitted. But that part never came to her in her sleep. It was always her time spent captive that manifested itself, never the rest. It was as though her brain had sealed the doors to her unconscious to protect her, even while she rested. Sandrine had to admit it was better that way. To convince the others, she had to forget that part of the story. She needed to truly believe that it had never happened, that it was just a nightmare conjured by a weary mind.

But would they believe her?

What would happen if the police found out about the rest? How would she survive if they forced her to emerge from her real refuge, the one she had just shared with the psychiatrist?

She would go to jail.

Could she take that risk now that she had finally escaped from her own prison?

No.

There was only one solution: the island.

"Yes, the island," she mumbled.

Why not go back there? Forever. The Erlking was gone. She had killed him. The photograph was proof of that. Everything must be different now: the sky, the plants . . . and the children. Had they returned? Had they survived and not drowned after all? Would they dance around her and sing her songs of love?

Of course, there was still that one wandering feral cat whom no one could ever catch. But maybe after so many years he had died in his sleep under a bush . . .

The idea grew more and more tempting.

I have to go back, that's the answer.

She knew how. She had fled to the island so many times over the years, allowing her mind to explore beyond the grey walls and carry her to another life. It was like having the power to return to a dream whenever she wished. It hadn't been the perfect dream, with the Erlking on the prowl, but now that the boogeyman lay on the floor of the cellar with his skull in pieces, she was sure it would be different.

After all, what's a nightmare when it's no longer frightening? Just a dream.

Sandrine imagined the door of the blockhouse in front of her. She held out her hand to push it open and see the world outside. She could smell salt, and then the scent of the fruit trees and the vegetable garden reached her nostrils.

I had to forget them to escape that cellar, but now I can return. I can take refuge on the island without worrying about the Erlking or the feral cat. Nothing can hurt me now. I can learn to live there by myself, sheltered from the truth . . .

As Sandrine fell asleep, the first notes of a song from a dream jukebox filled the air.

2

Damian sat staring at the wall opposite for a long time. He didn't yet understand exactly what his discovery meant, but the fact that he had found an inconsistency in Sandrine's story had turned his blood to ice in his veins. He eventually walked around the cellar again, steering clear of the plastic numbers his colleagues had placed here and there to indicate areas and objects of particular interest for analysis. The mattress, the chain, the bathtub, the exact location of the corpse . . .

He climbed back up the stairs to the kitchen, where more numbers were scattered about. The smell of cat food dominated a collection of other, less identifiable odours. He explored all of the rooms, wandering aimlessly through the darkness and dust, but his mind remained preoccupied with the cellar. Outside it was still pouring. Damian felt like it had been raining for years.

Why would the victim lie? Maybe she just forgot? Maybe it's one of those memories her brain hid away to protect her? But why hide a harmless detail like the presence of a clock in the room? Why would she feel threatened by such a normal everyday object?

Damian opened a few cupboards. The house had been searched, but the process had been interrupted when it got too dark. The teams would tackle the attic and outbuildings next. It should have been done already, but Damian realized that the superintendent had decided to have the officers move the old files instead of coming back to the scene of a crime that required no further explanation other than those provided by the victim. For the super, Sandrine had been kidnapped and after many long years had killed her captor and escaped. The case was closed. End of story. Now it was up to the courts to determine whether there were any extenuating circumstances.

Damian was about to leave when he noticed several keys hanging from nails on the wall. He shone his torch on them and selected the smallest one, which looked like it belonged to the letterbox.

You never know.

He went out into the rain, walked past the weeping willow and unlocked the metal letterbox. Inside he found two utility bills, and, there, right at the back, as if a gust of wind had blown through the slit and glued it tight to keep it safe from prying eyes, was a brown envelope. The address on the front was written by hand, and there was no clue as to the identity of the sender. The detective hesitated, then opened it, fully aware that he was breaking the law. He decided that the ends justified the means in this case. If it came to nothing, he wouldn't mention it to anyone.

He pulled out a letter from the Normandy Agricultural Federation. It was an invitation to participate in the annual livestock show.

"As I suspected," he said with a sigh as he slipped the letter into his back pocket, leaving the others in the box. "Nothing special . . ."

A sudden movement to the right of the house caught his eye. It had been fleeting, but Damian was sure he had seen something. He slowly made his way back towards the front door, and saw the shadow slip through it ahead of him, obviously seeking shelter from the rain. He followed the wet pawprints into the kitchen, where he was surprised to see the cat looking so at home. The animal leapt up onto the sink and drank a little stagnant water before jumping back down and heading for the cellar.

This is clearly his home. And now he's making a beeline for the mattress, reassured no doubt by the scent of the person who used to stroke him on there.

But didn't Sandrine say all the cats drowned?

3

The next morning, Dr Burel pulled into the hospital car park at eight o'clock. The night had been too short. She had stayed up late listening to the recording and taking notes on details to clear up and potential wounds to soothe during the next therapy session. The first thing she needed to know was Sandrine's real name. Accessing that information would begin to reverse the dehumanization she had suffered at the hands of her captor. Then she would carefully guide Sandrine and help her to admit and understand the brutality he had inflicted on her. After that, she could finally begin working on acceptance, which would undoubtedly be the longest and most painful stage of the treatment.

Veronique stepped into her office, put on her white coat, checked her emails, and reread her notes from the night before. Of course, not everything would come out right away. It would take hours of analysis to get through each topic, but she was feeling fairly confident. The fact that Sandrine had shared her story so quickly was proof of her will to survive, which would be crucial to the success of her therapy.

Dr Burel left her office and headed for Sandrine's room. She wanted to talk to her as soon as possible. In most cases, she would have waited forty-eight hours before questioning her patient again, but Sandrine's state of mind the day before had been so encouraging that she felt she could speed up the process. What was more, though she couldn't wholly admit it, she wanted to give the detective the information he needed to close his investigation. She had only known him for a few days, but she could tell that this case troubled him deeply.

On the way, Veronique thought about what she would do after work—a relaxing bath and the latest David Mallet novel, which she had bought but hadn't yet had the time to read. And maybe, after a nice glass of wine, she would transcribe the recording from the session she was about to conduct. Then she would put the case aside until she returned from holiday . . .

When Dr Burel opened the door, Sandrine had just woken up and was clearly still groggy from the medication. Her light-brown hair framed her face like the petals of a wilting flower in need of sunshine. Veronique offered a kind, "Good morning," then asked how she was feeling and if she was still happy to talk about her story from the day before. Sandrine accepted and invited the psychiatrist to sit in a chair next to the bed.

"I've thought a lot about what you said yesterday," began Dr Burel enthusiastically.

"Yesterday?"

"Yes, you know, when we talked. Detective Bouchard was also in the room."

"No, I don't remember seeing you yesterday," Sandrine replied flatly.

Veronique kept quiet. She simply observed her patient, waiting for her memories to stir. *Maybe I came back too soon. She's tired, and still feeling the effects of the sedatives and her recent revelations . . . All of that must have shaken her, but I don't see how it could induce amnesia . . .*

"Well, you did," she continued. "The detective showed you a photograph."

"A photo? No . . ."

"That's okay, don't worry. It's perfectly normal. Your memories will return soon," Dr Burel reassured her. She had brought up the photograph because of its emotional weight, which should have been enough to pull Sandrine's brain from its torpor. She was surprised to see it had had no effect. She decided to forge ahead. "It was a picture of a man's body . . ."

"Really?"

"Yes, the one who hurt you, the Erlking . . ."

"Oh no," objected Sandrine, turning away from Dr Burel. "That's impossible. The Erlking isn't here, he's on the island . . ."

"Sandrine, do you know why you're in this hospital bed?" the psychiatrist asked, feeling increasingly anxious. The atmosphere in the room had changed drastically in the space of a few short seconds. Veronique felt lost. Her hope for Sandrine's recovery had evaporated. As she stared at her patient, she had the strange feeling she was talking to an entirely different person.

"Yes," Sandrine replied with a cold smile. "Because of the island."

"Is that the only reason? You don't remember a cellar or anything else?"

"The Erlking was on the island. He's still there. He killed the children," Sandrine explained. There was certainty in her voice but her eyes were bright with fear.

"Sandrine, I thought—"

"He never left that place. Who rides forth to-night, through storms so wild?"

Veronique was taken aback to hear her patient recite the poem again. Then, in a perfect monotone, Sandrine told the story of the island—the exact same story she had told upon arriving at the hospital. There were no cellars, no chains, it was as if the kidnapping and rape had never happened.

This isn't possible, not after yesterday's revelations.

Veronique wondered what other monster could have so abruptly forced Sandrine back into her refuge.

4

Nine o'clock.

Damian had just finished his fourth cup of coffee when he decided to listen to the tapes again.

After finding the cat some food in a cupboard, the detective had left the farm and gone back to the station where he decided to focus on some less serious cases. Thinking about something other than Sandrine and her refuge for a few hours had done him a world of good. He had also chatted with two colleagues who had subtly slipped their preferred transfers into the conversation. Damian had promised to talk to the super, though he couldn't promise them results. Officers had some say in their choice of transfer, but they were organized first and foremost according to the needs of the different stations in the region.

Then he had waved to the night shift officers and gone home. He said goodnight to his daughter's picture and got into bed to try to sleep. But, just like the night before, it had taken hours. He was certain he had missed something important, that the one clue needed to break open the strange case had escaped him.

This morning, determined to lay his doubts to rest, he had arrived at the station with a single goal: to find the truth.

He closed the door to his office to block out the sound of his colleagues who were still stacking boxes in the corridor and immersed himself in the different versions of Sandrine's story. He still couldn't put his finger on it, but as he listened to the victim recount her violent experiences, a fleeting impression— like the one that had kept him awake for much of the night—alerted him that there was something else that didn't fit with either narrative. He tried to read between the lines, tried to interpret Sandrine's individual words and analyse her tone, but the inexplicable feeling just kept growing.

What had he missed? What detail had he failed to see?

At the end of the second side, the *play* button popped up, signalling the end of the recording. Damian sat there in silence, lost somewhere between an island and a cellar, trying to drag the truth into the light. Because he was certain now that Sandrine hadn't told them everything. Listening to her speak, it sounded to him now more than ever like she was reciting a poem from memory, performing without conviction, and that in itself was enough to know she was concealing something.

But where could she be hiding the truth?

Under which sentences? Behind which words?

It felt like an unsolvable enigma. Damian didn't have the necessary psychological tools at his disposal—he didn't even know where to begin. He was going to have to do it his way, follow police procedure and attempt to track down a solid lead.

He put the first tape back in and pushed play again.

As Sandrine spoke, Damian was surprised to find himself mumbling along with her, as if her sentences were the expression of his own thoughts.

In deep shit, that's where I am.

I regretfully studied my trainers, which had sunk down into a mixture of mud and cow manure.

The farm. The part of the story where the only concrete leads came together: Wernst and the clock.

After a few seconds, Damian suddenly stopped the tape, pushed rewind, and started over from the beginning.

There. While Sandrine is in the field with the farmer looking at the spray-painted cows.

Three words began to echo in his mind.

The livestock fair.

Holy shit . . .

That was it, that was the inconsistency.

He jumped up and fumbled in the back pocket of his trousers. The envelope he had found in Wernst's letterbox was still there. He pulled it out and read the first sentence again aloud. The letter was signed by André Dubreuil, Chairman of the Normandy Agricultural Federation.

We are pleased to invite you to participate in the Étretat Livestock Fair, which will take place on the 21st and 22nd June.

Bloody hell.

Damian put in the second tape, where Sandrine told the story of her captivity, looking for the right passage.

Sometimes my captor would disappear for a few days. I don't know where he went . . .

Why hadn't he clocked this sooner? He grabbed the phone, dialled the number in the letterhead, and waited for someone to pick up.

"Normandy Agricultural Federation, how may I help you?" asked a woman's voice.

"Hello, this is Detective Damian Bouchard of Villers-sur-Mer. Could I please speak to Mr Dubreuil?"

"I'm sorry, but he's not currently available. Is there anything I can help you with?"

"I need some information about one of your livestock fair participants. Mr Wernst."

"Oh yes, he's a regular! He comes every year."

"Do you know him?" Damian asked hopefully.

"Not personally no, but I organize the booths for the exhibitors, so his name is familiar. Mr Dubreuil will be able to tell you more. He knows everyone. Our local farmers are like one big family! He'll be back in about an hour. Leave me your number and I'll have him return your call."

Damian gave her the number and hung up. He closed his eyes to think things through. Was exhaustion taking him down the wrong path? First the clock and now another inconsistency . . . But why would Sandrine lie?

The detective could think of only one way to uncover the truth: he would have to talk to the victim again. He would make her face her lies, even if that upset her, even if her screams shook the hospital walls. He needed answers and he needed them quickly, before the station was emptied and the case was handed over to someone else.

He had just stood up to get another cup of coffee when someone knocked on his office door. Antoine stuck his head in without waiting for a reply.

"Boss?"

"Yes, Antoine. Do you need help emptying the storeroom?" he joked, noticing the officer's flushed cheeks and rolled-up sleeves.

"Uh, no . . . It's the psychiatrist . . ."

"What about her?"

"She's here and she wants to talk to you."

Veronique stepped into Damian's office and sat down across from him. Her pale complexion and the dark circles under her eyes made it clear that she hadn't slept any more than he had. Her blonde hair, usually swept up in a tidy ponytail, hung unkempt around her face. As soon as she sat down, she nervously lit a cigarette and inhaled deeply. "Moving, are we?" she asked, surprised.

"Yes, something like that," Damian replied evasively. "What brings you here?"

"We have a problem," she replied dryly.

"What's going on?"

"Sandrine. She doesn't remember yesterday. She says we never came to see her. I just spent an hour with her, and she has no memory of anything that happened yesterday, including what she told us."

Damian was taken aback. He finally felt like he was making progress, like he had found the clue that could untangle the mystery, but this regression would make it impossible to get the truth out of Sandrine. "Could it be the drugs?" he asked, trying to stay calm.

Veronique didn't hesitate. "No, that's impossible, the dosage is carefully calculated to avoid inducing amnesia or any other side effects. And that's not all. She's gone back to the island."

"The island?"

"Yes, she's gone back to her original story. No more mention of the cellar or her captivity. If I didn't have the recording, I would think I had dreamed it all up!"

"How could she have forgotten our visit? Jesus!"

"At first I thought maybe she was just exhausted, but that wouldn't have been enough to completely erase such an emotionally charged conversation," explained the psychiatrist, just as distraught as Damian. "It was hardly small talk! We showed her the dead body of her abductor, and it troubled her so much that she revealed what she had been through before we even asked!"

"So, what happened?"

"There's only one reason Sandrine would go back to the island. She doesn't feel safe here, in the real world. She's scared."

Damian studied Veronique. The psychiatrist was looking down at the floor, her thoughts elsewhere, far from this office. For the first time since they'd met, he sensed that she had lost her confidence. He even wondered if maybe Sandrine wasn't the only one who was scared. "We showed her a picture of her captor lying dead on the floor, his skull smashed to pieces by a rock. What could she be afraid of now?"

"I don't know, detective. But the fear has to be powerful to cause such a regression," said Veronique.

"How long will it last?" asked Damian frustratedly.

"Until the fear subsides, I assume. We're back at square one. Wernst's dead body only freed her for a few hours."

The detective lit his own cigarette. He had quit years ago

but had started smoking again when Melanie had disappeared. He had been promising himself to ditch the pleasureless habit ever since. "Has it . . . Has it occurred to you that she might be lying?" he asked cautiously.

"What do you mean?"

"I don't know . . . Maybe she's hiding part of the truth . . ."

"What makes you say that? I think I would have noticed if she were a pathological liar," she exclaimed in irritation. "Besides, everything you found in the cellar confirms her account."

"I'm not saying she's deliberately trying to fool us. But there are inconsistencies in her second story . . ."

"It's normal for details to be . . . modified or glossed over to dull the pain," Veronique objected. "They're usually insignificant, small 'blips', if you will, which the brain will correct during treatment."

"These aren't blips . . ."

The sentence hung in the air for a few seconds—a truth no one wanted to acknowledge.

"All right," said Dr Burel tersely. "You appear to think you've found some sort of irrefutable proof, is that right?" She clearly didn't like to be contradicted.

"There's no clock in the cellar," Damian said, levelling with her now. "And nothing to indicate there ever was one. The clock plays a key role in her story: the passage of time, 8:37 p.m. . . . How could she know the exact time he came down in the evenings without a clock?"

"Are you absolutely sure?"

"Yes. I spent hours hunting for one. I looked everywhere, even in the bins, just in case . . . Nothing."

"Why would she have made it up?" asked the psychiatrist, perplexed. "I mean, why would she consciously lie?"

"I don't know, but that's not even the most worrying bit. The only clock I found in the whole house was in the lounge."

"In the lounge?"

"Yes. So, since there wasn't a clock in the cellar, the only way she could have known the exact time he went down the stairs is—"

"Is if she was in the lounge, not the cellar," mumbled Veronique. She frowned in confusion. "That makes no sense!"

"I thought about this all morning and much of the night. What if . . . Let's say she's not lying. Could her memories of the cellar be another refuge of sorts?"

"A second refuge? But to protect her from what?"

"From the truth. Though I'm not sure what that is yet."

"But what could she have possibly been through that would be more traumatic than what she already told us? We're talking about a teenager being locked up and sexually abused for years! The evidence you found in the cellar matches her story! The chain, the dead cats, her blood! She explained all of that!"

"Not the clock."

"Maybe she just forgot! A . . . An object her mind imagined to consolidate all her memories! A simple building block to strengthen her refuge!"

"There's something else," Damian said gravely. "She said she didn't know where her captor went when he disappeared."

"That's right, that's what she said yesterday."

"I found an invitation to a livestock fair in Wernst's letterbox."

"A livestock fair," she repeated. "Yes, that's plausible. That would explain his absences. There are several in the region each year."

"She knew," Damian pointed out. "She lied about that, too. She knew exactly why he was away."

"How can you be so sure?"

Damian stood up, put the recording of Sandrine's first story in the recorder and hit *play*.

"Because she mentions it in her first refuge."

I turned to listen to the farmer standing a few metres ahead of me (who had cleverly chosen to wear high-topped wellington boots) as he pointed with his thick finger at the herd of cows gathered behind a barbed wire fence.

"What did the police say?" I asked as I took pictures of the animals.

"That it was probably kids. That they were just having fun . . . But what am I going to do about the fair now?"

"The fair?"

"The livestock fair a week from today," he explained with a slight accent.

Sandrine had done it.

She was back on the island.

She stood looking at the ocean and could sense the angular outline of the former blockhouse behind her. Her grandmother and the children in the water were gone. Mother Nature and her colours had returned, reclaiming the landscape and banishing the monotone shades of grey.

She walked to the forest and felt safe as she stepped into the trees. Bushy alders caressed her body with their leaves and the thick grass muffled the sound of her footsteps. Sandrine felt calm and serene—a feeling she hadn't experienced in years. She reached the clearing and Suzanne's house. The windows were wide open to let in the mild weather that had replaced the rain and threatening clouds. She could just make out the words of a song on the gramophone, and the sound accompanied her as she approached the front door.

Speak to me of love . . .

Sandrine went inside and found her grandmother sitting at the table, a cup of hot chocolate clasped in her hands. "There's one for you, too," said the old woman, nodding towards a second cup sitting on the table in front of an empty chair.

Sandrine smiled and sat down opposite Suzanne.

"What are you doing here, dear?" asked her grandmother.

"I'm hiding, Granny. I'm safe here, on the island."

"Weren't you safe in the cellar?"

"Not safe enough. They'll uncover the truth. The refuge wasn't sturdy enough."

"Do you remember the story of the three little pigs that I told you when you were little?" asked Suzanne.

"Yes, Granny."

"You built a house made of straw and the psychiatrist blew it down, forcing you to leave the island."

"I didn't know I would have to face her," replied Sandrine. "I hoped the police would believe me. I thought the island was enough. It protected me for so many years . . . It was real to me, so why couldn't it be real for everyone else? I didn't think they'd find the farm and discover the body. When the doctor showed me the photograph, I realized I was in danger. The island couldn't explain the chain and the blood. So, I told them the truth . . ."

"But not the whole truth," Suzanne pointed out.

"No."

"Then the detective started to have doubts and blew down your second refuge, the one built of sticks."

"I could tell he was suspicious from our very first meeting. I had to create an acceptable enough version of reality to convince him and save myself. I included some of the truth, and hoped that would be enough to satisfy him. But I don't think I succeeded . . . I got scared and came back here," admitted Sandrine.

"Let them huff and puff. They can't blow the third house down. No one will be able to drag you away from the island this time. The blockhouse is made of concrete . . ."

"Just like the wolf never got to the three little pigs inside the brick house," Sandrine added, remembering the story.

"Exactly," Suzanne said approvingly. She smiled broadly. "It doesn't matter what they find out since they'll never reach you here. Are you ready to tell me what really happened now?"

"Yes. It will be our secret, do you promise, Granny?"

"Of course, I promise."

"I had no choice, you know. I wanted to save them all, like you wanted to save the children from drowning. But I couldn't."

"But one of the cats escaped . . ."

"Yes, I let her out . . . Was she the one I heard when I first came to the island? The feral cat no one could ever catch?"

"Maybe, my dear. But in this refuge, she's just a distant cry, a frightened ghost. In the real world, that cat is still alive . . ."

"She could be my undoing. She could tell them everything . . ."

"Come now," urged Suzanne. "Don't think of that anymore. No one can reach you here. Come, tell me your story and then we'll have dinner."

"It all started years after he took me," began Sandrine, clutching the mug of hot chocolate. "I'm in the cellar. I've been missing you so much since you died . . . You left us a week before that man chained me up, and despite the time that's gone by, I still think of you every day. I dream up a past for you on this island and invent a new life for myself. I believe in it so completely that I can sometimes feel the sea breeze on my face. I forget my captor and his ridiculous moans. The chain no longer exists, but I cover the scars on my wrist with a leather cuff. I'm a journalist, Granny, not for a big national daily yet, but I'm certain I'll get there one day. As for you, you're still dead, but your friends tell me all about you to prove to me that you're not the person my mother described. I've only just arrived on the island. Paul invites me to dinner. I can tell he likes me. The children and their gruesome fate don't exist yet; they join the story later. The cats are here, but I don't name them, to avoid getting too attached. I barely touch them. The door to the kitchen is always ajar. Nothing seems to have changed, and yet, nothing will ever be like it was before . . ."

7

From then on, my captor became less intrusive. He continued to visit me to satisfy his urges, but not as frequently as before. He regularly came down to the cellar just to stroke the cats. Afterwards, he would disappear back up the stairs and I wouldn't see him again until the next day. Sometimes I could hear him talking in the house. I didn't know if he was speaking to me or if the words had simply escaped from his thoughts.

One night, he brought me a tray and went back upstairs.

Five minutes later, he reappeared with a second tray and sat down on the floor not far from me. We ate in total silence. He simply smiled shyly at me as he chewed. It was the first time we had ever shared a meal. The first time I had ever been able to look at him without shaking. It was a strange feeling. A blend of latent anger and gratitude. Once he had finished, he stood up and asked if I was still hungry. I said I wasn't.

I would have liked for him to ask me more questions, for him to talk to me about anything at all, just so I would feel less lonely, less insignificant. But that didn't happen.

The next evening, we ate together again.

"I don't want to hurt you, you know," he said. "I . . . I just have these urges deep inside that call to me every now and again and force me to . . . Well, you know . . ."

I nodded. I didn't want to contradict him. I didn't want him to leave me alone in the silence. Could he tell? Did he understand me despite it all? He stayed until I had finished. As soon as he disappeared upstairs, I missed him. Just as his longer absences left me feeling abandoned, the fact that he left me alone after dinner made me feel useless, unworthy of keeping another person company. It was a familiar sensation. My mother had often made me feel that way.

From then on, he no longer forced me. Not because he didn't want me any more, but because he had decided to stop. I could tell when he was fighting his urges because he left the cellar before he had even finished eating, his steps heavier than usual on the wooden stairs.

We started having dinner together every night. Our conversations came to include a wider variety of topics. I told him about my friends from school, and he told me about his work on the farm . . . He grew gentler and more polite. His awkward kindness contrasted starkly with his savage behaviour from the first years. He made me laugh more than once, and I was shaken to hear such an expression of joy escape from my body after so many years of absence.

Then, one day, a few months after we began eating together, he asked me if I wanted to have dinner with him.

In the kitchen.

He mumbled the offer awkwardly, like a teenage boy inviting a girl to a dance. I smiled. At last, I was about to broaden my horizons and leave that place, though it had become less suffocating thanks to our discussions. He took his keys from his pocket, freed my wrist, and held out a hand to help me up the stairs.

No one had ever been so attentive with me. I had never held my mother's hand to cross the road or walk down the street. For her, I was the unwanted proof of a moment of weakness—a shame similar to that experienced by the women whose heads were shaved after the war. That's probably why the police never came looking for me. Did she even report me missing? Or did she just cry fake tears while secretly rejoicing at her good luck?

As I climbed the steps, I realized that no one was waiting for me outside. The only person who had ever shown me any love was you, Granny. But you were gone. And now, the only person who offered me any affection was the man holding my hand as gently as if he were tending to a tiny baby bird which had fallen from its nest. He had been my torturer. But my memories of the violence he inflicted had faded with time, blurring my perception of the unbearable, drowning my certainty and disgust.

No one was waiting for me outside.

No one . . .

My freedoms increased.

I was no longer chained up. The metal handcuff lay discarded on the cellar floor like an artefact from a bygone era—a fearsome monster's lifeless limb chopped off by a knight in shining armour. I discreetly found my bearings in his world as I began to spend more and more time by his side. We tamed one another like wounded wild beasts who had decided to band together to survive. He let me cook for him and ate my food without a second thought. He explained that the world outside had gone awry. That the farm was a refuge and that he regretted having hurt me. The sincerity of his apologies was so touching that I wondered if perhaps *I* was at fault for having judged him too quickly.

Then, one day, he led me to the front door and opened it for me. He held out his hand, inviting me to step outside, and said something I never expected to hear him say.

"You're free now. You can go and waste your time trying to get back to a life that no longer exists, or you can forgive me. I'll never hurt you again, I swear. This door will always be open, so you can come and go as you please."

I stared at the door for a long time without moving. We had been living together for months without any fear or mistrust between us. Free. Free to what? To wander indefinitely? To go to the police and accuse a man I no longer saw as a threat? A man who was now the only buoy for me to cling to in a stormy sea?

Outside I would be alone. Again.

Whereas here . . .

I slowly and deliberately closed the door and made my way back to the kitchen to finish the apple pie I was baking for him.

And this wasn't resignation this time.

This was acceptance.

Months went by. Sometimes we slept together, but only when I initiated it. This feeling of power gave me new confidence. I felt like we had switched places. At first, I was surprised by how distant we had grown sexually. I was afraid that it was because he was no longer interested in my body, which had changed over the years. I felt like I was in a precarious position, that I had outlived my usefulness. But he explained that his urges had simply vanished, that he no longer felt that furious need that had made him hurt me again and again.

I took unexpected pleasure in helping out with the daily chores. Every morning I collected the eggs from the hen house, then helped him feed the cows or harvest vegetables. There were hardly ever any visitors, and should anyone decide to stop by, we could see them coming from the far end of the access road, which left plenty of time to hide me away along with anything that might betray my presence in the house. The only place I wasn't allowed to go was the barn, because it sat at the edge of the property, where I could have been seen. That building, located at the far end of the farmyard, was the edge of my world—a boundary I was forbidden to cross if I wanted to keep my life there a secret.

Other than that, I could go where I pleased. I could watch the sky, breath in the fresh air, or enjoy the shade from the tall willow just outside the front door. Free from coercion and fear, I grew to enjoy my new life. I cooked stews, read the novels he bought for me, and kept myself busy reorganizing—slowly and carefully, not wanting to upset him—the house. He let me do as I saw fit, never questioning my choices. He was surprised to find his medals hanging in the lounge one day, and to see all of his books dusted and shelved in a bookcase alongside those he had given me.

Was I happy? I certainly thought I was at the time.

Even the numerous cats who wandered freely in and out of the house without paying me the slightest attention bothered me less.

I'm not sure how many years went by like that. Time was no longer of much importance. Its relativity had been replaced by the reassuring routine of a restful existence. Habits, rituals, kindness—these were all beacons that helped me find my way and forget the lack of affection I had experienced as a child.

Every night after dinner, at 8:37 p.m., he would put on his wellies and go out to herd the animals into the barn. He would gather the scraps from our dinner for the chickens and pigs, and I would watch him disappear into the night. He would come back an hour later, exhausted from the hard work. But he was brave and resilient enough to always get up the next morning and begin again without the slightest complaint.

But one night, this new, contented existence of ours fell apart.

I was sitting on the sofa listening to the radio when he came and sat down next to me. "It's back," he said, his voice hoarse from exhaustion.

Looking down at his feet, he confessed to me that his urges, which he had thought had disappeared for good, were growing more intense and more frequent. I knew exactly what he meant. I had noticed it several weeks earlier, especially at night, when I was half asleep and I could feel him edging away from me in bed, sighing heavily. But also during the day, when his eyes fled my body. He explained that he'd had these urges ever since he was a teenager, that it was a disease without a cure.

He swore he would never hurt me again, that he would rather die. But the feverish look in his eyes when he mentioned that time in our lives was proof that he was inhabited by a darkness capable of whipping his senses into a frenzy and was much more powerful than he dared say.

So, gradually, he began to introduce the idea of another

solution. A solution that would mean I could keep living as I had been since emerging from the cellar, free from pain and suffering, and that he could still satisfy his urges without ever having to touch me. He told me I was strong enough—we were both strong enough—to get through this hardship. He convinced me a little more each day, explaining that it was the only way, that our happiness depended on it, and that children whose parents were always hovering over them would never amount to anything anyway. That they would spend their whole lives cowering under their father's cape like the boy in Goethe's poem, taking advantage of the love and affection I had never known.

When do you become a monster, Granny?

Is it out of cowardice? Or the instinct to survive? Or love? I don't know why I became a monster.

But I know exactly when I put on the dark, murky cape of the Erlking.

It was a Sunday evening. He had been away for two days at a livestock fair where he planned to sell a few of his animals. The clock in the lounge read seven o'clock when I heard him park the animal trailer in the farmyard.

A few minutes later, he came inside the house.

I didn't dare look at him. I wasn't brave enough.

I turned away, crying in disgust at my weakness.

He went down to the cellar alone, carrying the sleeping child in his arms.

8

Because she mentions it in her first refuge.

That's impossible.

Veronique was having a hard time accepting these revelations.

Could everything that had happened in the cellar really be another refuge, a shadow of the truth crafted by a terrified mind looking for a place to hide?

She had never been confronted with such a realistic alternate reality before. There was always one slightly strange dynamic in her patients' stories. An imaginary friend, the perpetrator in the form of a mythical monster, like the Erlking, ghosts, unexplained noises or apparitions, imaginary places . . . The fantastical elements symbolized the victims' desire to flee reality. Their tales often sounded like nonsense to the casual listener but were easy to explain and incredibly meaningful from a psychological point of view.

But in the cellar, in Sandrine's second refuge, all of the narrated events had felt real and totally devoid of fantasy. Could the clock be the only fictitious part of the story? If so, was it the only clue to the truth?

Dr Burel wasn't put off by the work that lay ahead. Sandrine's treatment would be long, but the process of deconstructing one or several refuges was the same. What bothered her was who or what could have frightened her patient into this second refuge. And the more she thought about it, the less she wanted to find out.

Veronique realized that the multiple walls Sandrine's brain had thrown up were too much for her to overcome by herself. She was going to need help.

She sat in silence across from Damian, waiting for him to provide explanations he didn't have. "I . . . I'll have to think about all of this," she said as she stood, her features drawn. "Tomorrow I'll call a colleague of mine for some advice. This is all very . . . troubling. The complexity of this survival mechanism is beyond anything I've ever seen."

"I understand. Don't doubt yourself, Veronique. Don't give up. Are there any details you can think of that might be useful to me? Things like the clock or the agricultural fairs?"

"No," she replied, disappointed she couldn't help. "Nothing for now."

"That's okay. Your job is to treat the victims, not to uncover the truth. That's up to me. Don't worry about it any more. If the cellar is a second refuge, then the truth it hides must be truly horrifying."

"I agree, detective. But at some point, I will have to help her through that truth, and the only way is to confront it, to open the door to the refuge and reach her. It's a bit like dancing with the devil—no one ever wants to, but everyone circles the dancefloor at least once in their life . . ."

"I'm just warning you. This story is far from over, and whatever we find out might well be the stuff of nightmares. Just . . . Don't get too close. That's all."

"What about you?" she asked, turning back to face him in the doorway. "Are you ready to dance with the devil?"

"I had the opportunity once and I turned my back on him. I won't make the same mistake twice."

Veronique left Damian's office. Neither of them had any idea when they would meet again or under what circumstances. And the heavy silence during those few seconds when neither of them could find the right words was an ominous sign.

The detective waited for the door to close, then lit a cigarette. He hadn't eaten lunch yet, but he wasn't hungry. His body seemed to be too absorbed in the mystery to feel anything other than the drive to solve it. He regretted that he had been unable to reassure the young psychiatrist. But how could he relieve her of her anxieties, when he was lost himself, with no idea how to reach the truth?

Around two o'clock, the phone rang, pulling him from his thoughts.

"Detective Bouchard," he said into the receiver.

"Hello, detective. This is Mr Dubreuil. My secretary gave me your message. What can I do for you?"

"Do you know a Mr Wernst?" asked Damian, picking up a pen and pulling over a piece of paper.

"Yes, of course. Frank Wernst."

"Could you tell me a bit about him?"

"Well," began Mr Dubreuil, "he's rather reserved, but always friendly. He never misses our fair, and his animals are highly sought after, especially his dairy cows. We're expecting him next month. He's already reserved his stand, though as far as I know we haven't received his payment yet."

Damian had no intention of revealing that the farmer was dead. The press still hadn't got wind of it, so there was no need to make it easier for them. If he informed this man, he would be unlikely to keep the news to himself. *Our local farmers are like one big family.*

"Might you have the dates of the fairs he attended, the location of his stand and the names of the buyers who acquired his livestock? I'd like to talk to anyone who spent time with him."

"Of course, but . . . What's going on? Has something happened to him?"

"I'm sorry, Mr Dubreuil, but I can't say any more at this stage."

"Of course. In any case, I hope it's nothing serious."

"I'll let you fax all of that over," Damian said smoothly, before the man on the other end of the line could try and extract any more information from him. "Your secretary has the number. Thank you very much for your help."

"My pleasure, detective. Please feel free to contact me again if necessary."

"I do have one more question actually: how long has your fair existed?"

"It's been running for twenty-five years straight," he said proudly. "With the exception of 1982, of course."

"What happened that year? Was it the hormones scandal?"

Damian remembered the public outcry well. A consumer organization had revealed that most of the calves raised in France were given growth hormones and raised in abominable conditions. People were put off meat for a while and, as a result, many livestock farmers had gone bankrupt. The industry still hadn't fully recovered.

"Ah, I see you're not from around here, detective."

"You've got me there," conceded Damian without specifying where he had come from or why.

"In 1981," Dubreuil went on, "a child went missing on the last day of the fair. He was the son of one of our exhibitors. We were all shaken by the tragedy because we all knew little Fabian. We decided not to hold the fair the following year, out of respect for the family. We hoped the boy would be found quickly, but the police never found a single lead. The parents had separated not long before. A bitter divorce. The father was violent and an alcoholic, and his farm was going under . . . The sort of thing that happens all the time in rural areas. So, the authorities assumed the boy had just run away. We kept hoping he would come back. But he never did."

"And that's why you didn't hold the fair the following year?"

"Yes. That and the fact the boy's father hanged himself six months later."

Damian thanked Mr Dubreuil again and hung up. Something was troubling him. A detail he couldn't yet pin down had his senses on high alert. He jotted down some notes from their discussion on a piece of paper, determined not to forget anything.

Fair = 25 years
1982 = fair cancelled = 1981 missing child
Father of missing child commits suicide (violent, alcoholic, divorce)
Wernst = still listed as a fair exhibitor. Since when? (check the docs faxed by Dubreuil)
Discreet but friendly (check this out, speak to people who had contact with Wernst at the fairs)
Kid never found. Probably a runaway
　Name: Fabian

Fabian.

That was it.

The name.

In a frenzy, Damian opened Sandrine's file and looked through the notes he had taken when he had returned to the station.

"Shit," he mumbled under his breath as his head filled with the vibrations of a deep, cavernous voice.

He flipped through the report from the first refuge, the island. He remembered listing the names Sandrine had mentioned, the names of the children at the holiday camp. There had been ten of them altogether but she hadn't given all ten names.

Here it was.

Children of the war. Half-bloods. Victims of the Erlking.
Fabian.
The one who protected the others by drawing on their walls.

I told you we'd have fun this time, you bloody worthless father.

Three days, Granny . . . It took me three whole days to realize what was going on.

A lifetime.

That first night, I didn't go downstairs to see who he had brought home. I couldn't move, couldn't speak. All I know is that he left the child in the cellar. I heard the sound of the chain and the handcuff being locked.

But the next morning, I had to take down their breakfast.

I delivered the tray without a word, without so much as a glance in the direction of the child, behaving just as my abductor had done with me. I kept my eyes down, placed the tray on the floor, and hurried back up the stairs, fleeing their troubling presence. I closed the kitchen door to block out the screams, then leaned against the sink and clenched my fists so hard I could feel my nails breaking the skin.

Don't cry, don't lose it now. Remember what he said . . .

"It's not for long, just a few days, just long enough to satisfy my urges . . . That child is unsuited to life anyway. They're not like you. You're different—it's life that's unsuited to you. I know that now. No one else would have chosen to get back up after what I did to you. No one else would have had the strength to forgive. You're special. The world outside doesn't deserve you. This child is the opposite. Useless. A fleeting firework that will soon be extinguished. Missed by no one. Their sole purpose here is to help us live together. They're just a tool. A tool to free me from my needs.

The first days are the hardest . . . You're still having difficulty coming to terms with this new arrangement. But soon, over time, you'll realize that it's the only solution. Whenever you begin to doubt, listen to your song, the one about love, and think of our happiness. The world outside is on the road to ruin. But we're safe here. The farm is our refuge. Isn't that what you've always wanted, Sandrine? There's no need to think of the child in the cellar. We've found a balance, I've given you stability. Why risk losing it all now?"

So, I followed his advice.

Speak to me of love.

Dozens of times. I turned up the volume whenever I could hear crying from the cellar. And shouted the lyrics as if they could stifle the part of me that still had doubts . . .

Speak to me of love.

Just a coincidence?

Probably. But a troubling one.

The fact that a man found dead in his cellar after kidnapping a girl and holding her prisoner for years had been in the vicinity when another child disappeared was not to be taken lightly. And on top of that, the victim's name figured in both of Sandrine's stories.

Could the children from her refuge have been real? Could they be real ghosts amid the ramblings of a tortured, terrified mind? Could the children be beacons from the real world, like the clock?

It's true Fabian is a common enough name, Damian admitted to himself, trying to keep the monstrous theory that was coming together in his head at bay. *Maybe it's just a coincidence, but this case is so unusual that . . .*

He studied the list of missing persons in Normandy. The police didn't have a centralized register of missing minors. There were regional lists, of course, but the photographs of the victims rarely crossed administrative lines and weren't circulated to the rest of the country's police stations. He checked to see that none of the names matched those of the children from Sandrine's refuge. Fabian's name wasn't on the list because, as Mr Dubreuil had explained, the case had been classified as a runaway. None of the others matched either. Damian was relieved, but he was acutely aware that this dead end didn't mean his theory was unsound. There were livestock fairs held in every part of the country. Unfortunately, he couldn't do the necessary research alone with the scant resources left at the station and all of his colleagues focused on the move.

He knew who to turn to, though. They hadn't seen each other in years and the only contact they had was a brief, monthly phone call, but Damian was certain that his friend would never refuse to help him. He had already proved it by searching the streets for Melanie and then visiting him daily, checking in to make sure Damian wasn't going to do anything stupid alone in the empty house when his missing daughter's laughter echoed unbearably through the air, eliciting tears of regret . . .

Damian took a deep breath and picked up the phone.

Following this lead was terrifying. His priority was to find out whether the children from Sandrine's story had been kidnapped by Wernst, but to do so, he had to leave his own refuge. The refuge he had built to hide from the past, from the possibility that one of the names Sandrine had left out began with an M.

"Hello?"

"Patrice?"

"Hey, Damian."

"Any news?"

"No, still nothing."

"That's okay. Soon, maybe . . . Patrice?"

Their conversation usually ended there. And, Patrice noted with surprise, Damian didn't usually contact him so soon after his previous call. He only ever normally phoned at the beginning of the month. But this time, only two days had passed.

"Yes?" asked Patrice, intrigued.

"Could you help me out with a case?"

"Of course! Is everything all right, Damian?" he asked worriedly.

"If I give you a list of names," Damian went on without answering his friend's question, "could you tell me if they match any missing children you can think of? Not necessarily local, could be anywhere really . . . Old cases you may have heard about . . ."

Damian read the names out to his friend. Each time he said a name, Patrice whispered it softly to himself, searching his memory, trying to remember if he'd ever heard a colleague mention a missing child by that name. Damian prayed he was wrong. He closed his eyes and exhaled a sigh of relief every time he moved on to the next name.

"Wait," said Patrice. "Julie?"

Damian opened his eyes and felt the weight of an invisible shadow on his shoulders.

Tick, tock, tick, tock . . .

"A girl named Julie disappeared in the Vendée region this summer," Patrice said. "The case got a lot of attention. It happened in a seaside town during the school holidays . . . Yes, I remember now, it was in Saint-Hilaire-de-Riez, but they found the body on the beach and the perp is in jail. I remember because my brother was on holiday nearby. He told me about it."

"No, that won't work, I'm only looking for unsolved disappearances."

"All right . . . Well, I can't think of anything for the moment. I'll mention it to a few people. Have all those kids really disappeared?"

"No . . . It's just . . . a hunch," replied Damian. "I can't say more yet. It's probably a dead end. I just wanted to check with you."

"Of course, whatever you need, Astronaut!"

"I . . . I have one more question."

"I'm listening."

"When Melanie disappeared . . . Was there a livestock fair on at the time?"

"A livestock fair?" Patrice asked, surprised by the strange question.

"Yes, where farmers sell their animals."

"I know what a livestock fair is, Damian. But don't you remember? We had a drink there a few times after work . . . I mean before . . ."

"Where?" Damian asked, his throat dry.

"At the Sancoins fair. One of the biggest livestock fairs in the region. But what has that got to do with anything?"

Damian fell back against his chair. Tears came to his eyes. A host of images slammed against the rocky cliffs protecting his memory: Melanie, Berry, witches, the woods, the canal, the devil.

How could I have forgotten? Sancoins . . . A small town about twenty miles from Saint-Amand. That put the kidnapper dangerously close to a potential victim . . .

Fabian and now Melanie. Two children, two likely targets for Wernst. But no bodies and no tangible proof. Just a hunch, which his super would simply dismiss as he closed the Sandrine file for good. Before taking it to his boss, he had to make sure Wernst had been at the Sancoins fair that year.

"Damian? Are you still there?"

"Yes, sorry, Patrice. Could you do one more thing for me? Could you contact the Chamber of Agriculture in Bourges to find out if a certain individual attended the Sancoins fair the year Melanie disappeared? They should have a list of the exhibitors. They know you so they'll be happy to help."

"Of course. Are you sure you're okay, though? You seem a bit . . . off."

"I'm fine, don't worry," Damian reassured him. "Can you get back to me as soon as possible?"

"Give me an hour. What's the name?"

"Wernst. Frank Wernst."

"Got it. And Damian?"

"Yeah?"

"We should talk on the phone more often. I mean, much more than just once a month. You know, Linda comes over sometimes. She's not angry with you any more. She . . . She's moved on and no longer holds you responsible for what happened."

Really? thought Damian. *Who is responsible then?* He remembered that his ex-wife had always been quick to blame others, and that the hours after Melanie's disappearance had been no different. At first, he had accepted her criticism, which he could tell was motivated by fear and despair. But, as the days passed and Melanie still hadn't been found, her words became more biting, cutting into him like sharp knives. Every time she opened her mouth, she dealt a near-fatal blow, though he was already completely devastated by the thought that he may never see his daughter again.

"She says we have to accept that people sometimes dance with the devil—much to his delight."

11

In the days that followed, I tried to continue along similar lines:
take down the tray, ignore the child, come back up, and forget.
Quick, mindless movements devoid of humanity. It was the
only way for me to fight the feeling that I had become a monster.
I had to keep the time I spent down in the cellar to a bare
minimum so I could forget about it, so I could keep thinking
of that small person as insignificant.

But that's not what happened, Granny.

The second night, at 8:37 p.m., Frank went down to the
cellar with the child's meal and a mug of hot chocolate. I had
moved to the dining room—the part of the house furthest from
the kitchen and the child—to turn on the radio and keep myself
focused on the history programme that aired every day at that
time. I tried to reason with myself, to persuade myself that he
was right, that our happiness was so powerful that it would
erase my regrets, but I never really succeeded.

But the walls were closing in on me. Each passing minute
numbed my outrage a little more, eating away at my reason
like a small, patient animal, slowly but surely robbing the
child of their humanity in my eyes, robbing them of their
light . . .

The radio show was about experiments the Germans had
carried out during the Second World War. It made me think of
you, Granny, and the fact that you lived through that dark
period of history. I felt sad you were gone. I would have loved
to ask you what to do. I wanted so badly for you to take me
in your arms and block out the child's sobs.

That's when the solution came to me.

I hadn't been to the island in a long time. Not since he had stopped hurting me. Not since the fear had gone.

All I had to do was go back there to forget about this place. Why hadn't I thought of it sooner?

I closed my eyes, with the show host's voice in the background talking about the Lebensborn or the "Fount of Life" programme designed to give rise to perfect Aryan children, as well as the many experiments the Nazis had performed on soldiers, civilians, and children during the Occupation . . . One guest mentioned an orphanage in the Oise region called Le Manoir de Boiseries, which had been used as a maternity hospital for French women pregnant with German soldiers' babies during the last years of the war. The building and the surrounding land had belonged to a prominent family, the owners of a famous chocolate brand, and had been requisitioned to set up what could only be described as an Aryan baby factory. The coincidence made me smile: it was the same chocolate my abductor had served me every day.

Menier Chocolate: making the world a better place!

I felt myself drifting away as if I were falling down a well, all the while knowing I would land on a gentle pillow of kindness. When I opened my eyes, I was sitting across from Paul on the *Lazarus.* The sea was calm, reassuring even, and I could hear the old captain, Simon, cursing in the cockpit. I was happy to be back here with the young handyman, although stupidly I felt guilty, as if I were cheating on the man down in the cellar. But I kept smiling as I listened to Paul. His description of the island's inhabitants helped me to forget the farm and the child.

I woke up just as I stepped onto the island's dock.

Wernst had just sat down next to me on the couch. His presence pulled me from my dream. He was slightly out of breath and remained silent for a moment. Then he stood up to turn off the radio.

"These programmes . . . Who wants to listen to that? Don't they know that there is no more faithful companion than war? When war crosses your path, you're scarred for life."

Yes, I thought, *the painful memories and nightmares haunt us forever. As does the guilt. But I know a refuge where I can get away from all that . . . An island where nothing and no one can hurt me . . .*

But then came the third day.

12

Patrice called back two hours later.

"Wernst participated in the Sancoins fair that year," he announced. The certainty in his voice and the deliberate way he articulated the words left no room for doubt.

Damian listened to his friend, though part of him resisted really hearing the words and what they meant.

He heard Melanie's laugh.

He saw her smile.

He imagined her empty bed, where he had slept so many nights, hoping she would wake him in the small hours by laughing at the way his feet stuck out at the bottom.

Bucephalus continued and the images disappeared. He explained why it had taken him longer than expected to get back to Damian. "I decided to try and call all of the different fairs where he had exhibited. Well, most of them. The man must have attended at least twenty fairs a year!"

Patrice had been efficient. He had contacted the Chamber of Agriculture in Bourges right away, which confirmed that Wernst had been present that year and that he had sold three animals. He then asked them if there was a national register of livestock fairs. He was in luck—the person on the phone was able to give him the number of the French farmers' union and they in turn supplied Patrice with a complete list of all the livestock fairs in the country.

"It's not looking good, Damian. Too many coincidences."

"I'm listening," Damian replied hoarsely.

"Of the ten locations I contacted, four have had a child go missing in the last ten years. Albi in 1979, Grenoble in 1978,

Brest also in 1978, and Clermont-Ferrand in 1980. None of the children were ever found, and your suspect attended each of those fairs. Maybe it's time you told me what's going on?"

Damian struggled to assimilate the information Patrice had shared with him. His fears, which had been no louder than a whisper before, barely noticeable, were now bloodcurdling screams, escaping from the lungs of drowning children.

"Two days ago," he began, "we found a young woman on the beach. She didn't remember anything except an island and a holiday camp where experiments had been carried out on children. The psychiatrist on her case diagnosed her with post-traumatic stress disorder. According to the doctor, the story about the island and the children was just a 'refuge' the victim had built in her mind to escape a traumatic reality. We managed to gain the patient's trust, and she eventually told us the truth: she had been kidnapped and held against her will for years. She finally escaped by killing her abductor. Wernst."

"Bloody hell! But what does Melanie have to do with all this?"

"In her first story, Sandrine mentioned the names of the children at the holiday camp. There were ten of them, but she only gave eight names. One of them was Fabian—the name of a boy who disappeared at a livestock fair near here which Wernst attended. And the other names are the ones I gave you earlier."

"Jesus . . . So, you think there are other victims? And that Melanie might be one of them?"

"I don't know, but the fact that this bastard wasn't too far away from my daughter when she disappeared isn't nothing. Maybe Melanie is one of the two unnamed children."

"Have you spoken to your super?"

"I'm going to. Given what you've just told me, we've got five disappearances that correlate with Wernst's movements. That's no longer a coincidence . . . After that, I'll head back to the farm where he lived. If he held the children there, there has to be evidence somewhere."

"Hasn't the place already been searched?" Patrice asked, surprised.

"Not all of it. The teams focused on the main house. The rain meant they didn't get to the outbuildings."

"Christ, Damian, this makes no sense . . . Your victim must have seen the kids. The four disappearances I just told you about happened ten years ago!"

"I know, but the problem is that the victim no longer remembers anything. She's gone back to her island, presumably to protect herself from the horrific truth."

"Anything else I can do for you?" asked Patrice.

"You've done plenty already, thanks," said Damian. "And . . . I'm sorry I left."

"We'll talk more about that another time, Damian. Keep me updated on your investigation and be careful."

"Will do."

Damian stood, gathered up his files, and stepped into the superintendent's office without knocking.

"There are some new leads."

"What do you mean? Which case are you talking about?" asked Fourier, surprised to see Damian looking so agitated.

"The woman on the beach," he explained, doing his best to keep from shouting to convey the urgency of the matter. The superintendent was sorting papers on his desk. A pile of documents sat in the corner of the room waiting to be filed.

"You told me yesterday that she had told the truth, and that you'd get me the full report soon!" replied the superintendent, his brows furrowed now in confusion.

"She's changed her story."

"What do you mean? Which story? Damn it, Bouchard, I asked you to handle this as quickly as possible!"

"She's returned to her island. She doesn't remember being imprisoned any more."

"What the—"

"Sir, I need all available men."

"I'm sorry?" Fourier said in wide-eyed astonishment. Of course, he was only in charge of a tiny police station that had nearly outlived its usefulness. And his men weren't the cream of the crop—just good men who were happy to have jobs in such a quiet part of France, far from the vendettas between rival gangs and drug trafficking found in big cities. But the superintendent knew enough to know conviction in a man's eyes when he saw it. And here the conviction was positively shining with an incandescent glow he had never seen in one of his officers before.

"We have new leads," repeated the detective. "If they're solid, this is a big case. Huge. And believe me, if I solve it, no one will ever be able to question the legitimacy of our existence ever again. But to do so, I need all of the men on duty to come and help me search the farm."

"Christ, Bouchard, slow down. Take five minutes to explain it all to me."

Damian gave the superintendent all the details. The first refuge, the truth, and the suspected second refuge: the story about Sandrine's time in the cellar. The clock, Wernst's presence at the livestock fairs, and the disappearances of Fabian, Melanie, and the others.

Fourier listened attentively, but his unmoving eyes betrayed his incredulousness. He asked every possible question from every possible angle, but each time, Damian provided an answer that steered them back to Wernst and the children.

"Do you seriously think . . .?"

"I'm more convinced of it by the second. We need to do this. Before it's too late."

The superintendent didn't hesitate for long. He ordered all of his men into the field and contacted the regional commissioner in Caen to ask for reinforcements and a dog team. But the commissioner refused. Another case in the area required all of the dogs they had, as well as the forensics team.

"For Christ's sake, we might as well already be closed!" shouted Fourier as he hung up. "No matter. We'll go it alone."

Damian and the superintendent told the rest of the team to follow them, leaving a single uncomprehending officer at the station.

"We'll be back! Patch all calls through to my radio!" shouted Fourier as he disappeared into the rain outside.

When they sat down in the police car, he turned to Damian. "Bouchard, even though this case could save us, I truly hope you're wrong . . ."

Half an hour later, the police vehicles stopped at the turn-off to the access road, their blue flashing lights piercing the rain and gloom.

"Find me proof that there were children here. I don't care what, just bring me something!" roared the superintendent.

The officers split up to search the premises. The largest group headed to the main house while the others hurried through the rain to the outbuildings. The generators hummed to life, disturbing the apathetic silence of the surrounding countryside. A few birds took flight, and the herd of cows gazed placidly in their direction before they lowered their heads once more to graze. A few chickens wandered aimlessly around the farmyard.

Damian searched the lounge. He had no desire to return to the cellar. The smell of death had clung to him since his last visit. He looked for the cat but couldn't find him.

Did I imagine him? he wondered as he removed the drawers from a heavy wooden dresser and placed them on the floor. He went through the same process with each piece of furniture. He didn't really know what he was looking for—photographs, drawings, objects?—but he emptied out everything in sight.

"Look, detective," said an officer.

Damian walked over to inspect the wooden frame hanging on the wall that had caught his colleague's attention.

"German medals," observed the officer.

"There's no more faithful companion than war," mumbled Damian, remembering Sandrine's words.

"What was that?"

"Nothing. Wernst must be a former soldier. Boys were enlisted in the Wehrmacht at sixteen. Sandrine explained in her story that he had a slight accent. And the name Wernst doesn't sound particularly French."

The next frame held a black-and-white photograph that looked like it had been taken just after the war. In it, a young, smiling Wernst with short hair stood beside the lake with a large spade in his right hand. His sleeves were rolled up, revealing the muscles in his forearms and reminding Damian of a Greek statue. *The kids didn't stand a chance.*

Two hours later, they were still searching, but their initial optimism was fading. The bedrooms, the kitchen, the bathroom, and the cupboards had all been thoroughly checked. Drawers and boxes lay on the floor. They had even tapped on the walls looking for anything hidden behind the plasterboard. They moved the refrigerator and bookcase but found nothing other than dust and grime. They even rolled up the sticky rugs and put them outside so they could inspect the individual wooden boards in the oak floor, but none of them revealed a trap door.

The sun went down and the darkness gradually invaded the horizon, like a hungry carnivore carefully closing in on its wounded prey in the dusk.

"There has to be something here!" muttered Damian desperately. "There just has to be!"

He pushed aside all thoughts of failure, of having missed something, of not looking in the right place at the right time. He chased from his mind the memory of the faces that had blamed him for not finding his daughter, though they never said as much. He turned a deaf ear when his ex-wife's voice shouted through the time and distance between them that his choices had led to their daughter's disappearance, that he was supposed to wait for her after school that day, that he never should have volunteered for that training course in Paris. He tried not to see Melanie's last smile, the joy on her face when he had given her the pair of red trainers she'd wanted for months, just two days before she disappeared.

Not now, there's no time for that. Focus . . .

Suddenly, there came a shout from behind the house. All of the men went still. "This way, hurry!"

Damian ran outside, doing his best to avoid the muddy puddles, and joined the group that had gathered near the barn. The wooden building, which was as tall as the main farmhouse, was about twenty metres long. The air was thick with the smell of cow manure and damp hay.

"Over here!"

Damian turned towards the far end of the barn and saw a wooden ladder that led to a trapdoor in the ceiling.

"Upstairs!"

He climbed up and poked his head through the small opening. He used his arms to hoist himself up into the attic, then dusted his hands on his trousers and turned on his torch. He had to stoop to keep from bumping his head on the beams above. Ornate spiderwebs clung from the rafters. With no window or opening, the air was suffocating. The detective made his way through the haphazard collection of objects on the floor and headed towards the officers' torch beams which were trained on a corner of the loft Damian still couldn't see.

"What is it?" he asked when he reached the superintendent and the officer with him. "What did you find?"

But neither of them had the strength to reply. They only looked at Damian with the utmost horror in their eyes.

13

You know, Granny, I'm convinced that time numbs you.

Love, life, smiles, and anger. My feelings were numbed when I locked eyes with that little girl. My humanity, my reasoning, and my soul—all numbed by the passage of time.

It wasn't supposed to happen like that.

I should have brought the tray, ignored her, and gone back up to forget her by travelling to the island. That was the plan. But as I bent over to place the tray on the floor, I heard her ask, "Do you know the cats' names?"

I looked up, surprised to hear her speaking to me so kindly. I expected words tinged with hatred and anger. "They don't have names," I replied in a troubled voice that I hoped sounded distant yet firm.

"They do."

"I never named them."

"But they do have names," she insisted as she swallowed a mouthful of food.

She was a beautiful girl. She had long brown hair and pale freckles dotted her face like stars in a summer sky. Her irises were like two wells overflowing with gold. I admired her beauty for several minutes as she ate, fighting the growing urge to take her in my arms.

When she had finished, she curled up into a ball with her knees against her chest and her back against the wall. "I miss my dad," she said.

"I'm sorry . . ." I said, finally expressing a sentiment that had echoed through my mind all too often.

"He always said to never lose hope," continued the girl.

"That's what he said when he finally bought me the pair of red trainers I had been asking for. 'You see, sweetheart, never lose hope!' So, I won't lose hope. I know he'll save me."

"That's a lovely memory," I said. I could feel the tears welling in my eyes.

"Did your father say that, too?"

"I . . . I don't know."

"I like talking about my parents. It makes it feel like they're here with me, sort of."

So, I asked her questions about her mother and father. As she talked about them, her eyes sparkled with pride. I had never met anyone who thought of their parents in that way. Had I been living in a parallel universe? Could everything I had always taken for normal simply be the product of a total misunderstanding created by a mother unfit to raise a child and a cruel farmer offering a poor imitation of freedom?

She told me about the region where she had grown up, where ancient superstitions still held sway. When people got lost in the fog, they trembled at the invisible but tangible presence of witches on the prowl. Books like *The Devil's Pool* alluded to things people didn't dare say aloud. She admitted she had been thinking about the stories a lot since she'd been in the cellar. They had become a precious refuge—much less hostile than reality.

I picked up the tray and headed towards the stairs. *The process has begun,* I thought. *She's building her own refuge. That's the magical power children possess. They create to forget and use the relative nature of time to survive a world that strives to devour them . . .*

I turned away and awkwardly tried to hide my tears. Halfway up the stairs, I said, "If you like, I can bring down some books or a deck of cards."

"Could I have some chalk?" she asked.

"Chalk? I . . . I don't know. I'll see if I can find some. What will you do with it?" I asked, intrigued.

"I want to add a little colour and sunlight to the room. And draw the cats," she said shyly.

"That's . . . That's a lovely idea."

Wernst had left for the day, saying he wouldn't be home until that evening. I knew he wouldn't approve, but I was confident I could make him see that it wouldn't change anything, that it was just a present, like the books he had brought me.

An hour later, I took down an old box of chalks I had found in one of the many drawers in the lounge. The girl's smile warmed my heart and tore down the remaining walls.

I had to talk to Wernst. I had to convince him. I had to tell him I didn't want to live this life, which wasn't preserving our happiness after all. He could have his way with me as often as he liked. There was no need for another body; I was his. So, he could let her go. She wouldn't talk, we'd make her swear. As for me, I'd promise to never leave him, to never seek refuge on my island again, to live there with him, to be enough for him, like before . . . If he truly loved me, he would understand. I was so sure it would work . . .

But like I said, Granny, time can have a numbing effect.

And humans are weak.

I left the door to the cellar open all day so she could listen to the music playing in the lounge. The cats took advantage of the opportunity to venture down the stairs and keep her company. Deep down, I still hated the cats for the way they showed off their insolent freedom and carefree existence, but they certainly seemed to raise her spirits that afternoon. I was surprised to see how quickly they adopted her. It had taken me some time to win them over.

Another reason I disliked the cats was because of the growing interest their master was showing them. Over the past few months, he had begun staying with them when I went to bed, stroking them, talking to them, giving them all the attention he had stopped giving me.

When I took down her dinner, the girl had drawn all over

the wall she was chained to. I was taken aback to find a huge rainbow arching over a radiant sun, flowers with multicoloured petals, a forest of reassuring trees, and a nearby house with its windows open. I stood there admiring the scene for several minutes, amazed by the bright colours on a wall that had never been anything but grey.

But what struck me most—to the point I had to put the tray down on the floor to avoid spilling its contents—were the children. Stick figures, like I had drawn years earlier to count the days. A name sat above each head. They all held hands in a perfect line. Each child seemed to have a cat sleeping peacefully at their feet.

"Are these your friends?" I asked curiously, as I stepped closer to the wall.

"No," she said simply, her eyes focused intently on mine.

"Who are these children then?" I asked. "Where are you?"

"I'm here," she said, pointing to one of the figures.

"And that's your name above?"

"Yes."

"Melanie?"

"Yes."

"And Fabian and Julie, were they school friends of yours?"

"No."

She kept staring at my face. I had the unwelcome impression that she was watching for my reaction. "Imaginary friends then?" I asked again.

"No. They're the others."

"The others? What others?" I asked, surprised, rereading the names.

"The other children the Erlking has killed."

14

Veronique went home after her meeting with Damian.

As she drove, she regretted leaving so abruptly. She had heard so much about him. His daughter, her disappearance, his self-imposed exile . . . But she hadn't dared bring any of that up. Was that why he seemed to be so awkward in her presence? Was he afraid she saw him as the sad excuse for a father the rumours made him out to be?

But then again, what must he think of *her*? Would her failure to find the key to Sandrine's final refuge make him believe she was incompetent? She had correctly interpreted his disdainful look when they had first met. It was a look she had come across many times in the eyes of the patients and other doctors since she had accepted the position at the hospital.

Too young to have any experience. Well, at least in a place like Villers-sur-Mer, she won't come across anything too serious. She'll have time to learn . . .

But now, less than two years later, a woman had turned up on her ward with a story full of inconsistencies and she would have to prove herself all over again.

Veronique couldn't wrap her head around the detective's most recent discoveries. A second refuge? But who was she hiding from? Was there another Erlking in Sandrine's story? Another monster Veronique had missed? How could she have made such an egregious mistake?

It was plain to see that the detective didn't believe Sandrine's story. And that upset her, because his doubts felt like they were aimed at her abilities as a psychiatrist as well as at the victim's tale itself. But wasn't that his job, after all? To doubt everything until he reached the truth?

She poured herself a glass of wine and swallowed it down in a single gulp. She sighed heavily. Outside, the rain was lashing down on the apartment building across the street. It was still early, but the cloudy skies had already reduced visibility considerably. *Like on that bloody island*, thought Veronique as she poured herself a second glass, which she drank more slowly.

She wanted to get back to Sandrine's stories, to draw diagrams, develop theories, and prove both the viability of the psychological theories she had studied and the value of her own expertise . . . But she had to admit she didn't have the strength. Not now, not after so many disappointments.

She finished her glass and made her way to the bathroom. She took off her clothes and turned on the taps, then sat down on the side of the bathtub, thinking through Damian's assertions. Why did she feel so uneasy about it all? Was it because she was starting to doubt her own judgment as well as her patient's claims? If Sandrine was lying—consciously or unconsciously—there was only one course of action. Veronique would have to prove to her that she was no longer in danger. But she couldn't do that until the detective discovered the ultimate source of her fear . . .

She closed her eyes and went over Damian's arguments in her head. But as soon as she replayed their conversation, Sandrine's words blended with the detective's, forming an absurd dialogue.

She's lying.

8:37 p.m.

Time is relative.

There was never a clock there in the first place.

As empty and useless as a clock without hands.

The livestock fair.

Sometimes my captor would disappear for a few days. I don't know where he went . . .

★

Veronique got into the bath and decided to forget about the events of the past forty-eight hours for a while. She stretched out her legs and savoured the moment. Then she immersed her head in the water, putting the questions off until the next day.

Relax, take a step back from all this, like they taught you in school. You don't have to prove anything to anyone . . . You've already committed a misstep by getting too close to the victim, you even embraced her for goodness' sake. So, get a grip now, forget her, at least for tonight. Have a good soak in the warm water, relax and—

Veronique's head shot up out of the water as she sat upright again and pushed her hair out of her face. *Shit! A beacon, another bloody beacon!*

She immediately got to her feet, hastily dried off, and put on the bathrobe hanging behind the door.

Shit, shit, shit . . .

"Are there any details you can think of that might be useful to me? Things like the clock or the agricultural fairs?" Damian had asked before she left.

But at that moment, and right up until she had put her head underwater just now, she hadn't been able to think clearly or even use her intuition to help the detective. Veronique pulled the tapes from her leather handbag and listened to them one after another, noting each time Sandrine mentioned a detail which corroborated her new theory.

Battered by the surf, come rain or shine.
The cold, apathetic sea . . .
Rainy weather . . .
All of the children fell into the icy water . . .
I drank. Long, deep sips.
Paul's body floated to the surface like a stuffed toy forgotten on a bed . . .

She counted no fewer than forty words and expressions from the same lexical field. A detail which wouldn't be of much interest to a detective, but which should have been glaringly obvious to a psychiatrist . . .

Beacons placed throughout the story, like breadcrumbs leading the way home in a fairy tale. Veronique rushed to the phone.

15

"You know the Erlking?" I asked.

"Yes, he often recites the poem."

"Who?"

"The man who touches me," she said, gesturing towards the area between her legs. Would you like to know the cats' names?"

"No."

"He gives a cat to each child, so they feel less lonely," Melanie continued.

"What?"

"Then, when the child dies, the cat stays, and gets their name, like a trophy. That's why he loves them so much."

"You're not making any sense. I've never seen any other children here . . . I was the only one . . ."

"There's a hidden room . . ."

A hidden room.

Now I stared at her. What did she mean? I noticed her bare feet and searched the room for the red shoes she had mentioned. Nothing. Where had they gone? Had they been forgotten in the trailer? This girl seemed to know an awful lot. The poem, the children, the cats . . . They had taken to her immediately, as if they'd known her for some time already.

"Where were you before this cellar?" I asked eventually.

"In the secret room."

"Where is this secret room for fuck's sake?" I shouted as loud as I could. Sensing that I was capable of violence, she huddled closer to the wall, sending the cats that had cuddled up next to her running.

"In the barn . . ."

Dr Burel called the Villers-sur-Mer police station and learned that Detective Bouchard and the rest of the force were out at a crime scene. She asked if she could contact them over the radio.

"May I ask what this is regarding?" asked the lone desk officer.

"I'm calling about an ongoing investigation. The woman found on the beach the day before yesterday," she explained.

"Ah, yes. I can pass on a message if you like."

"Is that where they are? At Wernst's farm? Have they found a—"

"I can't share that information without the superintendent's approval," replied the officer.

"Listen," continued Veronique, trying her best to keep calm. "The discovery I have just made might help solve this case. It's urgent and the detective and superintendent need to hear it. So, either radio them right now, or you'll have to explain yourself when they get back!"

"All right, all right. No need to get so upset. I'll call them now."

A few minutes later, the officer phoned her back, intrigued by the exchange he'd had with his boss. "I've just heard from the superintendent," he informed Veronique. "He says they would welcome some help from a psychiatrist."

Dr Burel jotted down the address and quickly threw on a pair of jeans and a jumper. Forty minutes later, she drove through the roadblock in the pouring rain and made her way up the battered access road.

The farm slowly came into view, isolated amid the fields, like an island lost out at sea. Dark, heavy clouds filled the sky over the house and its surroundings: it was an ominous introduction to the uncomfortable revelations to come. Spotlights dotted around the property shone in the darkness like huge, unmoving fireflies. Veronique parked behind a police car, opened her umbrella, and walked over to the nearest officer.

"Hello, I'm looking for Detective Bouchard, please. It's urgent."

"He's inside . . . But I'm not sure it's a good time . . ."

"The superintendent asked me to come. I'm a psychiatrist."

"Well in that case, you'll find them both in the lounge," said the officer, changing tack and gesturing towards the front door to the house.

"Did you find something?" she asked, noticing the officer's drawn expression. The man seemed indifferent to the rain streaming down his face.

"We did, unfortunately," he said as he turned and began walking round towards the back of the house.

Veronique hurried over to the farmhouse, pleased to get out of the rain. She was welcomed by Antoine who immediately led her into the kitchen and took her aside. "We've found evidence that several missing children were here."

"How many?"

"Ten. From all over France."

"My God . . . Sandrine wasn't the only one. Ten . . . Like the children in her holiday camp."

"We still don't know why they were here or how long they stayed, or even when it started. But we know what Wernst did to Sandrine, so . . ."

"You think he kidnapped and sexually abused the others, too?"

"Yes, that's the theory, unfortunately."

"I need to talk to the detective," said Sandrine, looking for Damian.

"He's no longer on the case," Antoine informed her, hanging his head.

"Why?"

"Conflict of interest," he replied vaguely.

"For heaven's sake, could you please just tell me what the hell is going on?"

"Dr Burel?"

Veronique turned around to see the superintendent standing in the doorway, watching her impassively.

"Yes, sir?" she replied.

"This way please."

She followed him to a bedroom where the mattress and blankets had been pushed into a corner. Drawers and their contents lay sprawled across the floor and the huge wardrobe had been emptied. The only window in the room was open to let in the cool, fresh air, though it failed to disguise the smell of mould that clung to the walls. Veronique noticed that the colours were fading fast as the sunlight disappeared behind thick clouds. Fourier himself seemed to be undergoing the same process; his skin, his face, his hands and even his hair were ashen. She couldn't help but think of the Goethe poem: *It is but the willows, trembling and grey.*

The superintendent sat down heavily on the empty bed frame. Veronique knew nothing about him other than what Damian had shared, but she could tell he was exhausted, both physically and emotionally. She wondered when Sandrine had taken over his thoughts. How many nights had he spent thinking of her? What kind of hell had she led him into?

"What's going on, sir?"

"We . . . We've found hard proof. In the loft above the barn."

"What kind of proof?"

"A chain and a mattress, like in the cellar. And a dozen pairs of shoes hidden in a suitcase. Sizes 2 to 4," explained Fourier finally.

"Children . . ."

"Forensics should be here in a few hours. They're likely to

find more evidence which won't leave us in any doubt as to what happened here."

"What about Damian? Antoine told me he was off the case . . . What does that mean?"

"It means that for the devil, distance is no object. Even when his prey is hundreds of miles away. Did you know Detective Bouchard had a daughter, Melanie?" he asked gruffly.

"Yes, I've heard the story, like everyone else in Villers."

A story unfit for children, she thought to herself, *but that people tell in the hospital corridors, at café tables, and while waiting in line at the market.* A story people seemed to loathe but felt compelled to share. *That worthless father. He left to forget about his daughter. Sad excuse for a man.*

"Wernst kidnapped the children while he attended livestock fairs all over the country. He probably locked them in his trailer to get them home. The forensics team will confirm that once they've inspected the vehicle. Damian is the one who figured it out, and he of course checked to see if Wernst had been in the area when Melanie disappeared. It turns out he attended a fair just twenty miles away from their town . . ."

"My God . . . So, you mean to say—"

"We found the shoes she was wearing the day she disappeared," Fourier went on. "Red trainers with an M written in permanent ink on the inside. Damian marked them himself. Old habits die hard. Since our equipment is all identical, we always label it to keep from mixing our things up. That's why I had to take him off the case. And that's why I asked you to come. Damian will need your help over the coming days . . ."

The superintendent stood up and placed his thick hand on Veronique's shoulder. She could already see in his eyes the tears that would undoubtedly come when he was back home and could process his feelings about the tragedy alone. Veronique swallowed her own sorrow, reminding herself that she had a job to do. "Can I see him?" she asked.

"Yes, follow me."

*

Damian was sitting on a chair in the lounge, staring blankly out the window, though it was difficult to see anything in the pouring rain. Veronique walked over and gently placed her hand on his. "I'm so sorry, Damian," she said.

At the far end of the wooden table sat a suitcase full of shoes waiting to be bagged and labelled by the forensics team, and then shown to the parents for the purposes of identification. Veronique glanced fleetingly at the evidence, but immediately regretted it. It reminded her of a documentary she had seen about the Nazis' "final solution" and the huge piles of shoes belonging to concentration camp victims.

There is no more faithful companion than war. When war crosses your path, you're scarred for life . . .

Melanie's red shoes sat in front of Damian. She would never tie the laces again.

"Damian?" Veronique ventured.

"I looked for her for weeks," he replied, his voice distant. "Everywhere. In the woods, the streets, abandoned houses, parks . . . But she was here, in this house. I thought I was escaping my pain, but I was actually getting closer . . ."

"It's not your fault. You couldn't have known that this bastard—"

"Where I come from, they say the dead guide the living. That they impact our choices for their own amusement, or occasionally to help us. Melanie probably led me here, making me look like a worthless father, like a man who gave up on the hope of ever finding his daughter and fled all memory of her by moving hundreds of miles away. But in the end, she did it to help me find her."

"Damian, maybe we should get out of here. We can talk at my place. You shouldn't be alone," she suggested now in a voice she hoped sounded soothing.

"I'm sorry Wernst is dead. I'm angry at Sandrine for killing him, for robbing me of the opportunity to do it myself. I warned you she hadn't told us everything."

"Yes, you were right," agreed Veronique with a sad smile.

"They're looking for the bodies now. I'm not allowed to help."

"Yes, the superintendent explained."

Damian suddenly realized how unusual it was for Veronique to be present at the crime scene, where civilians were never normally allowed. He stared at her in surprise. "What are you doing here, Veronique?" he asked.

"The superintendent . . . He asked me to come and help. I was home and . . ." Now Veronique remembered the real reason she had come. The horrific turn of events had made her forget all about the beacon she had discovered in the bathtub. Was now the time to share her news? Or should she focus her efforts on helping Damian overcome his grief? Maybe she should mention it to the superintendent instead? *No,* she finally decided, tightening her hold on Damian's hand. *He's the one who came with me into Sandrine's refuges, and now he's paying the price. If anyone deserves to hear my hypothesis, it's him.*

"I think I've found another beacon."

Damian's eyes lit up at her words. She was surprised at first, but quickly realized that his daughter's death wasn't news to him. In some ways he had known for years, once all hope had deserted him after his fruitless searching, the sleepless nights, and the even darker days. *His worst fears have simply been confirmed, he knew that it was inevitable. Now he'll be able to grieve his daughter without fleeing reality. He's broken, but now he can look himself in the mirror and confront the truth.*

"In which refuge?" Damian asked.

"Both. In the cellar and on the island."

"Go on."

"Throughout her stories, Sandrine constantly alludes to water: the rain, the sea, the shipwreck, the cats drowned in the bathtub . . . I think it's deliberate in some way, that a part of her unconscious wants to express something through this image."

"You're right," he agreed, recalling the victim's words. "I hadn't noticed before."

"And, I'm not sure what it means," continued Veronique,

"but there's an inconsistency tied to water when she visits her grandmother's house on the island. She even uses the word 'strange'."

"Remind me."

"The dried-up pond next to the house. The map didn't match what Sandrine saw," she said, trying to jog his memory.

"No, I don't—"

"This is strange, according to the map the solicitor gave me there should be an outbuilding here . . ." said Veronique, reciting Sandrine's exact words.

Damian frowned as he thought back. "Yes, right," he said. "Now I remember. And you think that inconsistency somehow leads to the truth?"

"I don't know, but if we found something related here, it might help us figure out what Wernst did with the children," suggested Veronique.

"Could the missing building symbolize the barn where he hid the evidence he didn't want to get rid of? Killers often keep personal objects as trophies . . . Oh, shit . . ."

"What?"

"The shoes, Sandrine mentioned them, too."

"When?"

"When she left Wernst's farm after interviewing him! Wait, let me think. Yes. *As I closed the front door behind me, I bent down to put on my trainers. I stopped short when I saw that the old man had cleaned them* . . . It's as if she barely recognized her own trainers. The care Wernst took with them left her feeling uncomfortable . . . That's definitely a beacon we should have noticed!"

"My God, I wonder how many other details slipped past us!"

"She only mentions it once, in passing. How could we have known that such a simple sentence contained so much truth?" argued Damian, as if reading Veronique's thoughts. "As for the water, it must be of critical importance since it appears so many times in both stories."

"In that case, if the barn was a trophy room of sorts, what

could the dried-up pond next to Suzanne's house represent? What if . . ."

"What?"

"Symbolism! First the disappearance of the outbuilding found on the map and then the dried-up pond . . ."

"Where are you doing with this?" asked Damian, confused by Veronique's sudden excitement.

"What do you notice when you look at a dried-up pond?"

"Uh . . . I don't know. The lack of water?"

"Exactly! Not the lack, but the *disappearance* of the water! The disappearance! Its presence symbolizes disappearance!"

Damian leapt to his feet, sending the chair crashing to the floor. "He drowned the children! Like on the island! That's how Wernst got rid of them!" he shouted before running out the door.

17

"What's in the barn?"

"More drawings, done by the other children."

"How do you know that? You only arrived a few days ago and . . ."

"Because I was there. I've been here for a very long time . . . Just climb the ladder and go to the far end of the loft. You'll see."

I rushed back up the stairs. Wernst could come home any minute. The sun was already dangerously close to the horizon. I ran out of the house, around the willow, and headed for the barn without worrying about who might see me. *There's no way. That girl is making it all up*, I kept thinking as I set up the ladder. When I reached the loft, I walked towards the far end, being careful not to step on the various objects scattered about, which the dusk outside had turned into deceitful shadows. I caught sight of a skylight near the far wall. The weak glow coming through it was like my lighthouse, guiding me to an alcove I couldn't have imagined was there from where I came up. That's when I saw it: the mattress. Just like the one I had spent so many nights on. I fell to my knees. A chain identical to the one that had bound me to the wall lay on the floor, with the same metal handcuff at the end.

"This can't be," I whispered. "It just can't be . . ."

I looked up slowly to study the wall.

Here and there stickmen had been drawn using a small stone or some other hard object. No colour. Just grey lines and circles.

The names had been written in different handwriting, by different little hands. Ten names, including Melanie. Ten cats . . .

I pummelled the mattress with all my strength. I stifled my screams by shoving my fist into my mouth. *This is why that bastard stopped touching me! It wasn't because he felt bad! He just quelled his urges in secret . . . This is why I wasn't allowed near the barn! He never stopped being a monster . . . Every night. 8:37 p.m. He kidnapped more children to fulfil his needs, so . . . so he wouldn't have to hurt me any more. My God . . . He did it to protect me. It's all my fault . . .*

My tears and shaking intensified as I realized what a monster I had become.

I left the cursed place and returned to the house. I reached the door and rifled through the keys. The spare key to the chain lock was easy to find: it was the smallest one of all. I remembered, because I had watched each time my captor had freed me temporarily so I could stretch my legs. I had always been disgusted by its size. Such a tiny thing responsible for my freedom or lack thereof. A big, heavy key would have been more fitting.

Melanie watched in fear as I stormed back down the stairs a few seconds later.

"What's going on?" she asked as I slid the key into the lock on her handcuff.

"What happened to the other children?"

"He . . . He killed them . . . He drowned them," she stuttered. "That's what he said when I screamed on the first night. 'Do you want me to drown you right away like the others?'."

"Oh God . . . You have to run . . . You have to escape the forest . . ."

"What forest?"

"The Erlking's forest. Go now and never look back."

"But . . . What about you?"

"I'm going to leave, too. Don't worry."

"We could go together," said Melanie, in tears.

"No. I have to kill the Erlking, or I'll never be able to get back to the island."

"I don't understand . . ."

"Run, Melanie. Quickly, before he comes back . . . Run back to your life!"

She hesitated for a moment. Then, realizing there was nothing more to say, she ran quickly up the stairs. The last thing I remember saying to her was to put on my trainers, which were beside the front door, and to run and keep running until she found her parents. And to never doubt that they were waiting for her.

I screamed, Granny.

So loud my throat burned. I hit the floor so hard that my knuckles started to bleed. I hated myself for being so cowardly, for giving up on hope and letting myself become the monster I had despised. How had I ever believed him? How had I accepted his crimes as normal and stifled my humanity, taking refuge in such abject detachment? I hadn't just caused those children's deaths, I had also killed and buried the girl I had once been. The girl who smiled at shop owners, who dreamed of kissing Paul and holding his hand, the girl who hoped that one day her mother would see her as a joyful extension of herself rather than a consequence of a deadbeat father.

I stayed there on my knees, my forehead resting on the rough concrete. I could have killed myself then, using one of the knives from the kitchen. I could have slit my wrists, opening the scars left by the chain back when my childhood innocence was still intact, back when I rebelled against my captivity until I bled. Instead, I nervously rubbed my scars against the floor to feel something, anything—pain, of course, but also just to feel alive.

Because I realized then that I had died the day I had agreed to live with that man. The feelings of safety and happiness I cherished were just a new prison—a place that was much more dangerous and definitive than the cellar, which in the end seemed like a refuge from the way Wernst had twisted my mind and soul.

> *My father, my father, and canst thou not hear*
> *What Erlking whispers so low in my ear?*

Then I heard a noise behind me and spun around. They were nearly all there. Drawn by my intense emotions and the smell of blood. They came closer, rubbing against my legs.

His cats. His children. His trophies.

I went back upstairs. I had one last thing to do before fleeing to the island for good. I fought my trembling as I searched the cupboards for the magic powder that made the world a better place. *Soon, I'll be there soon. I'll find you, Granny. I can already see the* Lazarus *in the harbour and feel the way it rocks when I step onboard . . .*

I felt the sea breeze as Paul stood next to me, pointing at the island in the distance.

I filled up several bowls as I stepped onto the island dock.

I added the sedative as I studied the photographs from the old holiday camp on the walls.

I went back to the cellar, where I watched the cats enjoy their last meal. And somewhere, an invisible hand put a coin in the jukebox.

They fell asleep quickly. Even the sound of the running water didn't disturb them.

And then I picked them up, his children, one by one, and I held them under for a long time, until their immobile bodies floated on the surface.

The island. Forget everything else. Seek refuge there. You'll be so happy. Use the power of your childhood. Go back to being that girl . . .

> *Speak to me of love,*
> *And say what I'm longing to hear . . .*

When I opened my eyes, I saw a cat at the top of the stairs. He was studying the cellar wearily, unwilling to come down any further, probably alerted by the death of the others. I decided to spare him, that tenth cat. I didn't call to him. I scared him away, giving him a chance to live. I thought of Melanie. Would she find her way over the fields to a house? Would she get lost in the foggy night? Would she make it to the other side of the Erlking's forest?

The cat fled from the house. He turned back one last time, crouched in the long grass and peered back through the tiny window into the cellar before disappearing.

An hour later, I heard his car outside. I heard him call me. At first his voice was calm, but after a while it was tinged with fear. He appeared at the top of the stairs, his face pale. I smiled flatly at him, my face as grey as the wall behind me, where Melanie had drawn to her heart's content. He quickly realized I had let her go and ran towards me intending to give me a hard slap. He tried to pull the cats from the bath, hoping to save them.

But it was too late, the boat had sunk, and his children had drowned.

I don't even remember picking up the stone from behind the bathtub. All I know is that he turned his back to me, and I seized the opportunity. I hit him once. His scalp was bathed in blood. He stared at me, an uncomprehending look in his eyes. Before he could gather his thoughts or even move, I slammed the stone into the top of his forehead. Once. Twice. He collapsed on the floor, but I kept hitting him. I couldn't stop. His skull cracked with each impact, covering my clothes, my face, and the cement with its contents. When it was over, I sat down next to him for a long time.

Then I went to the island to find you, Granny.

18

The superintendent had a hard time keeping up with Damian, who was running towards the field, ignoring his boss's shouts. He watched as Damian stepped through the gate and ran to the lake. When he reached the edge, the detective took off his shoes and jacket.

"Christ, Damian, what the hell do you think you're doing?!"

"They're here," he shouted, pointing at the dark water. "He drowned them."

"How . . . How can you know that? You're not going to—"

Too late. Damian had just dived into the water.

All of the officers at the site gathered around the lake waiting for Damian to wear himself out trying to drag the bottom by hand. They all knew that their colleague had just learned his daughter was dead, and that sometimes it was better not to keep men from their madness. Veronique stood to the side, not sure whether to pray that he was right or wrong. The rain had stopped, but the grey clouds hovered in the sky, as if to enjoy the spectacle beneath them, and gathered right above the farm as the men one by one went still and quiet, until the place resembled a graveyard.

Damian kept diving down, again and again. His silhouette would appear against the artificial glow of the spotlights then plunge beneath the surface until he came up for his next breath. This continued for some time. The superintendent feared the detective might decide not to come back up after a while. But, just as he was about to give the order to drag Damian out, the detective swam over to the side and collapsed into the mud.

"There are . . . There are bags down there . . . But they're too heavy for me . . . Much too heavy," he explained as he gasped for breath.

The men moved the spotlights to the edge of the pond, then laid down planks to stabilize the area. Antoine found a hook and a long rope in the loft and suggested using it like a fishing line. He asked the superintendent if they should wait for the forensics team, but his boss, who was busy rolling up his trouser legs and taking off his shoes, gestured for them to carry on. "We're alone on this. We've always been alone . . . Let's get it over with. Bring those children up."

Damian dived back into the freezing water, armed with the hook, which he attached to what he imagined must be a canvas feed bag. The men at the surface pulled as hard as they could to extract it from the thick sediment.

The first bag emerged slowly but surely from the murky water.

When the forensics team reached the crime scene, all of the bags had been pulled up to the surface and laid out on the planks. The police had dragged the bottom with shovels and rakes but found no more.

"They're going to open them," the superintendent said as he watched Damian dry off and put on the spare clothes he always kept in the boot of his car.

"There are only nine . . ."

"Damian, the bodies are going to be in a real state . . . It will be hard to identify them," Fourier warned.

"If he didn't undress them, their clothes will be helpful, even if they're partially decomposed."

"I know, but . . . Don't hope that Melanie—"

"I have to. Hope is all I have."

Veronique managed to convince Damian to wait indoors. She gave him two sedatives, which he reluctantly accepted. He said he was certain he could handle the truth. But the superintendent intervened, ordering him to stay inside.

"She was wearing jeans and a blue hoodie," said Damian as he gulped down the pills with a glass of brandy he'd found in the kitchen.

"All right," Veronique conceded. "Stay here. I'll handle the rest."

"Veronique?"

"Yes?"

"She really fooled us with her island . . ."

"She did indeed."

Veronique watched and tried to contain her disgust and anger as the forensics team cut open the bags and removed the bodies. She was surprised they hadn't decomposed more. A police officer explained that the temperature of the water, the absence of carnivorous animals, and the lack of current had most likely preserved the children longer than would have been expected.

"If the bodies had been thrown into the sea or a river, they would be unrecognizable," he added, blowing into his hands to warm them.

By around two o'clock in the morning, the nine bags had all been opened. The forensics specialists were collecting various samples before placing the remains in black body bags. An hour later, their vehicles left the site and headed for the nearest morgue. The recent reinforcements would stay until late morning so the Villers squad could go home to try to get a little sleep. They all welcomed the superintendent's order with sighs of relief, as if they feared they might be losing bits of themselves with every second spent at the farm.

"So?" asked Damian. He was clearly feeling unwell and his grey features made him look like a zombie. His brain was no longer supplying the precious adrenaline that had allowed him to hold on for so long, and the sedatives had done the rest by anaesthetizing his emotions.

"They didn't find a tenth bag," she replied. "They'll search again tomorrow, in the daylight, with help from a professional diver."

"Melanie?"

"Nothing, for the moment. The clothes are pretty well preserved," she explained with a nauseating taste in her mouth. "But none of them match your daughter's outfit."

"She must have got away, like that cat," whispered Damian.

"What cat?"

"The one I saw yesterday. Another inconsistency. Sandrine told us Wernst killed all the cats."

"If Melanie got away, Sandrine must know. I'll ask her about it tomorrow."

"She won't say anything else," countered the detective. "No matter what proof and reassurance we provide her, she'll stay on her island. She's clever."

"How do you know?"

"Because being on the island allows her to forget all of this ugliness. It protects her from reality—and from any legal repercussions."

"What?"

"Well, any defence lawyer worth his salt will plead insanity. She won't be held accountable for her actions, and will remain free, in an institution where people like you will waste their time trying to treat her."

"Do you really think she consciously created her refuge to avoid prosecution?" Veronique asked doubtfully.

"Maybe it's not the only reason, but I'm sure it occurred to her . . . I think that's why she went back to the island. Because we were too close to the truth. She could sense the danger. We became her new Erlking."

Veronique thought back to the first time she'd seen Sandrine, less than an hour after she'd arrived at the hospital. She had trusted the victim when she'd shared her first story, and she had felt a dull pain in her stomach when Sandrine had explained what she had really been through. But now she didn't know

what to think of her. No theory had prepared her to come face
to face with the devil so convincingly disguised as a wounded
angel.

"What will you do now?" she asked, sitting down next to
Damian.

"Look for Melanie. And find her."

"She disappeared years ago . . ."

"I'm certain she's hiding somewhere. Somewhere Wernst
couldn't reach."

"How can you . . .?" Veronique couldn't finish her sentence.
How could he still imagine a happy ending? It had all been lies
and deceit from the beginning. No amount of light could pierce
those thick grey clouds . . . Could he not live without hope?
Was hope the only way to defeat the Erlking?

"Because I can't hear the devil any more," he admitted, tightening his hold on her hand as if to comfort her. "And I think
he's done dancing with me."

THE FINAL BEACON
"Sandrine's Refuge"

I

September 2019

François Villemin finished speaking and studied the students' reactions.

As he had expected, they remained silent, though they all seemed to be waiting for him to add something, anything that might answer their unspoken questions. But the professor enjoyed letting them stew. He said no more and left them with their thoughts. He went over to his computer and removed the PowerPoint slide showing the Moritz von Schwind painting, inspired by Goethe's poem, that had been projected on the large screen as he spoke. Then he stepped around his desk and leaned back against it, contemplating his audience, satisfied with the impact he'd had.

"Questions?" he asked eventually.

Dozens of hands instantly shot into the air of the lecture theatre. He couldn't help but smile at the future specialists who, once their long years of training were complete, would be among those answering other people's questions. But he wasn't surprised by their inability to analyse the complex mechanisms of the refuge. The story he had just told them contained so many secrets that he had known full well his students would need explanations. He ran his knotted fingers through his beard, then pointed to a young man sitting three rows back. He stood up.

"What happened to the detective? Did he find his daughter?"

"Ah," replied the professor with a soft laugh. "You want to hear the end of the story . . ."

Multiple heads nodded in unison. During his talk, the room

had been silent. The students had all been completely absorbed in Sandrine's story. But now, no longer spellbound, they found themselves contemplating a refuge to which they did not have the key.

"Well, if you had listened carefully and properly analysed the materials for this week, you would already know the answer," chided Villemin.

"What do you mean?" asked the student.

"Think hard and you'll figure it out."

The young man's brows furrowed in incomprehension as he sat down. His classmates didn't look any the wiser either.

"You there, in the second row," said Villemin.

"What is Sandrine's real name?" a young woman asked shyly, her cheeks flushing a bright shade of red.

"That's a rather impertinent question!" the professor exclaimed with a smile.

The auditorium filled with muffled laughter, which momentarily dispelled the uncomfortable atmosphere created by the professor's evasive answers. He was the type of teacher who always encouraged his students to think for themselves. And sometimes—rather often if he was honest with himself—he enjoyed playing with them, pointing out their inability to find the answers that were right there in front of them.

"Could one of you please tell me the topic of today's class? Yes, you."

"Psychological refuges?"

"Precisely! That's exactly right! You'll be a renowned psychiatrist one day!"

More laughter, although the awkwardness and anxiety still lingered.

"We all use refuges," the professor began. He had decided it was time to elucidate at least part of the mystery. "Usually without realizing it. A smile can be one. For example, when someone asks you if you're all right when you're going through a hard time—a break-up, an illness, anything really—you'll take refuge behind a smile, a shield you hold up to keep the person from seeing your pain, to avoid acknowledging it yourself. *Yes, I'm good thanks. Look at this smile I'm hiding behind, isn't it proof enough that I'm doing fine?* Lies can also constitute a refuge. *Did you knock over this glass? No, Mummy.* Children hide behind lies to protect themselves from punishment. Reading a book is a refuge, really. Escaping one's daily life to experience borrowed adventures . . . But writing a book is one as well. Behind all those words on the page, the author often projects his or her deepest fears, hoping to exorcise them, to be rid of them for ever more. Authors narrate their most terrible demons to keep from seeing them when they look in the mirror. Intense admiration of a band or a football team, that's a refuge too. As are hostility and violence, which mask our own weaknesses . . . Pulling the covers over your head to keep from seeing the monsters in the dark . . . Playing with figurines or imaginary friends. Drugs, alcohol, religion . . . They're all refuges we turn to at some point in our lives. Consciously or unconsciously, we build up a system that helps us to get through the trials and tribulations of life. You see?"

"But those are just small . . . adaptations of reality, not serious problems or diagnosable conditions," a young woman objected.

"That's true. Because these refuges are temporary and under control. But imagine a little white lie that turns into a series of lies that then grow so powerful that the liar can no longer differentiate between fantasy and reality."

"Mythomania?"

"Exactly. And there are plenty of examples. In the case I presented today, the refuges were born of an extreme situation—rape and imprisonment. In such circumstances, we know the brain uses a neurobiological mechanism to 'force' the victim to abandon reality."

"But in Sandrine's refuges, there were also beacons placed carefully throughout to remind her of reality," continued the young woman, clearly puzzled by the professor's explanations.

"Ah, Sandrine . . . Intriguing, isn't she? Yes, in this case, part of the refuge was latent, set off by her brain during periods of intense stress. But when the stress dissipated and she was still in the cellar, her consciousness had to find someplace to escape the monstrous nature of her situation. It was the only way to escape madness."

"So, there are refuges we willingly create and others that are forced upon us?"

"Yes, and Sandrine used both, placing beacons from her experiences—her autobiographical memory and her semantic memory, like the island, the poem, the children's names . . . All of that helped her to build a solid refuge. She didn't incorporate all of the details at once, though. They were added over time, consolidating her refuge until it was sturdy enough for her to escape to. According to her story, it took years. But the initial trigger was of course the violence inflicted upon her. That was the foundation of her refuge, its framework."

"So, as time goes on, refuges become more complex?" asked a student sitting right in front of Villemin.

"Yes. Much like for a simple lie, the more time you have to come up with it, the more credible it becomes. I'm surprised, though. I wonder if you'll ever ask the question I've been waiting for since I finished my story."

"What will you be teaching next semester?" asked another young man. His question was met with laughter from the others.

"Very funny, but that's not it. Come on . . . I hinted at it at the beginning of class . . . Yes? Deliver us from our ignorance, my dear Padawan," he chuckled, encouraging the young woman at the back of the auditorium to speak.

"Why aren't there any references to 'Sandrine's Refuge' anywhere?"

"Hallelujah!" exclaimed the professor, opening his arms wide like a messiah. "*That* is the question! Why *aren't* there any references to this case? What do you think?"

"I'm not sure . . . Because the professional community refuses to recognize it? Or maybe the psychiatrist who worked on it hasn't yet published their conclusions?"

"If that were so, why would I be talking to you all about it today?"

"True, I hadn't thought of that."

"But you're not far off . . . The real reason you'll find no mention of 'Sandrine's Refuge' in your textbooks or online is simple: Sandrine never existed."

2

The students were dumbfounded.

Sandrine never existed.

What did he mean? Was this another joke? Another technique to get them to think for themselves? A test?

They turned their heads to look at one another, searching for answers, but saw their own surprise and confusion reflected back at them on their classmates' faces.

Villemin typed something on the keyboard of his MacBook and pulled up a new image on the screen. "What do you see?" he asked.

"A drawing?" asked a young man.

"That's a start, yes. It's a child's drawing. As you'll notice, it's a drawing of an island surrounded by a blue sea. And what do you see now?" he asked as he changed the image.

"A group photo?"

"Yes, a photograph taken at a birthday party for the girl who drew the picture. You'll notice there are exactly ten children who all look to be around fifteen years old. And now, here's the last image."

The final stanza from Goethe's poem appeared in a large font they could all read. The students mumbled the lines under their breath, pronouncing the boy's terrible fate, as Sandrine had done in the horrific story they still didn't understand.

The father shudders, he speeds o'er the plain,
The child he is holding is moaning with pain.
His home is reached, mid fear and dread,
And in his arms, lo! the child is dead.

"*In seinem Armen das Kind war tot*," said the professor, reciting the final line in the original German. Now that I've shown you these three beacons, can you uncover the truth?"

He watched as his audience tried to find the key to the enigma he had placed before them. He could have just laid it all out for them, of course, highlighting the remarkable ingenuity of refuges and revealing the truth about Sandrine's. But why bother teaching if he was going to handfeed them information? He strived to *train* his students. Villemin wanted to prove to them how difficult a refuge—not a smile or a lie, but an elaborate refuge developed by the victim over the course of years in response to intense emotional trauma—could be to decipher. He often compared refuges to palimpsests. The patient's story—the refuge—was the visible text, while the truth was hidden beneath it, out of reach for all but the most astute readers.

The professor also knew that he was asking too much of them. His students didn't yet have enough experience to distinguish reality from fiction. He himself had spent a great deal of time combing through the materials. Dozens of hours listening, asking questions. Long, difficult therapy sessions. Had the victim left the refuge to accept the truth?

No, regretted the psychiatrist turned university lecturer, recognizing his failure.

"Professor?"

"Yes?"

"Do the three beacons you've just shown us belong to Sandrine?"

"Not exactly."

Confusion and excitement filled the auditorium once again.

"Did Sandrine draw the picture?"

"No, but keep the questions coming."

"You said there were ten children in the group photo. Are their names the same as those of the Erlking's victims?"

"They are indeed."

"But if this story never happened, why show us a real drawing and a real photograph?"

"Because these beacons tie reality to the lie. These beacons are real. You can't accuse me of inventing the Goethe poem!"

"So, they belong to someone else!" exclaimed a young woman. "Sandrine isn't the victim. She's not the one who suffered the trauma that triggered the refuge."

"So, who is?" asked the professor with a smile.

"Veronique? The superintendent? It can't be Wernst because he's dead . . . One of the children? The one who got away?"

"You've never been so close to the truth. What type of trauma might trigger the creation of a refuge, do you think?"

"One involving terrible suffering, of course. Rape, imprisonment, physical and psychological violence . . ."

"You're forgetting one," Villemin said enigmatically.

"I'm not sure what."

"The refuges victims build to protect themselves include pieces of reality alongside the fiction. And in most cases, the fiction protects them from a traumatic event they want to forget. By sharing this particular case, I wanted to show you that you can't believe everything your patients say, that you must look for the truth and light in the darkest places. The trauma is the key. In this case, it's grief."

"Grief? But there is no loss . . . The only person who could be grieving is Damian, but that's not possible—Melanie was never found . . . And the detective seems to be full of hope. They never found her body, so he could still believe he could save her, even though the chances are slim . . . If Melanie had been in one of those bags, *then* we could consider that the refuge was built by a man who'd lost his daughter. But that's not the case."

"Well, that's just it," explained the professor. "None of this story was ever Sandrine's refuge. Sandrine is just a part of the real story. Just a paragraph written over the original text of the palimpsest. Because Melanie *was* found. A long time ago. And her father is the one who found her . . . That's why I showed you the third beacon. *In seinem Armen das Kind war tot.*"

3

Meillant Wood was slowly waking up. Sunlight struggled to reach the forest floor through the dense leaves of the tall oaks. The thick carpet of undergrowth was enveloped by the half-light and the fog, which had inspired so many of the legends in the Berry region.

Patrice had passed out coffee to volunteers as Damian equipped each of them with a whistle. He knew most of them. Friends, neighbours, Saint-Amand residents saddened by the tragedy. The town had been searched thoroughly. The streets, the surrounding fields, abandoned houses, the canal—none of these places had led them to a body or a clue to the girl's whereabouts. The woods were the only place left to look.

The search had been organized two days after Melanie's disappearance. There had been so many volunteers that the police had been forced to turn down many of them.

"We'll form a human chain at first, then we'll spread out, leaving a few metres between us," Patrice explained to the thirty people gathered around him. "We'll head north, and we'll check in with everyone on the hour. It's a large wood, but it's well maintained, so by working this way we shouldn't miss anything.

If you think you've found something, anything at all, use your whistle to call us over. Let's spread out now and form a line. Thank you all for coming."

The superintendent waited for the line of volunteers to establish the proper spacing before giving the order to advance. As planned, Damian took up his position on the far left, nearest to the edge of the forest.

He hadn't slept in two days. Every time he closed his eyes,

he heard his daughter calling for help. He hated himself for not having been there, for failing to protect her. He wasn't worthy of being someone's father. He regretted refusing to buy Melanie the red trainers she'd been wanting for so long. Regretted not hugging her close more often.

The search got underway. The line of volunteers moved into the forest where they had all previously enjoyed walks, hunting, or fishing. They had never imagined they would someday be back to search for a missing child. Over the course of the morning, the search party wandered its paths, visiting its darkest corners, travelling its topography like passengers on a ship caught up in a terrible storm out at sea. At lunchtime they gathered for sandwiches that had been donated by a local baker. An hour later they returned to the task at hand.

Not a single whistle disturbed the silence that day. Damian felt his heart begin to race when he noticed movement in a bush a few metres away. He ran over to find it was only a feral cat. The animal quickly scampered off. The detective clenched his fists to contain his mounting despair as he watched the feline disappear into the ferns.

At six thirty, Patrice asked everyone to head back to the main road that ran along one side of the wood. Buses provided by the local authority were waiting to take the volunteers home. Regretfully, they placed their whistles in the box and climbed aboard. They glanced at Meilland Wood a final time on their way past, hoping that the trees had never seen a frightened young girl, praying that she had found some other place to hide. The forest was the site of enough terrifying legends; it had no need of one more.

Damian waited for the buses to drive off, then lit a cigarette. He inhaled deeply and blew his smoke up towards the greying sky.

"We'll start again tomorrow," said Patrice. "Let's go now, though. It's about to start raining."

"She's here somewhere. I can feel it."

"Damian, I know . . . I know it's not easy, but you have to

go home and rest. You'll pass out next time if you keep on like this. Linda needs you too."

"She won't even speak to me, you know," Damian confided in his friend. "She doesn't say it openly, but she thinks it's all my fault. I chose to go on that training course. I insisted when she asked me not to go. She asked me to stay and spend time with our daughter, to surprise her after school."

"It's not your fault. Get that idea out of your head," Patrice advised him with a friendly pat on the shoulder. "We'll find her. I'm sure of it."

"There's a small lake, not far from here," Damian remembered, turning towards the setting sun. "We should have a look . . ."

"Tomorrow a dog team will be here from Orléans, and divers will be dragging the lakes and rivers on Thursday. Let's just focus on the forest and— "

"Did I ever tell you my grandfather fought in the war?"

"Yes," Patrice replied with a smile, remembering the long evenings they had spent drinking and talking before Damian got married.

"He didn't talk about it often. As a kid I dreamed about it, though. I imagined him running through the fields, dodging bullets left and right, shooting down German planes . . . But all he ever really said was that there is no more faithful companion than war. That when war crosses your path, you're scarred for life."

"I didn't know that part," conceded Patrice.

"He also said he was only truly afraid once. It was at the end of the war, when the Wehrmacht was retreating. He was on patrol in the Oise, looking for deserters. A fair number of German soldiers had fallen for French women and were refusing to leave them to return home. His unit had been ordered to search a forest like this one, in Chantilly. They had been walking for hours when they happened to come across a magnificent estate that had once belonged to a prominent family of choc-olate manufacturers. It was completely deserted. They searched the perimeter and then the big house as well. There was a strange atmosphere inside: there were bassinets and cots, rooms with medical equipment, and classrooms, but no people. Then they discovered the lake behind the main building. And you know what they found there?"

"What?"

"Children. Tiny bodies floating on the surface of the water. Dozens of them. The soldiers removed them one by one. Some of them were around four years old. Others were still infants. That's when he got scared. As he carried away the bodies of those innocent children, the war truly terrified him. Much more than it ever had on the front lines."

"That's a horrific story," mumbled Patrice, already heading towards his car.

"I just want to check one last thing before we go."

"What's that?"

"The lake. After that, I promise I'll go home and rest."

The police van struggled to avoid the potholes littering the gravel track, which was more like a narrow ravine than a proper road. The lake slowly came into view, the light of the moon reflected in its dark surface. The first raindrops began to fall as the two men got out of the car. They turned on their torches and began walking along the lake's edge. The undergrowth was denser in this part of the wood, and they had to swerve regularly to avoid thickets and deep puddles of mud. The oak trees and swampy alders grew side by side, creating a compact, oppressive atmosphere. The darkness drew closer. They were about two-thirds of the way around the lake now.

"I should have spent more time with her . . ."

"Damian, don't torture yourself like that."

"*Who rides forth to-night, through storms so wild?*"

"What?"

"It's Goethe. She had a test the day she disappeared. I helped her study for it, but she couldn't remember the last lines of the poem. I told her to recite them over and over again, to try and absorb the words until she could feel the damp forest and hear the Erlking's ghostly voice . . . I can see us now sitting on the sofa in the lounge with the poem on her lap. I think that's the last time I hugged her. The next morning, I left for my training course in Paris. It wasn't just a quick hug. It was a real cuddle like when she was little and she would run to me at the slightest little thing, when she looked to me to soothe away all her fears. I learned the lines with her, to show her it was possible. To show her she must never lose hope. But I should have spent more time with her . . ."

"Damian, you are a fantastic father. You never could have imagined for one second that . . . Damian?"

When his friend stopped moving, Patrice understood. Even before the screams that came next as he fell to his knees. All the oxygen seemed to have been sucked from the air, leaving the superintendent unsteady on his feet. He closed his eyes to try to keep his balance. When he opened them again, he noticed that nature's colours had fled. The greens, browns, and other forest hues had disappeared, leaving behind only a light grey, like ashes carefully scattered over a doomed world. He looked towards the lake. There, just a few metres away, lay Melanie's naked body, which glowed a nearly phosphorescent white in the moonlight. Her torso emerged from the depths and an arm reached towards them, as though the girl had used up the last of her strength to drag herself out of the water.

Patrice slowly walked over to his friend, ignoring his own tears and his growing panic. But he couldn't contain the violent spasm that made him double over. He fell backwards and found himself on the ground not far from the body.

Memories of Melanie swirled in his head, leaving him stunned.

The first time he'd ever seen her, in her bassinet at the hospital.

The first time she'd said his name.

Her birthdays.

Her smile.

The way she called him "Uncle Pat" even though he wasn't a blood relative.

The times she came to the station to wait for her father's shift to end. Sitting in his office and pretending to answer urgent calls, imagining herself bossing around a squad of police officers.

Melanie.

"Oh God," Patrice whispered.

The body's translucent skin was dotted with wounds clearly inflicted after her death by hungry scavengers. Her face looked down into the dirt. Long, slimy clumps of hair were spread out on the ground around her head.

Patrice struggled to his feet and took off his coat. He used it to cover the body, then staggered over to his friend. "I . . . I'm so sorry. Da . . . Damian . . . I have to . . . call the station. Don't move, I'll be right back."

Patrice hurried to the car and got on the radio.

His message was interrupted several times by uncontrollable sobs. He could hardly get the words out, words which he couldn't bring himself to believe.

Melanie.

The desk officer listened and took notes, his hand trembling. When he asked the superintendent to confirm the exact time of the body's discovery, Patrice looked at his watch as the rain hurtled down and battered the cursed alders.

It was 8:37 p.m.

4

The lecture theatre was silent. No one dared raised a hand.

The students waited for the professor to speak again.

"That is the real story," he said sadly. "That was the trigger for 'Sandrine's Refuge'. Just a few days after the funeral, Damian fell into a deep depression. He tried to kill himself by slitting his left wrist—which figured prominently in the refuge, if you'll remember. He was sent to a psychiatric hospital. It was hoped that given time, his pain would ease. But he refused to leave his room. That's where he created the refuge, to hide from his grief. He spent a year there.

Then, one morning, when the psychiatrist came to see him, Damian told him the story of Sandrine, as I told it to you. He used the drawings he remembered from his daughter's room, like the one of the island I showed you. The poem they learned together. The red shoes he finally bought her after she had pleaded with him for weeks. The song from the 1920s that she loved so much. Her friends from her last birthday party. The difficult relationship Linda's mother had had with her daughter, and the father his wife had never known. He used the blame she placed on him after Melanie disappeared. The strange feeling he got that his wife wasn't only speaking to him, but to the ghost of her own father, calling him worthless as her mother must have done, reproducing her behaviour the way Sandrine reproduced Frank Wernst's . . . He added many other details as well to strengthen his refuge.

That's when the director of the hospital, an old friend of mine, asked me to come and see his patient. I spent years separating the truth from the lies, tracking down the real biographical links, excluding the elements of pure fiction, and finding the beacons. I explained to Damian how mental refuges work, to try and help him understand what he was going through. I never imagined that my words would become more bricks in the foundation of his utopia. All I wanted was to treat him, to help him accept his grief and encourage him to leave his refuge."

"Did you succeed?"

"No, young man. I failed. Despite the thirty-six years that have passed since the tragedy, Damian is still living inside his refuge. And I now think it's the best place for him."

"What a terrible story."

"It is. But the smiles that hide the truth are terrible, too. On a smaller scale, of course. They also hide pieces of tragedy. Damian believes his daughter is still alive. She escaped the Erlking. He continues to look for her, scouring newspapers and websites. Every day he goes to the café on Place Carrée in Saint-Amand-Montrond, where he sits for hours, oblivious to the curious looks from passers-by. The locals watch him sadly— some of them still remember the detective and his daughter. And if you ask him who he's waiting for, he'll tell you that the dead from the old cemetery below the town square speak to him. And that none of them has ever mentioned Melanie . . ."

Author's note

"Erlking" is a poem written by Johann Wolfgang von Goethe in 1782.

The poem and its interpretations are divisive. Some people suggest that it represents the passage from childhood to adulthood, while others see it as a description of illness (arguing a fever caused the boy to hallucinate), and yet another school of thought contends that it describes the nightmare of a victim of sexual abuse in which the Erlking symbolizes the paedophile.

I employed all of these different interpretations in the novel.

Translator's note

There are many English translations of "Erlking" available. The translations in the novel are cited from *Poetry and Philosophy of Goethe*, edited by Marion V. Dudley, S.C. Griggs and Company, 1887.

Acknowledgments

I would like to say a big thank-you to Philippe Robinet and Caroline Lépée for their support, encouragement, and kindness.

Thank you, Melanie, for your hard work and advice.

Thank you to the rest of the Calmann-Lévy team, and special thanks to Antoine.

Thank you to my first reader, Sophie, and to our little king, Loan.

Last but not least, thank you to those of you who read my books, who come to meet me at events, and who send me lovely messages. An author often has doubts when he is sat alone staring at a computer screen. Thanks to you, those doubts now often fade.

In many ways, you are my refuge.

Thank you.